An OATH TAKEN

Also by Diana Cosby

The MacGruder Brothers:

His Captive

His Woman

His Conquest

His Destiny

His Seduction

His Enchantment

An OATH TAKEN

DIANA COSBY

KENSINGTON BOOKS
KENSINGTON PUBLISHING CORP.
www.kensingtonbooks.com

KENSINGTON BOOKS are published by

Kensington Publishing Corp.
119 West 40th Street
New York, NY 10018

All Kensington titles, imprints, and distributed lines are available at special quantity discounts for bulk purchases for sales promotion, premiums, fund-raising, educational, or institutional use.

Special book excerpts or customized printings can also be created to fit specific needs. For details, write or phone the office of the Kensington Special Sales Manager: Kensington Publishing Corp., 119 West 40th Street, New York, NY 10018. Attn. Special Sales Department. Phone: 1-800-221-2647.

First Electronic Edition: December 2014
eISBN-13: 978-1-60183-307-5
eISBN-10: 1-60183-307-5

First Print Edition: December 2014
ISBN-13: 978-1-60183-308-2
ISBN-10: 1-60183-308-3

Printed in the United States of America

At times in life we meet the most amazing people. This book is dedicated to Cindy Baker, an incredible woman, my sister, and a woman who is my hero. I'm blessed to have you in my life.

Acknowledgments

I would like to thank members of the Society for Creative Anachronism (SCA) for answering numerous questions and their insight into medieval Scotland. The SCA is an amazing organization where reenactors help to keep our history alive. I'd also like to thank The National Trust for Scotland, which acts as guardian of Scotland's magnificent heritage of architectural, scenic, and historic treasures. In addition, I am thankful for the immense support from my husband, parents, family, and friends. My deepest wish is that everyone is as blessed when they pursue their dreams.

My sincere thanks to my editor, Esi Sogah, my agent, Holly Root, and my critique partners, Shirley Rogerson, Michelle Hancock, Karin Story, and Mary Forbes. Your hard work has helped make the magic of Nicholas and Elizabet's story come true. A special thanks to Sulay Hernandez for believing in me from the start.

And, thanks to my mom and dad, my children Eric, Stephanie, and Chris, the Roving Lunatics (Mary Beth Shortt and Sandra Hughes), Nancy Bessler, my family and friends in TX, and The Wild Writers for their friendship and continued amazing support!

CHAPTER 1

England/Scotland border, August 1291

Sir Nicholas Beringar, castellan to Ravenmoor Castle, halted his steed near the sheer cliffs. Streaks of afternoon sunlight collided to create a prism across the narrow inlet, igniting a wash of purple and gold across the savage land. "'Tis magnificent."

"Indeed," Sir Jon, his most trusted knight, replied as he drew his mount to a stop alongside. "'Tis understandable why men would lose their hearts to the Scottish borderlands."

"And fight with their last breath to keep it," Nicholas added, in awe of the beauty of this untamed wilderness, a land torn asunder by the death of King Alexander III. "How tragic that in the Scots' strife to name their new king, clan has turned against clan. Only through the church's intercession does the fragile bond of unity exist."

Jon grimaced. "For now."

"Indeed. I pray King Edward's intervention will aid the Scots in choosing their next king. Meanwhile, my duty remains to rebuild Ravenmoor Castle and end the restlessness of the Scots along the western border."

"As well as the reiving."

"Aye," Nicholas agreed. "God's teeth, I have added patrols, yet sheep and cattle are disappearing at an alarming rate. Within the past two days, the reivers are growing bolder, and have robbed travelers on Ravenmoor land."

Jon nodded. "It makes no sense. The increased guard should have quelled their thievery, not incited further plundering."

With a grimace Nicholas glanced toward his knights resting their mounts a short distance away. "We will uncover no answers bartering words. 'Tis time to return to Ravenmoor Castle. Take the men and go. I shall be along posthaste."

Concern darkened his friend's eyes. "I will leave two knights to accompany you."

"No." Nicholas studied the chiseled landscape to the west that transformed into rolling fields of thick grass and peat. "We completed rounds over Ravenmoor's land but moments ago. No one is about." And he needed time to think. Alone.

"As you wish." Sir Jon cantered to the waiting knights, waved them to follow.

The clatter of hooves softened, becoming muted as his men reached the turfed lowland. Several moments later they became but a distant fleck, then disappeared into the dense swath of forest beyond.

Nicholas rubbed his brow to quell the throbbing in his head. He must halt the lawless acts of the reivers. As well, he must win the trust of the Scots who remained in Ravenmoor Castle since King Edward had claimed it for his own over a year ago. A challenge, considering the reception he'd had this morning. Before he and his men had departed on rounds along Ravenmoor's border, he'd made a point to speak with several of the remaining Scottish tenants. Their responses had been clipped and cold. All had eyed him with distrust. A reaction that, however much he'd worked to change since his arrival a sennight past, remained.

Sadly, the reason was damnably clear. As the new castellan of Ravenmoor Castle, he'd taken a brief tour of their living quarters. Rotting boards and crumbling foundations were only the beginning of the deplorable conditions.

Closer inspection of the castle revealed a general state of disrepair compounded by the people's inadequate clothing, meager resources, and empty larder, barren except for a few containers of herbs. A quick review of the ledgers revealed misappropriation of funds and abuse of power by the previous castellan, Sir Renaud. Had the knight stood before him, Nicholas would have shackled him and hauled him before King Edward to answer for his gross neglect.

The detailed reports Sir Renaud had sent to the king bespoke his pious efforts to strengthen relations with the Scots and rebuild Ravenmoor Castle. Had he used the money for his own greedy ventures instead? Or did another reason lay behind the previous castellan's betrayal to his king? Whatever the reason, Sir Renaud chose to ignore King Edward's command to appear before him with a detailed report of the castle's status.

And had paid with his life.

A death served by the neighboring Scots during the latest attack.

Perhaps justice existed after all. With a grimace, Nicholas turned his steed toward Ravenmoor Castle. Mud sucked at his mount's hooves as he skirted the bog, rich with the fragrance of sedge and peat that bordered the marsh. Then he guided him up the gradual incline toward a stand of trees.

However long he pondered his findings, Nicholas discerned no motive as to why Sir Renaud would lie to their king except greed. Neither could he determine the reason for the escalation in the number of attacks on Ravenmoor's borders in recent days.

God's teeth, 'twas a mess. He needed time to rebuild Ravenmoor Castle and gain the Scottish residents' trust, except the deteriorating state of affairs between England and Scotland usurped that luxury.

So, he would focus on what he could control. With the outer defenses in place, over the next few days he would review the castle's ledgers in depth. They should provide a degree of insight into the actual state of affairs. Or, at least a clue as to how to approach the wariness of the surrounding Scots.

A light breeze sifted over the hills, spilled through the stand of thick elm and oak in his path. He glanced west. His men should be arriving at Ravenmoor Castle by now and plenty of work remained to be done. Enjoying the beauty of the borderlands would come later.

Nicholas donned his helm and kicked his mount into a canter.

Without warning an arrow hissed past his head, missing him by inches.

"Bedamned!" Turf flew as Nicholas reined his steed hard to the left. He yanked his sword free and scoured the dense stand of trees for charging men.

Naught.

The hair on the back of his neck prickled. Precious seconds passed. The expected attack, the clank of metal and the flash of blades as warriors stormed from behind the trees, never came. Who'd fired the arrow? Nicholas kicked his steed forward. He'd bloody find out.

"Halt or the next arrow will find its mark," a lad's rough burr commanded.

"State your name!" Nicholas called as he reined in his mount. He scanned the leaf and branch shield to pinpoint the youth's position. Was he alone? If not, how many others held their bows trained on him?

A branch quivered.

Nicholas searched the limb.

The tip of a black boot peeked from the leaves.

"You are surrounded," the lad warned. The leaves on a nearby tree shook in confirmation. "Throw down your gold and you will nae be harmed."

Nicholas scoured the nearby elm to locate the would-be accomplices, and paused in disbelief. Entwined within the branches and extending through several surrounding trees ran a network of blackened string, all leading back to the youth. A clever ploy to convince his mark that additional men filled the trees.

Compassion for the Scottish lad assailed him. He understood all too well how hard times could alter a life irrevocably. Where were his parents? Had they been killed during the siege on Ravenmoor Castle more than a fortnight past, or during a previous battle in the fight to claim land along the border by both Scotland and England?

"Toss down your gold!" Nervousness crept through the youth's voice.

The tree branch trembled, this time allowing Nicholas a better glimpse of the reiver. The youth was draped within a large black hooded robe two times his size, yet Nicholas made out the shadowy outline of his face.

Though the lad may be a victim of the times, Nicholas refused to tolerate any lawless acts on land beneath his responsibility. "I am Sir Nicholas Beringar, castellan of Ravenmoor Castle. 'Tis upon my land that you brandish your thievery. Come down. Now!"

Lady Elizabet Armstrong tugged the folds of her cowled hood closer to her face and sunk deeper into the thick, green shield of leaves. Mary, Mother of God, of all people to rob, why did he have to be the new castellan?

Sweat beaded on her brow, and her hands grew clammy. She should have followed her instincts and returned home with this day's spoils. Except as she'd started to climb down, she'd spied the single rider in the distance and believed relieving him of his coin 'twould be simple.

The castellan's steel-gray eyes locked on hers.

Sensation swept through her. His aura was magnetic, yet lethal. Broad shoulders needed no gambeson or hauberk to increase their dimensions. His trim, well-muscled body attested to his physical adeptness. And he sat upon his steed with the confidence born of years of battles.

Shaken by her attraction to her enemy, she forced her attention to his mail, his chestnut warhorse, and the finely-tooled broadsword. His trappings bespoke wealth. If he held but even a few coins, she would take them. And if he carried none, she would relieve him of his weaponry. They would bring a fair price at the market.

"If you carry nay gold, leave your sword and dagger," Elizabet demanded, keeping her voice low.

A deep, impatient sigh rumbled from the castellan's chest.

A slap of anger streaked through her. The Englishman would take her seriously! She nocked an arrow and drew the bowstring taut.

"Such a move would be unwise," Sir Nicholas said, his voice disturbingly calm. "I know you are alone."

Her hand shook as she sized up the large man, too confident for her liking. She bluffed. "Obey my command or my men will kill you."

The castellan's expression darkened. "I see the blackened string threaded through the trees."

Blind panic shredded her last ounce of calm. What was she going to do? She couldna obey his command. Believing she was a lad, he would most likely punish her, mayhap sever her hand or worse. And what if he discovered she was a woman? Terror raced through her. Before he would touch her, she would fight to her death!

Body trembling, Elizabet lowered her bow. She shifted on the limb to steady herself, and the branch gave a traitorous groan. With a gasp, she caught a nearby limb. She must get rid of him! "I have decided to allow you to pass."

The foreboding knight studied her a long moment. "Come down, I wish to speak with you."

She edged closer to the trunk. Why couldna he react like any of her previous targets over the past couple of days? If given the opportunity, each would have fled like the spineless fops they'd been. Instead, Sir Nicholas was proving to be a formidable challenge.

What was she going to do?

A lonely wind howled through the trees, batting the newborn leaves with a careless hand. The scent of peat, tinged with fresh, mountain-fed water, sifted on the breeze. She took in the darkening sky, wishing she was home, safe in her chamber. Again she cursed herself for nae returning to Wolfhaven Castle when she'd had the chance.

"Lad, I will not harm you."

Though several feet separated them, she sensed his frustration. And resolve. "'Tis a trick. I know the penalty for thievery."

The castellan kicked his mount forward.

She held her breath as he halted beneath the branch she stood on, his gaze straight at her. If he'd stared at her in anger, that she could ignore. But the intensity of his gray eyes probed her as if seeing straight to her soul. Shaken, she pressed farther into the leaves.

"I would offer you a job as my squire."

A trick! "I am nae a lackwit. If I climbed down you would cut off my hand." And God help her if he discovered she was a woman.

A frown creased his brow. He lowered his broadsword and laid the flat of his blade across the withers of his mount. "You have my word as a knight that my offer is sincere."

Hope ignited. What if he spoke the truth? Elizabet ached at the thought of her family and people trapped within Ravenmoor Castle. Were they wounded? Suffering? She hated nae knowing. Worse, with each passing day her belief that they lived dwindled. The coin she'd stolen these past few days was far from enough to bribe a castle guard at Ravenmoor to set her family and people free. If she agreed, could she successfully play the role of a lad?

'Twas unthinkable.

A fool's lot to consider his offer. As if she could ever trust a Sassenach? The slang name for the English suited their lie-infested statements.

Even as she pondered the reasons why such a decision would be dangerous . . . if the castellan's offer was sincere, she must use this opportunity to gain entrance to Ravenmoor Castle. Her family's future depended on it.

"Lad?"

Fighting her nerves, she nodded. "I will be your squire."

Satisfaction shone on the castellan's face. "Come down. You will ride with me to the castle."

"Nay. I will make my way on the morrow, at first light."

A muscle worked in his jaw. "I have given my word that you will not be harmed."

She tightened her grip on the nearby branch. "And I have given mine. I will arrive at Ravenmoor Castle at first light."

"I could come up there after you," he said with challenge.

She darted a glance to the nearby tree then back to him. His well-honed muscles left no doubt of his prowess. In which case, she would jump. Then, if she didna break her neck, she could outrun him, as he would be slowed by the weight of his armor.

Leather creaked as he shifted in the saddle.

Instinct assured her he knew exactly of her thoughts to escape. Irritated, she tilted her chin in defiance.

Mirth flickered in his eyes. "At first light, then."

She released a slow breath.

"I would have your name."

A name? Of course he would expect a name. "Thomas," she replied before she could change her mind.

"Thomas," he said without preamble, "if you have not reported to me by Terce, I will track you down." His brow furrowed. "'Twould serve you well to heed me. I do not make false claims."

Of that she had little doubt. "I will be there."

With a nod he turned his destrier, kicked him forward, and cantered toward Ravenmoor Castle.

Elizabet swallowed hard as her enemy's daunting outline melded into the trees. She'd made the right choice. To doubt herself now could only lead to disaster.

As darkness consumed the last flicker of sunlight, fatigue weighing on her, Elizabet halted halfway up the tower steps of Wolfhaven Castle and faced her steward, Lachllan.

Torches set in nearby wall sconces illuminated his wrinkled face, laden with concern, love, and anger. "You will nae pretend to be the castellan's squire. I promised Giric that I would keep you safe. I will nae break my word to your brother." He shook his head with disgust. "That you sneak out to reive by yourself is enough to set my blood afire. Can you nae see the folly of your going to the castle alone? What were you thinking, lass?"

The frustration simmering in his voice endeared him to her even more. Elizabet laid her hand on her steward's shoulder. "If I thought there was any other way to free my family and our people, I would seek it. There is nae. The few pieces of coin I stole this day couldna feed a goat much less bribe an English guard." She dropped her hand. At the moment all she wished for was a few hours of sleep. "Once I am inside, I am confident an opportunity to aid our people will arise."

Lachllan eyed her skeptically. "Even if I were to agree with your foolhardy plan, how will you convince the castellan that you are a lad? Half-hidden within the leaves and your face shielded is a far cry from being in his service where you would work at his side."

She frowned, having pondered that exact question the entire ride home. "The duties of a squire are familiar to me. As for my attire, I will borrow an old set of clothes from Giric's chest." If her brother knew of her intent, he would be furious. With the discord between her and her father, she doubted he would care, but she still loved him.

Except with them both locked inside Ravenmoor's dungeon, neither Giric nor her father had any say in her decision.

Lachllan gave an unconvinced snort. "You will need more than a change of clothes to convince the new castellan that you are a lad. You look too much like your mother." His face softened. "And a beautiful woman she was as well."

Warmth swept her cheeks. "My mother was a strong woman who fought for what she believed in. I am going. I canna let her memory or our people down."

Red flushed his weathered cheeks. "Did you nae hear a word I said? This time you will nae have your way." Lachllan lifted a finger in warning. "Your father would skin me hide if I allowed you to leave, nae to mention Giric. And I love you too much, lass, to allow you to take such a risk."

She threw up her hands, understanding too well—her father would nae care. He'd wanted a second son, nae a daughter. Since her birth, he'd given all of his lauds and attention to Giric. It hurt to think about the years she'd tried to gain his praise.

And failed.

Pointless or nae, she must try. "I will nae stand here and do naught."

Her steward scowled. "You have tended the wounded below, and over the past few days have spent countless hours reiving. You canna do more."

A cool breeze tumbled down the carved stone stairs and the flames of the torchlight from the sconces above her danced, casting long shadows along the walls.

They were at an impasse.

Elizabet released a slow sigh, saddened that even from her home, she would be forced to slip away like a thief. But to save her people, she would do what she must. In the morning before she snuck out the escape tunnel, she would pen her steward a note. "I bid thee good night."

Wizened eyes studied her as if trying to deduce her mood. Regret shadowed his face. "Lass, I wish it could be different."

She gave him a hug; a silent good-bye. "I as well." Elizabet started up the stairs. Why couldna he understand why she must take this risk? Even if she could have explained, what assurance could she offer? The answer was simple.

None.

The venture ahead of her lay filled with danger.

She entered her chamber, and memories of her childhood, of those happy times with her mother, filled her. For a moment she reveled in their warmth. Then the reality of her father's coldness erased the comforting thoughts. If nae for Giric's aiding her in her grief when her father would nae, she didna know what she would have done.

Elizabet shoved the door shut. She refused to think of sad memories this night. The past was behind her, and her focus would be on the morrow, on saving her family and the people of Wolfhaven Castle.

On edge, she crossed to the chest at the end of her bed. After pushing past several worn woolen dresses, her hand rested on cool, smithed-steel. Her fingers trembled as she withdrew the shears. With firm resolve she ran her fingers through her long black hair. Nay longer was she a child, but a woman with responsibilities.

If Sir Nicholas saw her now, would he see her as a woman, or an enemy to be conquered? What was she doing thinking of the castellan as anything but an obstacle to be overcome? Elizabet positioned the shears. Like the last tie to her youth, she severed the first strands. Inky wisps spiraled downward and spilled onto the floor.

She'd made her decision.

There was nay turning back.

CHAPTER 2

Stripped to his waist, sweat rolled down Nicholas's chest as he, along with several of the other men, lifted the heavy wooden beam. "Now." Grunts echoed around him as they shoved.

The log toppled onto the roaring fire. Sparks shot up, entangled with the thick, black smoke, then flames spewed from the dismal cloud, engulfing the dry timber within seconds.

The stench of wool, wood, and other mangled items that Nicholas didn't wish to identify crackled and popped in the convoluted heap. Except for the castle walls and the keep, the rest of the shops and homes were unstable, pathetic shacks not fit for vermin. Once they were torn down and burned, his knights and the tenants would begin to rebuild.

At news of his plans, the Scots within Ravenmoor Castle had eyed him warily, more so when he'd announced they were to live inside the keep until each home was rebuilt. The suspicion reflected in their eyes was as searing as the heat of the flames before him; both must be watched and carefully nurtured.

After several days, their skeptical glances were becoming the norm, but he refused to let their distrust dissuade him from his goal. He would rebuild the homes as well as a foundation of trust. When the routine of the castle allowed, he would review the castle's ledger to discover the extent of Sir Renaud's betrayal to their king.

He bent and caught hold of the next piece of timber, then nodded to the others. Together they lifted the wood and turned toward the fire.

"Sir Nicholas," a knight called from behind him.

"Heave," Nicholas ordered as he shoved. The termite-infested wood clattered into the flames. With a scrape, it tipped and became wedged in the inferno. Satisfied the rotting log would remain, he turned.

The knight who'd called him gestured toward the portcullis. "A Scottish lad who states his name is Thomas requests to speak with you."

So he had come. Satisfied his intuition had served him well, Nicholas caught sight of the slender figure shifting nervously at the gate. "Bring him to me."

"Aye, Sir Nicholas." His knight strode toward the entry.

Nicholas wiped his forehead as he took in the youth's appearance. Still garbed in over-large clothes and his face half-shielded by a ragged hood, the lad presented a pathetic sight.

"Sir Jon," Nicholas called. "Take charge."

"Aye, Sir Nicholas."

As Nicholas headed toward his new charge, the lad darted a desperate glance toward the gates. "I would catch you."

Anger flashed in Thomas's eyes. "I was nae leaving."

His too-quick response told them both the truth. And why wouldn't the lad be afraid? By law, for Thomas's attempted robbery upon Ravenmoor lands, Nicholas could have ordered his hand severed or the lad hanged. That Thomas had kept his word and come to the castle was enough for now. Although with the way his new squire shifted beneath his gaze, how long would he remain?

Nicholas halted within an arm's length away. "Remove your hood. I would see your face."

Thomas's fingers trembled as they paused at the edge of the cowled garment and pushed. Aged, brown wool tumbled back exposing a hacked crop of shoulder-length raven black hair, framing his too-small face. An almost feminine face. The lad's mouth tightened, then he lifted his chin in a defiant tilt.

He owed the soft curves of the lad's face to his youth. With dirt slashed across one cheek and his arrogant stance, Thomas appeared as if a Scottish warrior readied for battle. But it was his eyes that held Nicholas. Emerald. A deep, rich shade as green as Scotland's rolling hills, and the lad's expression as fierce as its untamed firths. No words were needed to declare his strong will; it emanated from him in waves.

Timber crashed.

Nicholas grimaced at the fallen heap that had once housed the blacksmith. Men converged on the rubble and began to haul the splintered timbers toward the fire.

The time, manpower, and expense to raise Ravenmoor Castle to its full potential would be enormous. Most would consider taking on a wayward lad amidst the chaos ridiculous. In truth, with the sad state of relations between the borders, Thomas was the key to proving to the tenants of this castle that Nicholas was sincere.

"Follow me." Nicholas headed toward the back wall where men were beginning to tear down the barracks.

As Elizabet followed the castellan through the courtyard strewn with piled wreckage toward the keep, she took in the sleek play of muscles rippling across his back, finely honed power that could aid as well as wield death.

Fighting for calm, she scanned the grounds, astonished by the mass destruction within the castle's interior living quarters and shops. She acceded that the few buildings standing were safe. The castellan had made a sound decision to demolish the haphazard structures. His interest in rebuilding Ravenmoor Castle seemed genuine. Or, were his acts merely a ploy to gain the trust of the Scots living within?

She studied the knight ahead of her who moved with a steady, catlike grace. He was a man used to being in charge—and obeyed. Apprehension trickled through her. What if she or another Scot revolted against him? Would his actions be fair, or would his resulting decisions be as self-serving as the previous castellan's?

Uneasy, she scanned each of the four towers on each corner of the castle walls. Her throat tightened. In one of them her family and people were imprisoned. Until she found and freed them, she would do what she must to survive within Ravenmoor.

Instead of leading her to the large amounts of debris needing to be hauled to the fire, the castellan headed toward the keep.

Panic swept her. "Where are we going?"

Sir Nicholas kept walking.

Doubts rekindled. Her knees quivered with each step. Did he regret his decision to ask her to be his squire and had he decided she would be punished? Or, had he realized that she was a woman and now was taking her to his chamber?

"Watch out!" a stocky man yelled as he blundered toward them.

A fat pig, squealing and smattered with dirt, bolted ahead of its pursuer and straight toward her.

Before she could move, the bristle-haired beast shot between her legs. With a yelp, Elizabet tumbled to the ground.

Several feet away, the pig squealed its outrage as a sandy-haired youth headed it off. The stocky man ran past her and grabbed the swine's feet. With a grunt, he lifted the sow and glanced toward the castellan. "Sorry, Sir Nicholas. The bloody beast must know his fate."

"Aye, Ihon." Mirth sparkled in the castellan's eyes as he shot Elizabet a knowing look. "'Tis the ones you underestimate that give you the most trouble."

"It is at that." With a laugh, the man lumbered back toward what must be the kitchen, the squealing pig secured under one arm and the sandy-haired boy following a pace behind.

The lad stole one curious glance toward her, then hurried to catch up to the stocky man.

Heat burned Elizabet's cheeks at the mirth on Sir Nicholas's face.

"Are you hurt?" Nicholas asked.

Only her pride. She hurried to her feet and began to dust off her oversize trews, all too aware of him as a man. "I am nae a wee lad who needs to be coddled."

The laughter in his eyes faded. "My question was out of concern," he said with cool authority. "I will not tolerate disrespect from you nor any other who serves me."

Elizabet dropped her gaze, her mind frazzled, her nerves more so.

"I am sorry. 'Tis an unsettling day." The truth. At dawn she'd snuck from beneath Lachllan's vigilant watch to enter the enemy's castle pretending to be a lad. In addition to all of her fears for her family and doubts that she could pull off this masquerade, it helped little to discover that the man who held the greatest threat was a man she could admire.

After a long moment, Nicholas nodded. "Aye, 'tis at that. Come. There is much to be done."

In silence she followed, thankful when they passed the entrance to the keep and headed toward the back of the curtain wall.

The stench of smoke and dust permeated the air as they made their way to where five men worked, ripping out boards from the decrepit stable.

She frowned. "You said I was to perform the duties of a squire?" Which, in her experience, involved grooming the horses, cleaning the mail, and other tasks that served the knight.

"A squire's job involves whatever his knight tells him to do," Nicholas replied. "We will begin by helping the men tear down the stable. After that, we will work our way back toward the fire."

Elizabet nodded and moved to the far end of the stable. The castellan halted by her side and tugged a board loose. She watched the play of his muscles and admired how, with sheer brute strength, he ripped the plank loose. How would those powerful hands feel if they touched her skin?

Shaken by her unwanted musings, Elizabet grabbed an aged bar of steel and worked on loosening a nearby plank. She was here for her people, her family, nae to swoon like a lackwit over a brawny Sassenach whose loyalty belonged to the murderous English king.

Wood groaned as it broke loose. She tossed the board onto a growing pile, then shot a covert glance at each of the four towers. A thought she'd nae considered eroded her fraying nerves. What if her mission here was folly and her people and family were dead? Her body trembled. Nay, they were alive. She refused to believe otherwise. Elizabet pried beneath another rotting timber and pulled. Once she discovered their location, she would set them free.

* * *

The August sun crawled high in the sky, its rays relentless on Nicholas's back. Ignoring the heat, he assessed their progress. Three more hovels to raze and burn, then the rebuilding could begin.

A movement to his right caught his attention. Tugging on the end of a plank, Thomas struggled to free a stubborn piece of wood.

"Hold fast, lad." Nicholas walked over and caught hold on the end of the thick board beside his squire. "Let me help you."

Sweat streaked the dirt on the youth's face as wary eyes met his. Thomas shrugged, focused on the board, and began to pull.

The plank gave way.

Thomas stumbled back, and Nicholas caught the lad before he fell to the ground. The youth froze in his arms. Nicholas stilled. Beneath the massive folds, the lad was reed thin. Blast it. Considering he'd been taking foolish risks robbing travelers, why had he not guessed Thomas would be starving! Within his protection, he would eat his share each day. That he would see to personally.

His squire struggled. "Release me!"

Nicholas let him go.

Eyes wary, Thomas stepped back.

Nicholas tamped down his frustration. Trust would come, but something about Thomas pulled at him, made it important to gain the lad's faith in him, a reason that extended beyond this castle and these lands. Confused by his strong feelings toward his squire, Nicholas gestured to the bucket twenty paces away. "There is water in the pail. Get a drink."

"Aye." With a cautious glance, Thomas left.

Nicholas rubbed his chin as the lad hurried off, pleased by his squire's diligence. Throughout the morning Thomas had worked as hard as any man. And without complaint. But, he'd noticed his squire maintained his distance from the other men. A smile tugged at his mouth. Stubborn pride.

Would the lad also eye him with skepticism if Nicholas suggested he head to the kitchen to break his fast? Likely. Thomas reminded him of his only brother, Hugh, during his youth.

Nicholas frowned at memories of their adolescence. After their father's death, because of Nicholas's younger age, he had been offered a home with his uncle. As the elder, and given their family's connections to the king, his brother, Hugh, had traveled to become the squire to the young Prince Edward.

Tarnished by their father's shame due to his disobedience to the king, their family had lost its title, castle, and lands. Hugh had withdrawn until his only passion was for that of a blade. And his pride.

Now before Nicholas stood another lad afraid and alone, his pride his only shelter. Just like Hugh, a man who suffered to this day.

No, Nicholas vowed. He would guide the lad past whatever atrocities lay in his past. Thomas would not suffer the same lonely fate as his brother.

First, he needed to find a way to break through the lad's misgivings. But how? With the passing hours, he'd hoped to chip away a fragment of his squire's cool reserve at least, except his wall of distrust stood firm.

Thomas set the ladle in the bucket. With hesitant steps, he walked to where Nicholas stood.

Blast it. "Time to return to our task."

Tight-lipped, his squire nodded.

The clatter of wood and shouts of men sliced through the thick silence as they worked side by side. Thomas gave him a wide berth as he hauled each load of debris to the fire. By the fourth trip, Nicholas's irritation grew.

On his squire's return, he stepped into his path. "Why do you avoid me as if I carry the plague?"

The glint of fear returned in Thomas's almost feminine eyes, but the flash of anger erased it. "Silence is nae a crime."

" 'Tis not." He paused. "Does your family know you are here?"

His squire's expression grew guarded. "My family's needs are nae your business."

Nicholas studied Thomas, again caught by the similarity of the lad's circumstances to his own traumatic youth. Were his parents dead? Was he surviving on his own? If so, 'twas no wonder he'd turned to thievery and was half-starved, or that he was suspicious of every offer.

At the empathy on Sir Nicholas's face, Elizabet wished it away. She wanted none of the castellan's concern. Hours after her arrival, she'd hoped he would have forgotten about her. Instead, he'd studied her throughout the day. Now, it seemed her plight only served to endear her cause to him more.

Nor had submersing herself in the backbreaking task erased her awareness of him. 'Twould seem with each hour they spent together, Sir Nicholas intrigued her more. Blast it, why did he have to care? More confusing, why did it bother her that he did?

A wave of tiredness enveloped her, and with a frustrated sigh she stepped around him and resumed working. A light breeze tumbled through the bowels of the castle, laden with the hint of the moors she so loved.

As she reached for the next plank, the rough timbers bit into her blistered hands, and her back screamed from the strain. She forced herself to push through the pain. Only after the bells of Vespers began to chime did she glance at the cloudless sky.

"Enough work for the day, men," Sir Nicholas's voice boomed. "A good start."

With nods, the men within the castle and his English knights nae on sentry began congregating in the courtyard near the well. Boisterous laughs met with friendly greetings.

Elizabet swayed with exhaustion as she watched the smiles, the shared laughter, remembering all too well the heartwarming camaraderie between her people, wanting back what no longer existed.

Rubbing the aching muscles in her arms, she stole a glance at the towers, where her family, as her hopes for the future, lived.

The ringing of the bell grew silent, but the passage of time rang all too clear in her mind. She must learn the inner workings of the castle and discover where her family and people, if they still lived, were being held. She'd counted on subtly questioning the people who lived within, an intent she'd nixed as she'd remained beneath the castellan's watchful eye.

Ignorant of her dilemma, Nicholas threw the timber in his hands to the ground, then gave her a scrutinizing glance. "Come."

Too weary to protest, she followed as he made his way toward the large gathering of men. Mayhap she could discover the location of the dungeon from the men during their upcoming meal? Her questions of the castle's layout would be those of any new arrival and shouldna arouse undue suspicion. Once it was dark, she could slip inside.

As they crossed the courtyard, she caught the scent of roasting pig. Her stomach growled, a reminder she hadna eaten in several hours. She couldna ever remember being so tired or hungry.

"You smell like a gutter whore, Sir Jon," an English knight called out, and the other men roared with laughter.

Heat burned her cheeks as Elizabet glanced toward the center of the bailey where the men jostled each other near the well, tossing out ribald jests.

Sir Jon reached down and grabbed a bucket of water. "No worse than you," he yelled, and gave chase.

Several men cut off the would-be escapee who yelped as the water drenched him. Mud and soot rolled off of him, and the group hooted with laughter. Mud-slicked, the men returned to the well, and began to strip their smoke-laden and sweaty clothes.

Panic swept Elizabet as creamy white buttocks and raw, hewn muscles strode about in a shameless, all-male display. She halted. 'Twould only be a matter of time before they saw her. As the castellan's squire, she would be expected to strip and wash as well. Heart pounding, she took a step back toward the keep.

Nicholas smiled at the men's antics as he began to loosen his trews, pleased with this day's effort. The last of the decrepit buildings lay heaped upon the ground ready to burn. Tomorrow, they could begin to rebuild. In time, like the castle, everything would fall into place.

He glanced at his squire, expecting to see the lad relieved that the day's labors had ceased and, like the other men, removing his filthy garb, anxious to wash away the day's grime. Instead, Nicholas spotted him slowly backing up and halfway to the keep. "Thomas?"

Fists tight at his sides, his squire halted midstep. The lad's gaze cut toward him, wide and unsure.

Confused and surprised by his squire's reaction, Nicholas started toward him.

If possible, the lad's face grew paler. Thomas held up his hand as if a shield. "Stay back."

What in Hades? "I will not harm you."

Fear raced in Thomas's eyes as he glanced from him toward the naked men then back. "Do nae come closer." His body trembled and he took another step back.

Anger stormed Nicholas as the realization of the lad's true fear slammed home. God's teeth, the lad had been raped.

CHAPTER 3

Nicholas fisted his hands in raw fury. Memories poured through him of how throughout the day Thomas had watched him, his gaze nervous and filled with suspicion. Neither had he missed how when he'd caught his squire earlier, the lad had stiffened in his arms. And with the youth fending for his own life, who knows what miscreants he'd encountered or what other nefarious deeds they'd served him.

Blast it! Why hadn't he considered the possibility of the lad being brutalized before? "Thomas," Nicholas said gently, "these men will not touch you in that way."

The lad's eyes widened, then his lower lip trembled. "Keep away from me!"

At the panic in his squire's voice, Nicholas's outrage exploded. If the perpetrators had stood before him, he would skewer their heads on a pike. Damn them and their perverse pleasures.

With effort, Nicholas held his emotions in check. Anger would do naught but broaden the void between them. The moment called for patience and understanding, strengths that had guided him many times over, qualities that would serve him now.

He unfurled his fists and shook his head. "I will not make you wash with the men."

Relief cascaded over the lad's face, but distrust lingered.

Holding his squire's gaze, Nicholas stepped forward.

On trembling legs, Thomas took another step back.

"I give you my word that you will not be harmed." Nicholas gestured toward the keep. "Follow me. There is a basin of water in my chamber. You can bathe there—alone."

For several moments, his squire eyed him, unsure. Then he nodded.

Guilt assailed Elizabet as she followed the castellan. She hadna meant for Nicholas to assume she'd been defiled. At his horror, she'd almost revealed the truth. In the end, she'd maintained her silence. With her family and people captured in his cells, their fate unknown, she couldna afford to tell him the truth until they were freed.

The aroma of roast pork, rosemary, and sage filled the great hall as she followed the castellan inside, trudging on legs that felt heavier than sacks of grain. With the few times she'd accompanied her father to Ravenmoor Castle, she doubted the women working inside would recognize her.

Moments later, they entered the turret and ascended the steps. The pad of her boots echoed around her as the flicker of torches sent long shadows dancing ahead.

At the third floor, the castellan headed down the corridor and entered a large chamber at the end. The few rugs upon the floor, the barren walls, bespoke a man nae drawn to wealth or luxury, but practicality.

A small table stood beside a massive bed. Heat warmed her cheeks as she took in the sturdy frame, the thick, feather-stuffed mattress covered with a woven wool blanket. She could easily envision him lying upon it, sprawled out, naked.

Naked? On a soft groan she closed her eyes. Was she addled! 'Twas wrong to think of him such. He was the enemy, the man who held her people and family. To soften toward him in any manner was dangerous.

Shaken by her untoward thoughts, she opened her eyes to find him kneeling before a well-polished trunk in the corner with iron hinges. After riffling through the contents, he pulled out a pair of hose and a long, linen tunic.

"These should fit you better than your oversize robe." He tossed the garments at her.

She caught the clothes. Hands shaking, she set them on his bed. "I do nae need them. After I rinse out my garb, it will serve me fine."

With a weary sigh he stood, folded his arms across his chest. "After you bathe," Nicholas stated, his each word crisp, "you will wear the clothes I set out, because you are my squire and I order it."

Elizabet glanced at the basin near the hearth. As promised, water stood readied. She faced him, nodded.

"In the future," he continued, "there is another pair of trews and a shirt inside the trunk that you will wear as well." After one measuring glance, Nicholas walked to the door. At the entry, he paused. "I have several tasks that require my time. Once you are finished, go to the great hall and eat. After, await my arrival. When I return, you will serve me." The castellan strode out, closed the door with a firm snap.

Her entire body trembled as she clutched the rough, homespun linen against her breast. She hadna considered her attraction to the castellan, but neither had she anticipated him to be a fair, considerate man.

This was supposed to be simple. Slip inside Ravenmoor Castle, find a way to free her family and people, then leave. Except the frustrating man was making it complicated. But standing here pondering what she couldna change wouldna help achieve her goal. With a sigh she began to remove her garb.

Nicholas shook the water from his hair, thankful to be clean at last. He donned his tunic and cinched his belt, eyeing the ledger on the desk in the small but serviceable chamber where the castle records were kept. Mayhap he could make a degree of headway reviewing the previous castellan's entries in castle's operations before the meal.

A knock sounded upon the door.

He grabbed a towel and wiped his face. "Enter."

The door groaned open and Sir Laurence, a slender English knight who'd served the previous castellan, entered. "Sir Nicholas."

He lowered the towel. "You have news?"

"Of sorts. 'Tis the prisoners in the dungeon."

"Prisoners?" Nicholas eyed the knight hard. "I have been here over a sennight. When I asked if there was anything of importance that I should be informed, why was I was not appraised there were prisoners?"

"My regrets, Sir Nicholas. Sir Renaud had issued strict orders not to be bothered by the prisoners' welfare, and I . . ." Sir Laurence cleared his throat. "'Tis an oversight that will not happen again."

Blast it, he'd believed he'd addressed all immediate issues. "Tell me."

"The healer requests that the bodies be moved."

Nicholas slapped the towel onto the chair. "Bodies?"

The knight shifted uncomfortably. "Sir Renaud—"

"I do not give a bloody damn about Sir Renaud. Tell me about the prisoners—no." Nicholas strapped on his broadsword, strode to the door, and jerked it open. "Take me there. I will see for myself."

"Yes, Sir Nicholas." The knight hurried through the entry.

After exiting the keep, they crossed the courtyard and entered the far turret. As Nicholas reached the top of the stone steps leading to the dungeon, the guard at his post snapped to attention.

Sir Laurence shoved open the aged wrought-iron door. "This way."

Torchlight sputtered as a cool slice of wind whistled through the dank confines. As he stepped inside, the stench of bodies and refuse struck Nicholas like a catapult. Within the broken cast of yellowed light, he found men huddled inside narrow cells no larger than a coffin. Some dying, while others lay unmoving, their gazes fixed.

Furious, Nicholas strode up the narrowed center path, repulsed by the foul conditions and the basic lack of respect shown to their fellow man. In his many years of service to the king, never had he witnessed such atrocities as those sprawled before him. 'Twould sicken the stoutest man.

"Sir Laurence," Nicholas boomed, "I want the dead removed from the cells immediately, and bid the healer to return. Those who live will be tended to posthaste."

"Aye, Sir Nicholas." The click of hurried steps against stone echoed as Sir Laurence rushed out.

With methodical precision, Nicholas scanned the cells. Three cells down, his gaze collided with a pair of ice-blue eyes bright with fever. The coldness in their depths pulsed with rage. Hair as black as soot framed the rigid determination set within the stranger's face, and several dark bruises with an angry purple-black hue cut across his cheeks and forehead. Though the prisoner only stared, his silence spoke volumes.

The man was dangerous.

Nicholas acknowledged him with a brief nod. As a warrior he understood the risks this man had taken in fighting for his beliefs. He also understood his part in this lethal game—as castellan, he must serve justice to those who went against his king. These men were prisoners because they'd broken the law in opposing England's rule. Still, he would ensure they were treated with respect.

Accompanied by the soft moans of the wounded within the cells, Nicholas walked over and stood before the dangerous man's cell. This close, he caught the sheen of sweat on his brow, the gaunt appearance of his face, and the tremors that wracked his body. A hand's length away lay the large frame of a dead, older man, the shaft of a broken arrow protruding from his back.

The prisoner's eyes narrowed.

As if living in these vile conditions the man didn't have cause to be furious? Nicholas nodded toward the dead man. "He shall be removed immediately and given a proper burial."

The prisoner lifted his jaw in defiance, and for a split second the gesture reminded Nicholas of Thomas. An odd thought. Or was it? Though the lad's struggles to fend for himself held not the bloodshed this man had witnessed, in a sense Thomas was a prisoner to the lessons of life as well.

The sounds of men climbing the steps echoed from the turret.

With one last look at the prisoner, he headed toward the door.

Sir Laurence entered the dungeon followed by several knights.

A pace away Nicholas halted and gestured toward the cell where the fevered prisoner still watched him. "Who is that man?"

Sir Laurence shot a curious glance down toward the cells, scowled. "Giric Armstrong. With his father having recently died during his incarceration, he is now the Earl of Terrick, a title that gives him the holding of Wolfhaven Castle, whose land borders Ravenmoor."

The Earl of Terrick. Bloody hell! "As if treating the noble with such contempt would help bring peace?"

Sir Laurence's face paled.

Frustrated, Nicholas held up a hand. "I know, the previous castellan's orders. Tell me what you know of him."

Sir Laurence shot the earl a cool glance. "Though loved by his people, many, along with me, think he is a thieving reiver just the same. Sir Renaud had him beaten for his insolence, and ordered that the healer leave him be." He shot Nicholas a cautious look. "After the castellan's death, I ordered that Lord Terrick be given extra water and food, but he has remained in a fevered state."

With the information he'd gathered, doubts assaulted Nicholas as to whether the noble had earned the beating or if the previous castellan meted out the punishment for his own corrupt pleasure. "And who is the dead man in his cell?"

"Lord Terrick's father," he replied. "Sir Renaud refused to allow dead prisoners to be removed from the cells." He shook his head. "I regret not having informed you immediately of the prisoners and their status upon your arrival. Sir Renaud was so adamant about not being bothered with the prisoners that I . . ." He lowered his head in shame. "'Tis no excuse."

Nicholas scanned the cells with disgust. "From this moment on, I will be informed of *every* aspect of running this castle. Is that clear?"

"Yes, Sir Nicholas."

"Begin removing the dead and start with Lord Terrick's cell. When the healer arrives, she is to tend to him first."

Sir Laurence gave a brisk nod, waved his men forward, and started the gruesome task.

The first star twinkled in the blackening sky as Nicholas glanced out the tower window, one of the two sources of fresh air in the soured confines. Drawing in a slow, cool breath, he understood Lord Terrick's anger and his pain, remembered too well the grief at his own father's death in addition to his resultant disillusionment. That moment, the happy life he'd coveted as a child had crumbled, his beliefs shredded by bitter tongues, lies, and deceit. From the dregs of tragedy he'd learned to fight for truth, to persevere, and to never give up faith.

He glanced toward the center of the courtyard. The bonfire from the destroyed huts still raged an orange-red. The thick swath of smoke stained the pristine night, which had grown quiet except for the footsteps of more of his men heading up the steps to the dungeon.

Nicholas looked at the window to his chamber where he'd left Thomas, and his throat tightened. With ease, the lad could've been one of the injured or dead locked within the cells. Through a miracle he'd been spared. By God he'd do right by the lad, teach him, guide him to a better life. With a hard swallow, he helped his men haul out the dead.

Dressed in her new garb, refreshed after having washed off the layers of dirt and soot from her body, Elizabet descended the steps to the first floor. The great room unfolded before her, rich with the scent of roast pig, fish, and ale.

The front door opened with a bang, and a knight entered. He glanced toward several knights near the hearth. "Simon and Giles, Sir Nicholas needs more men to haul the dead from the dungeon."

Air rushed from her lungs. On trembling legs, she pressed her hand against the stone wall.

The dead?

Giric? Her father? Their people?

Tears burned her eyes as she struggled nae to race down the last two steps of the turret. As she entered the great room, the knights were exiting the keep. Several lads, a few women, and three old men continued to set up trencher tables. Otherwise, the enormous chamber lay empty.

She must learn the truth! Ignoring a woman's call to assist her, Elizabet hurried to catch up to the knights. Outside, she followed at a safe distance, and with each step, prayed for her family's life.

Across the bailey, the knights shoved open a door and headed up a turret.

The dungeon! She gave a quick look to ensure no one noticed her, hurried to the entry, then pushed open the door. Heart pounding, she peered up the steps.

The scrape and shuffle of feet on stone and a grumbled curse echoed from above. A moment later, torchlight illuminated a stocky man descending the stairs, a body draped in his arms.

God no!

'Twas the butcher, a man who'd faithfully served her family for years.

"Move out of the way, lad," the man grumbled.

Panic swept her as she stumbled back.

The man shoved past.

More steps sounded from above.

On trembling knees, Elizabet glanced up. In the knight's arms lay the chandler, the man who'd gifted her with her first beeswax candle. Bile rose in her throat.

"Help or move," a man's curt voice ordered.

Tears blurring her eyes, she moved aside.

The man cursed and headed up the steps.

Elizabet swallowed hard. She needed to know. As she reached the landing, the door above shoved open.

A knight, with a body slung in his arms, stepped out. "Move back, lad."

Elizabet stared in horrified disbelief—her father! Bile welled in her throat and she almost retched. A tremor wracked her body, then another. Her father, a man whose love seemed elusive, a man whose respect she'd fought to earn, was dead. Grief for what would never be suffocated her.

What of Giric? Please, God, let her brother be alive.

Afraid to look, more terrified nae to, she gazed upward in anticipation of the next body.

And froze.

Halted several paces away, Sir Nicholas watched her with unfeigned interest. His eyes glittered with questions, questions she could never answer.

CHAPTER 4

As the guard departed the dungeon with the body of the previous Earl of Terrick, Nicholas analyzed the emotions he'd witnessed on Thomas's ashen face—shock, disbelief, and finally horror. And when his squire had lifted his eyes to meet his, he'd seen fear.

Why?

He glanced at the body of the noble a brief moment before the guard disappeared from sight, then back to Thomas. Unease sifted through him. Did his squire know the deceased?

Footsteps of an approaching knight echoed behind him. Nicholas needed to move, but he could not allow the lad entrance to the dungeon and witness the travesty above. "Thomas, return to the keep. Stay there until my return."

His entire body trembling, his squire held his gaze, but he didn't move.

God's teeth. What had the dead man done to the lad that would warrant such trauma? "Thomas."

His squire's lower lip trembled as he glanced up the stairs. "I-I came to help wi-with the dead."

Anger slammed through Nicholas. "Return to the keep now!"

Thomas held his ground as if he would challenge Nicholas. On a broken sob the lad turned and fled.

Blast it. Frustrated, Nicholas took the last few remaining steps to the bottom of the tower, then exited into the night.

He caught the lad's shadowy figure as he raced across the courtyard as if chased by the hounds of Hades. Near the center of the courtyard, Thomas halted and turned toward the gatehouse.

Nicholas froze. Was the lad going to forsake his vow and flee?

After a long moment, his squire glanced toward him, then sprinted to the keep.

Her each breath rough, Elizabet stumbled into the great hall, shoved the door behind her, then collapsed against the sturdy frame. Tears burned her eyes at the memories of her father's body slung in the guard's arms.

Dead.

Mary, Mother of God, what of Giric? Had her brother died as well? She wiped away the tears. Nay, he had to be alive!

"Get on with you, lad," a woman's voice scolded.

Dazed, Elizabet glanced behind her.

A plump, elderly woman, with her hands on her hips, stood several paces away scowling at her.

With a hard swallow, Elizabet fought for composure. "Yo—You asked me something?"

The woman frowned, her pruned face sagging with disgust. "The castellan and his men will return posthaste and they will be expecting their meal." She nodded toward a huge pot hanging above the flames in the hearth. "The meat needs to be ladled out. Go help instead of standing there dawdling. On with you now."

However much Elizabet wanted to escape and find privacy to try to come to grips with this eve's horrendous discovery, she'd aroused too much suspicion with Nicholas moments before. Like it or nae she must continue to play her part in this role to discover if her brother lived.

Fighting back the tears, she walked to the cook fire. The heat spewing from the hearth burned hot against her skin as she ladled out portions of roast pig, wild onions, and herbs onto the platters. Though she'd nae eaten for hours, her stomach rebelled at the idea of food.

A short while later, the keep door scraped open.

Her heart racing, Elizabet scoured the faces of the men entering the great room after their gruesome task, searching for one.

The castellan stepped inside, halted. He grimaced as he scanned the confines, and his gaze paused on her.

Unnerved by the concern in his eyes, she turned away and threw herself into her task, thankful when he didna confront her. And he would, of that she had no doubt.

As the evening wore on, she moved about her duties, serving Nicholas his food, refilling his goblet when empty. Throughout the meal she listened for scraps of information, but learned naught that indicated if Giric was amongst those who had died.

Frustrated by unanswered questions and exhausted from worry, she stood in the shadows watching Sir Nicholas, waiting for the moment he would signal her and she could leave.

The grumbles of his men and the clunks of their tankards as they ate echoed in the great hall as Nicholas speared the last chunk of meat. If only he'd known of the dead in the dungeon earlier. He chewed the meat, swallowed. And what would he have done? Besides removing the deceased earlier, naught. He shoved away his trencher. After wiping and sheathing his dagger, he signaled to his squire.

He studied Thomas's slow approach; exhaustion rode his fragile features and nervousness haunted his eyes. From the lad's strong reaction to the dead noble, at some point, the prisoner had played a significant part in his squire's life. But how? Had the earl taken Thomas into his home? Had he caught the lad reiving and cast him into the dungeon? Or was he the man, or one of many who had molested a homeless lad with nowhere to turn?

His squire set the basin of water before him. "Water for you to wash, Sir Nicholas."

"My thanks." He cleaned the grease from his hands then accepted the cloth. Nicholas handed back the linen. "'Tis all I will require for the night."

Relief washed over his squire's face. He retrieved the bowl, then started away.

"Thomas."

At the edge of the dais he halted, his expression guarded. "You wish for more food, Sir Nicholas?"

He shook his head. As tired as he was, he couldn't help feeling empathy for the stricken expression that shattered the lad's face. "You will accompany me to my chamber."

Thomas's fingers shook and water spilled over the sides of the bowl. "I-I thought I was to sleep in the stables." Defensiveness etched his whispered words.

"You will sleep on a pallet by the hearth."

The little color on his squire's face fled.

The last thing Nicholas wished was to add to the lad's problems, but in this instance there was no way around it. Thomas must learn to trust him.

Exhausted, Nicholas departed the great hall with his squire in tow. At the lad's hesitant step, protectiveness for Thomas overwhelmed him, the depth of it surprising even himself. 'Twas not uncommon to find tragedy striking families during this volatile time. So why did the misfortune of this one lad touch him as none before? The only reason that made sense was because Thomas reminded him so much of his brother, Hugh.

Nicholas glanced at his squire keeping pace by his side as he headed up the turret. God help him. If he had a say in the choices of his future, Thomas wouldn't live such a cold life or know its pain.

At the third floor, he headed to his chamber.After his squire had entered, Nicholas closed the door, then gestured to the trunk at the end of his bed. "You will find blankets inside. Make a pallet for yourself beside the fire."

The lad's gaze grew wary. "If nae the stable, I could sleep outside your door." Hope shone in his eyes. "'Tis commonplace."

He wanted to keep an eye on Thomas, for more reasons than he wished to count. "For now you will sleep here."

The lad's throat worked. "Aye." With forced movements Thomas knelt and began the task, slanting suspicious glances toward him every so often.

Nicholas poured a cup of wine, tried to focus on the warmth of the fire and the sweet scent of heather on the night breeze, welcome after the stench of death. As his squire glanced at him for the fifth time, Nicholas muttered a curse. "Thomas."

The lad jumped and dropped the blanket in his hands.

Nicholas grimaced. "I will not harm you."

His squire picked up the blanket, but his gaze remained unsure.

Frustrated, Nicholas walked to the bed. He couldn't protect him from all of life's horrors, but while the lad remained at Ravenmoor Castle, he would spare him a few. "You are to keep away from the dungeon."

The lad clenched the edge of the blanket until his knuckles turned white. "'Tis my duty to assist you."

His squire's courage was admirable but on this he would not relent. "Stay out of the dungeon."

"Sir Nicholas, I—"

"Enough!" he interrupted, confused by his squire's insistence to aid with the grisly task. "'Tis done." He raised his hand when Thomas started to shake his head. "Do not challenge me. As with any order I give you, 'twill be obeyed. Is that clear?"

Thomas's throat worked. "Aye," he replied, his voice barely a whisper.

More than ready for sleep, Nicholas turned to his bed. The day had been long, more so by the morbid discovery in the dungeon. The last thing he needed to deal with was a mule-headed lad who confused him at every step. With a tug, he removed his tunic and threw it on the floor. Warmth from the hearth heated his skin as he undid the laces on his trews and started to shove them down.

At Thomas's gasp, he turned.

The lad stared at him, his mouth agape and his eyes shimmering with fear. Slowly, a blush swept across Thomas's face, then he averted his gaze.

Nicholas swore softly, cursing the men who'd raped the lad. He hadn't thought twice about disrobing in his own chambers, but then again, it came back to the issue of trust. Regardless of the circumstance, his squire must learn that he would never do him harm. "I know your past has led you to distrust men, but I have given you my word that I will never harm you."

Silence.

As if he expected different? 'Twould take time. "Go to sleep, Thomas." The feather-stuffed mattress sank under his weight. He tugged the heavy wool blanket halfway up to his chest then closed his eyes. An owl hooted in the distance. A cow bellowed from the courtyard below. Wind blew in a quiet hush, the clean scent of the night and of the moors he was coming to love filled the chamber, but sleep evaded him.

Nicholas stared out the arched window to where stars filled the sky, exasperated by his inability to deal in the correct manner with this one lad.

Throughout the years he had handled numerous difficult situations with finesse. Often he would be called upon to end fights or to instill logic when none seemed about. On the Isle of Man after a major confrontation, through negotiations he had played a significant role in defusing conflicts that had cooled tempers and erased rumblings of further rebellion—the reason King Edward had chosen him to serve as castellan of Ravenmoor Castle.

In the past common sense had served him well, but 'twould seem on matters concerning his squire, his every gesture of good will ended up in shambles. Why?

The soft slide of the blanket sounded.

Nicholas glanced over. "I know you are awake."

The flames sputtered then swayed erratically in the hearth. An owl, closer this time, called into the night.

After a long moment, Thomas rolled over and faced him. "Aye?"

A thousand questions spun in his mind. Should he ask about his past? No, his previous efforts assured him 'twould serve to make the lad withdraw. Ask about his family? Nay. Mayhap 'twas their differences, or those perceived by the lad, that erected the wall between them. If his squire saw that his own path hadn't been easy, mayhap 'twould be the key to forming the all-important first steps to trust.

"When I was six and ten I had the fortune of being sent to a monastery to study." Nicholas smiled as the past tumbled into his mind. "I remember the pride of that day, of riding alongside my uncle into the grand courtyard surrounded by walls that had taught a myriad of students, diplomats from other countries, sons from influential families, and royalty. Only through King Edward's intercession had I been granted permission to attend."

"You are a priest?" Confusion and a touch of awe filled Thomas's voice.

Remorse tainted Nicholas's thoughts, and his smile fell. "Nay." The sense of loss after all of these years still cut deep. "I never finished my studies."

A log settled in the hearth. Flames skittered and danced around the thin column of smoke lazing up into the night. Silence, thick with unanswered questions, filled the chamber like the scarred memories haunting his mind.

He waited for the questions of why, but after a long silence he realized that his squire would not pry. If Nicholas chose to share the innermost secrets of his past, his pain, the decision would be his.

The revelation shook him. He'd not expected this depth of understanding, or mayhap deep down he'd known. That would explain the draw, the unexplainable need to share with this one lad more about his personal life than he had with anyone else—ever.

The moment grew thick with barely restrained emotion, a quiet force that threatened to consume him. The sharing of this tragic event to establish a venue of trust became more than an act of good will, it became a necessity. He couldn't explain it if asked, but the need to reach out, to reveal this life-altering issue of his past to Thomas was as essential as his next breath.

The anger, frustration, and despair that had simmered deep inside flooded through his mind. He'd believed himself far beyond the hurt of that tumultuous time so long ago, but here in the murky darkness tainted with smoke and the night, confessing his soul to a lad, he found the truth, the pain of emotions too long denied.

"For the first five months at the monastery my studies went well," Nicholas started, not surprised by the rawness of his voice, a pain he doubted would ever leave. "I enjoyed the lessons and appreciated the chance to learn. One day a young man from Gretna, a Scottish town not far from here, arrived at the school. Though there were many differences in our cultures, we became fast friends." He smiled, remembering the quick laughter in the young man's eyes, his loyalty given to his friends. "His name was Dougal, and he fared from the clan MacNaughton."

His smile fell away as the pain of the remembrance severed the warmth. "He came from a prominent home, was betrothed to a maiden whom he loved, and was to fulfill not only his own dream of attending his studies, but upon his graduation, his father's as well. Several months passed. . . ." His throat tightened, and he stared at the stars in the sky as they blurred before him.

"What happened?" Thomas asked.

Nicholas exhaled. "Winter swept in with a fierce abandon on that cold, blustery March day. Even the hounds shivered near the hearth. The day was long, the lessons intense, exhausting, and after being closed up with studies for months, tempers ran high. An in-class discussion about the lawlessness and heathens living in *The Debatable Land* escalated, ending up becoming a one-on-one confrontation between Dougal and our instructor."

He grimaced, remembering Dougal's passion, his determination to enlighten the priest along with others in the class of the true motivation behind the reiving along the borderlands.

"Dougal's eyes blazed as the debate grew. I remember watching him, envying his ability and quick wit, which in this case served him well; his points were clear, concise, and to summarize the argument, he outwitted the teacher."

"Nae the best decision, I bet," Thomas said.

"Indeed," Nicholas agreed. "Furious at being outmaneuvered, especially before a filled classroom, the priest called him insolent and ordered him from the room. Enraged at being punished for having done naught wrong, Dougal refused. The priest withdrew his whip, but Dougal stood his ground. He struck Dougal across the face, then again and again, and he told the class that he would not tolerate insubordination. As the priest raised his whip again, with Dougal's face, hands, and body cut and bleeding, I jumped up and grabbed the priest's wrist."

Embers crackled into the chamber, warmth against chill, sadness against memories.

"What happened then?" Empathy touched Thomas's quiet voice.

Nicholas glanced to his side, surprised to find Thomas sitting on his pallet staring at him. "For my actions, I was expelled."

Thomas leaned forward, his eyes wide with concern. "And Dougal?"

Fury tore through him. "Infection set in from the lashes. A fortnight later he died. I returned his body to his family and stayed until after his burial."

A deep ache filled Elizabet, as she understood the pain Nicholas must have borne, the hurt that time would dull but never completely erase. She knew the grief of losing someone you loved, and of wondering the fate of the same.

Her knees trembled as she rose and walked to the edge of his bed. She knelt and laid her hand upon his shoulder, feeling his strength and his tremors as well.

Now beside him, she hesitated, unsure of what to say of what to do. He didna need words of condolence, the time for those long past. "My mother died when I was but six." She closed her eyes as the faint memory filled her mind. "After, my father turned away from me because—" What was she doing? Elizabet jerked her hand from his shoulder and stood. "My regrets," she said, her voice shaky, her mind reeling from how close she'd come to revealing the truth.

Nicholas sat up. Firelight sharpened his face, touched by questions and concern. "Thomas—"

"'Tis late." She hurried to her pallet praying he wouldna ask any questions. For a moment she'd sensed a harmony, a peace between them, a rare unity until this moment that she'd shared only with her brother. A shiver stole up her spine. What was going on?

A long sigh came from Nicholas, then the bed groaned as he lay back. "Go to sleep, Thomas. 'Twill be a long day on the morrow."

The pop of the fire echoed in the silence.

Several moments later, Nicholas's breaths fell out soft and slow.

He was asleep. The relief Elizabet expected was replaced by regret. How could she nae? For one brief moment they had reached a plane of understanding, a friendship that would never be. For once she gained freedom for her brother and her people, Thomas would disappear forever.

CHAPTER 5

Elizabet's laughter, filled with childish delight, melded with the soft lyrical chuckle of her mother's. She leaned into her mother's embrace, loving these moments the most.

Her mother's warm, green eyes, like leaves in the summer, twinkled with mirth.

"And did the fairy princess indeed cast the prince into the bog?" Elizabet whispered, on edge to learn the prince's fate.

Her mother's eyes struggled for sincerity, but lost to humor. She laughed. "Aye, she did indeed."

The clatter of hooves echoed from the courtyard.

Her mother glanced toward the window, the smile never leaving her face. "'Twill be your father."

Anxious for his hug and whisker-roughened kiss that would tickle her neck, Elizabet jumped from her mother's knee to greet her father. She struggled to move forward. Failed. Panic swept her. Why couldna she move?

The faint smell of smoke wove through her mind, then the soft, deep even breaths of someone nearby entwined with the crackle of the dying fire a backdrop. She opened her eyes. The castellan's chamber came into view.

A dream.

She shut her eyes, tried to reclaim the dream of moments ago, but the last image of her mother faded.

A night bird cried in the distance, its mournful call fading into the eerie stillness.

Opening her eyes, she glanced out the window.

Gray hinted at the edges of the star-filled night.

'Twould soon be dawn. Careful nae to make a sound, she sat up, looked over.

Nicholas's chest slowly rose and fell.

The castellan was still asleep. She must slip out before he awoke. He would be furious to find her gone, but she would contend with his anger later. As she was banned from entering the dungeon to find out if Giric was alive, she would review the ledgers of the keep. Like the records maintained in her home, they should list the death of anyone of substantial importance. And she prayed she'd nae find her brother's name on the pages.

With care, she stood. The tunic Nicholas had given her to wear the night before concealed her curves as she gathered her clothes. The seconds it took to cross to the door seemed like hours. Holding her breath, she lifted the latch and pulled. The thick oak and steel door creaked opened. Heart pounding, she glanced back.

The castellan's eyes remained shut and his breathing even.

She hurried out, closed the door behind her, then scanned the corridor.

Empty.

Before anyone came, Elizabet slipped into her day's garb, then headed down the hallway. The aroma of baking bread filled the air as she ascended the turret, and her stomach rumbled. Moments later she entered the great hall. A few hounds lay amongst the rushes thumping their tails in welcome, their huge, sad eyes watching her, while the other knights and tenants visible slept. The men would soon awaken, and she didna have much time.

She hurried toward the tiny chamber off an alcove, where she'd learned the previous castellan kept his important documents. The castle ledger should be there.

Once inside, she positioned the door to where it blocked her from anyone's view, then she searched through the stack of books and documents lying on the top of the aged oak desk. Except for a quill, ink, and a number of personal effects, she found naught. She explored the top, righthand drawer, then the next.

Two unopened drawers remained.

Her fingers trembled as she reached for the next handle. It had to be in here! She held her breath and she pulled.

Wood scraped.

The ledger came into view.

Thank Mary! She set the thick book on the desk. Thin parchment crackled as she opened the leather-bound journal. She glanced toward the door.

She had to hurry. Elizabet flipped through the yellowed sheets, carefully reviewing each notation for Giric's status.

Precious seconds passed.

Grumbles of men stirring echoed from the great hall.

Blast it. Determination drove her as she scanned the entries in search of Giric's name.

"Have you seen Thomas?" Nicholas's deep voice sounded from outside the chamber door.

Elizabet froze. He couldna catch her here!

"Nay, Sir Nicholas," a man answered.

Heart pounding, she closed the ledger, stowed it in the drawer, then quietly slid it shut. She crept to the door, caught sight of Nicholas's sturdy frame through the narrow slit.

A scowl marred the castellan's face. "If you see my squire, tell him to find me immediately."

"Aye, Sir Nicholas." The man passed by the door.

Now you go away too, she silently urged as Nicholas surveyed the great hall before him. With a muffled curse, he turned and took a step straight toward her.

Nay! Elizabet staggered back. How could she explain her presence here?

"Sir Nicholas," another man's voice called from a distance away.

The castellan halted, his shadow stealing into the opening between the door to the chamber. "Yes?"

"Sir Jon would like to see you in the dungeon," the man said. "There has been another death."

A soft curse. "I am coming." The castellan's shadow slipped away.

Terror tore through Elizabet. Another man dead—who? Please God let it nae be Giric. She shot a desperate glance toward where the ledger lay hidden. She'd nae found her brother's name, but with Nicholas out of the keep, dare she go back and search more within the pages, or with the guard's news would her efforts be in vain?

A woman called for help bringing out the bread.

Her choice was made. The castle was beginning to stir. She couldna chance being caught. Elizabet slipped from the room.

The pounding of mallet to wood thudded as Nicholas departed the dungeon. He glanced across the courtyard. The new stable stood readied. Nearby, several men worked on the frame for the barracks. The pleasure over the rebuilding faded at the news of moments ago.

Another man was dead.

Mouth tight, Nicholas glanced toward the morning sky. Fingers of yellow and gold slid into the violet expanse. He drew in a long, cleansing breath, savoring the soft dewy scent of grass and the morning sifting on the breeze, needing to rid his senses of the stench of death.

Lord Terrick's fever still raged. As Wolfhaven Castle bordered his land to the north, good relations between the two were imperative. He needed Lord Terrick to live. The father having died within his dungeon, if his son passed as well, 'twould prove difficult—if not impossible—to reestablish any fragment of an alliance with the bordering Scots.

"Sir Nicholas," one of his knights called.

Nicholas halted as his man approached. "What is it?"

The knight gestured toward the far side of the courtyard. "If you have not found your squire, he is in the stable."

He glanced toward the newly constructed building. The disappointment he'd experienced at waking to find his squire gone from his chamber resurfaced. After the shared confessions between them last night, and learning a slice of Thomas's past, he'd believed they had reached a crossroads of sort. To awaken and discover Thomas gone without a word was a slap to his pride.

"My thanks." Frustrated he'd not read Thomas better, Nicholas strode toward the building. Had the similarities between their youths clouded his normally keen judgment, leading him to make decisions with his heart instead of his mind? The shortcomings in this instance could very well be his—a hard fact to consider or accept.

Straw crunched under his feet as he entered the stable and the scent of hay and horses greeted him. A gelding whinnied, another snorted and pawed the earth. Near the back, he caught sight of Thomas grooming a steed.

At his approach, Thomas glanced over, paused midstroke. Shimmers of early morning light flickered over his face, illuminating the apprehension in his eyes.

Doubts toppled over frustration as Nicholas neared. Had anything truly changed between them? What had he expected, a day of setting an example and Thomas would understand that he was a man of his word, someone he could trust?

Tension knotted in the back of his neck. Yes, 'twould seem he had. Who better than he knew the true meaning of having someone care for you enough to take the time to make a difference? And how dare he become secure in this arena and believe he could walk into this lad's life and ease his high-strung emotions with meager effort. Hadn't he experienced firsthand the torrent of emotions one could feel, the pain, the angst, and the long years of work involved to overcome the challenges faced?

And he'd been fortunate. Through it all his uncle's strength and love helped to keep him focused as to his true reason. Shame washed through him. Yes, he was indeed a fool to expect so much so soon from a lad who believed him to be his enemy.

Humbled, Nicholas drew in a deep breath, focused on the positive progress made. However much the lad seemed to deny the fact, a bond existed between them, a connection he would nurture.

He halted before Thomas. The lad shuffled uncomfortably, bringing Nicholas back to his purpose. Whatever his emotional oversight, it didn't forgive his squire for vanishing from his chamber this morning without a word. A fact the lad would learn now.

He stepped closer.

Thomas's breath caught, his eyes darted toward the exit, but to his credit he held.

"Why did you leave the chamber this morning without my knowledge?"

The lad's fingers tightened on the curry. "I—I . . . I had much on my mind and I couldna sleep."

"Your place is to serve me, not traipse about on a whim. If you needed to talk, you only had to wake me."

A flush stained his face. "I am sorry."

Though his squire's eyes portrayed sincerity, Nicholas pressed on. The lad must fully understand the consequences his irresponsible actions could yield. He took another step bringing him inside the stall and a pace away from his squire. Close enough to see the flecks of gold shimmering in the emerald depths, to be caught by their secrets, secrets Thomas seemed bound and determined not to share. "If you cannot perform your duties as your position requires, you will be released."

Thomas's face paled.

Nicholas continued, resolute to press his point home. "A disobeyed order or act of negligence during combat could cost us our lives. If you cannot even perform the simple task of remaining in my chamber to aid me donning my garb, how can I entrust you to guard my back in the heat of battle?" He shook his head. "The answer is simple. I cannot."

The lad swallowed hard. His lower lip trembled. "I didna think—"

"No," Nicholas interrupted with a hard edge. "That you did not." His temper rose another notch as he remembered that none of his guards had witnessed the lad's departure. "If you had you would not have slipped through my castle like a thief. I refuse to tolerate further insolence, however slight." He curled his hand on the hilt of his sword. "If you wish to remain as my squire, you will pledge your troth to serve me faithfully from this moment forth. If you cannot do that"—he glanced toward the portcullis—"the gates of the castle are open." He leaned down to within an inch of Thomas's face.

The lad's eyes widened.

"But I warn you," Nicholas said with a dangerous calm. "If you leave, and if I catch you reiving again, you will not have a second chance. You will pay the price for your crimes to their full extent." He straightened. "'Tis your decision. Make it now."

Fear tore through Elizabet as the castellan's ultimatum to pledge her troth to serve him faithfully now or leave echoed in her mind. She couldna leave now. Nor could she tell him the truth. If he found out she had searched through his ledger to find her brother's name, he would toss her out on her ear, and rightly so.

Mary, Mother of God, when had this entire situation gotten so out of hand? The last thing she wished to do was to care about an English knight who served as a pawn for King Edward. She should hate the castellan, despise him, but instead she found herself beginning to trust Nicholas, to respect a man who should by all rights be her enemy.

"'Tis the decision so hard?" Nicholas snapped.

She jumped as heat stole up her cheeks. The turmoil roiling through her threatened to shatter her fragile hold on her riotous emotions. "I—I will stay."

Nicholas gave a dissatisfied grunt and slid his hand up his leather baldric halting midway. "I am not asking you if you will stay. I am asking for your loyalty. If you are someone I can count on." He paused, his gaze searching, probing with a fierce intensity. "Are you someone I can trust?"

This was the only way to save Giric. "Aye. I swear to you, while within your employ, I will serve you well." The roughness of her reply revealed more of her upset than she wished. She prayed he would take her anguish for shame, her hesitation for humility, and nae ascertain the truths she concealed.

As he studied her, her respect for the man grew. Though she had pledged fealty to the enemy, he was a man whose word she felt she could trust, and a man whom, if he went into harm's way, she would follow without question. The castellan's mouth thinned into a tight line, then he nodded. "Upon my return from morning rounds you will begin training with arms." He arched a brow. "Do you have a sword?"

Elizabet shook her head. She couldna tell him that in Wolfhaven Castle, a claymore crafted especially for her sat readied.

He nodded. "Upon my return I will find you a weapon."

She cleared her throat. "Thank you, Sir Nicholas."

The tension creasing his face slowly ebbed. A twinkle stole into his eyes. "Mayhap by the end of our first session you will not be so quick in your thanks."

At his unexpected teasing she found herself charmed. Shaken, she crossed her arms over her midriff, an ineffectual shield to her growing fascination toward him. Elizabet forced her mind away from this dangerous ground, remembering all too well the aches and pains to be found with the training of arms. The tangible reminder would be as welcome as necessary. She needed to keep her perspective.

"Mayhap you are right," she replied.

A hint of a smile touched his lips, then faded.

The sense of loss was immediate. Elizabet wished things were different, the time, the setting, but she might as well wish for the fairies to appear before her eyes.

Suddenly, a shaft of sunlight danced in a darkened corner, raced up the sturdy wood wall of the stable, then disappeared.

Stunned, she glanced to see if Nicholas had witnessed the miracle of light, but his unmoved gaze assured her he had nae. *'Twas but an errant ray of sunlight reflected off of the hilt of his sword*, but she couldna dismiss the shiver or apprehension racing through her or the question of if a fairy had indeed listened to her plea.

"Upon my return then," Nicholas said.

She nodded. Her mind a mix of worry for Giric and intrigue for Nicholas, Elizabet saddled his horse.

After mounting his steed, the castellan, along with a small division of his men, cantered through the gates. Dust swirled in their wake, clouding their exit like the confusion muddling her mind.

Rubbing her temple, she stared at the dungeon on the opposing end of the courtyard. Sunlight shattered across the quarried stone filled with macabre blends of grays, browns, and blacks. She frowned, remembering her promise given to Nicholas only moments before. Aye, in the future she would serve him well—except in matters concerning Giric.

Her loyalty toward her brother must come first.

How was she going to gain entrance into the dungeon? She released a frustrated sigh. And when she tried, would the guards let her in? Had Nicholas passed orders to his men to forbid his squire entry?

Hope sliced through her. What if he hadna?

She glanced toward where the errant beacon of light had shimmered with magical promise moments ago. "Please, if you are listening, let his men be ignorant of this fact." And she prayed the fairies were listening.

Elizabet glanced toward the exit.

The sun's ray now streamed through the crenulations, streaking swaths of golden light along the opposite stone wall toward the earth.

Nicholas would be gone a few hours. She needed to gain access before his return, but how?

"What are you doing?" a curious but cautious young voice asked from her side.

Startled, she turned. About four paces away stood the lad who had chased the pig around the courtyard upon her arrival. In his eyes she read adoration, the kind she'd held for her brother and other men who had commanded respect from her father. Mayhap because of her position as squire, the lad now put her in such a light? The youth's misguided respect left Elizabet feeling all the more a fraud.

"Yo—You were staring at the corner." He dropped his gaze and shuffled nervously.

She nudged a strand of her unruly hair behind her ear. Had he witnessed the glimmer of light? "I was dreaming." In reality, with the odds of her getting into the dungeon, she may as well be. But, 'twould behoove her to make friends while she was here. "My name is Thomas."

The youth lifted his eyes to her. "I am called Malcolm. My position is to assist the cook, but one day, I, too will become a squire and learn to wield a sword."

"Indeed you will," she agreed. "Where are you headed?"

"I am on my way to fetch the healer." He shot her a glance of pure envy. "But I would rather be tending the horses, or another task." He paused. "When I was walking past, I saw you and . . ."

"I understand," she finished as an idea formed in her mind. This could be the opening she needed. Mayhap besides bringing the healer to the dungeon, she could aid her as well. That would allow her to discover if Giric still lived. "I am finished here and could fetch the healer for you."

He grimaced as he mulled the idea. "'Tis my responsibility."

"Indeed, but I have seen you about the castle. You are kept busy."

"Aye," he said as if pondering the validity of having another do the task. "The cook is always wanting something, and I still have to chop wild onions and mushrooms for the stew and haul wood for the cook's fire."

She smiled. "Let me do this for you."

Malcolm hesitated, then nodded. "'Twill give me a few extra minutes to gather some meat from the larder. It would nae be like I was shirking my duties."

"I did ask," she assured him, finding herself won over by his indecision, remembering herself at his tender age.

He eyed her a moment. "I doubt Ihon would ever know."

"Nae from my lips."

A smile touched his mouth, and his blush deepened. "My thanks."

Elizabet nodded. "You are welcome."

After giving her instructions on how to reach to the healer's hut, Malcolm turned as if to leave, then hesitated.

"Was there something else?" she asked.

He shuffled his feet then drew in a deep breath. "After you learn how to fight . . . I mean, one day when you are a knight . . . Could you . . ."

She smiled. "When Sir Nicholas teaches me to handle a sword and once I am proficient, I will train you."

His eyes widened. The respect in his gaze grew. "Th—Thank you. You will nae regret your offer." A smile pasted on his face, he darted toward the keep.

With a sigh she watched him go. Perhaps she could train him with a sword, but nae here. Neither could she let on that she already knew how to wield a blade.

Setting aside her brush, Elizabet picked up a bucket and walked to the well. Before the round crafted rock, she looked down. A bottomless vat of inky blackness swam before her. Her fear of the dark, of confined spaces, swept over her. Shaken, she shoved aside the horrific event of her past, filled the bucket, and hauled it to the horse.

She glanced toward the still-darkened corner where mayhap a fairy indeed had listened to her plea. She smiled. 'Twould seem an opportunity to gain entrance into the dungeons had been delivered after all.

CHAPTER 6

The pungent aroma of sage stood out among the numerous scents as Elizabet stepped inside the healer's hut. Bundles of dried herbs hung from the ceiling on forged hooks like a ragged, storm-fed sky. The musty green leaves of sage billowed amidst the faded white flowers of catmint, then entwined with the spiraled tendrils of mandrake and sheaths of horsetail to blend in with a rich myriad of many other herbs.

On an old, roughly crafted table, a ceramic bowl sat on its side, yellowed from use over time. Alongside lay a pestle chiseled from stone. Small ceramic pots, some open and several sealed with wax, sat nearby. In the corner by the hearth, a thick wool spread, void of design, draped over the small, narrow bed of straw shoved against the wall.

"Hello?" Elizabet called.

"I will be right there," an old woman replied from the back.

Elizabet peered toward the sound. In the far corner, kneeling between dense bundles of herbs, an elderly woman was bent over a basket. Curious, she crossed the room then watched as the healer plucked dried peppermint leaves at a brisk rate.

"I told you I would be right there," the woman said without turning, irritation sliding through her voice.

"I am sorry."

The old woman glanced back. Shrewd brown eyes canopied by flesh and time studied her without apology. With a humph, she returned to her task. She pulled several more leaves from the stem. "I have never seen the likes of you before."

"'Tis my second day at Ravenmoor Castle."

The healer tossed the stripped branch of peppermint into a growing pile on the dirt floor, then grabbed another leaf-filled one. "So why are you here, lad?"

"You are needed at the dungeons to tend to the prisoners. I was sent to bring you."

With deft hands, she removed the last few leaves, tossed the barren stem aside, then stood. "A sad state of affairs it is," the healer grumbled as she wiped her hands against her course brown tunic. She shot Elizabet a shrewd glance. "Squeamish about going in?"

"Nae, I have . . ." What? Explain she had nae seen the prisoners but feared for the life of her people? Coldness stole over her, and Elizabet fisted her hands at her side.

"'Tis all right, lad." A heavy smile worked its way into the healer's pruned face. "You would think I would be immune to the sight of blood and death by now, but at times I find myself sickened."

The grim image of her father's body carried from the dungeon haunted her mind, and Elizabet shuddered. God in heaven, what were the conditions within the dungeon? However horrific, as long as Sir Nicholas didna discover her plans, she would soon find out.

The elder moved with surprising agility and picked up her basket, then set it on the aged table. "Do you have a name, lad?"

Elizabet unfurled her fists. "Thomas."

"Call me Deredere." With efficient movements, she packed a small leather pouch between two vials of oil separated by clean cloths, then secured the wicker lid. "Thomas? From where?"

"Wolfhaven Castle." Why had she given her the truth! 'Twas too late to change her answer now. Regardless, she and the healer were but talking. Nicholas would never learn of her answer.

The healer gave a slow nod. "I have tended to a few people within the castle."

Nerves slid through Elizabet. "We should be going," she urged, needing to circumvent further discussion of this topic.

The old woman nodded, but her eyes held Elizabet's a moment longer as if reading her soul.

Trying to shake off her unease, Elizabet gestured toward the basket. "Would you like me to carry that?"

"Nay." She slid the basket onto the crook of her arm. "Your escort is enough."

"I am here to assist you."

Deredere lifted a doubtful brow. "What would a lad like you know about healing?"

"Let me help, please. Herbs and healing are of great interest to me." A glint of softening lit the healer's eyes, and Elizabet pressed her advantage. "If I get in your way, I will leave. I swear."

After a slow, decisive exhale, the healer nodded. "I willna be having you beneath my feet." She narrowed her thick dapple-gray brows. "The men need to be treated, nae gawked at and pitied."

Elizabet gave a solemn nod. "I understand."

"See that you do." She ambled toward the door. "Let us be on our way then."

Excitement filled her. Soon she'd discover if Giric was alive! She followed the healer outside, and prayed the guards would allow her in the dungeon.

The sun inched higher into the morning sky as Elizabet, riding beside the healer, cantered toward Ravenmoor Castle. She searched the rolling fields and scoured the dense forest beyond, half-expecting to see Nicholas and his men returning early and catch her.

Naught.

It should be another two hours before his return, but she stole one final glance behind her as they headed through the gates.

The clatter of their mount's hooves thrummed the ground as they rode into the courtyard. The dungeon loomed before them. The weathered rock seemed to whisper of secrets, torture, and death. Trembling, she dismounted and tethered their horses.

Her expression tight, the healer headed toward the tower.

On edge, Elizabet followed. The shadow of the circular stone turret engulfed them in a cool, dismal swath, and a tremor prickled over her skin.

"Lad," Deredere said.

"Ay—Aye?"

"You are white as sun-bleached cloth. 'Tis nae a problem if you decide you canna face the wounded. One of the guards can assist me."

"Nay," Elizabet said quickly, her breathing shallow, her heart pounding. "I must . . ." She paused and tried to calm her fears before she gave herself away, but flashes of her father's body ripped through her mind. "I am fine." Before the healer could question her further, Elizabet jerked open the door and hurried toward the dungeon.

"The lad has nae a wit of sense," the healer muttered in her wake.

Elizabet's steps echoed around her as she moved up the steps, each haunting her like a drum of death. In moments she would know. Please let Giric be alive!

"Halt." The guard blocked her path as she reached the landing.

Sir Nicholas had ordered the guard to nae allow her inside! Frantic, she stepped closer. "Please, I—"

"Enough!" The guard frowned at the healer struggling up the steps. "You should be helping the healer instead of worrying about yourself." With a sharp look he stepped past her, lifted the basket from the old woman's hands, then he made his way to where Elizabet stood. "Where is Sir Nicholas?"

"He is out on rounds." She held her breath and prayed he didna refuse her entry.

The guard studied her as if unsure. "You are here to escort the healer?"

Her every nerve sang. "Aye."

"Next time, carry her basket," the guard snapped. "'Tis heavy."

Relief filled her. The guard had stopped her because she'd nae aided the healer. "The healer said she could carry it."

He frowned. "Aye, she is a stubborn one, but 'tis your duty when you are escorting her here."

"In the future I will." As he handed her the basket then stepped back, any worries of Nicholas's having left orders for her to be banned entry from the dungeon fled. But the castellan would find out. 'Twould nae matter at that point for she would know the fate of her brother.

Elizabet took in the thick wrought iron door. Please, let Giric be in there and alive.

Metal scraped as the guard pulled the entry open.

Shabby sunlight sifted through the dank chamber in faded streams, and the faint odor of death permeated the air.

Nausea swept her, and she almost wretched. Mary, Mother of God, how could anyone remain in these inhumane confines and survive? Dread filling every step, she scanned the narrow cells. A wash of faces, all familiar, swam into view: several archers, knights, the master of the hunt.

All except Giric.

The air grew thin, hard to breathe. He must have been the man who had died this morning.

"Lad?"

The healer's hand touched her shoulder, and Elizabet jumped. She tried to quell her rising fear. "I . . . I didna expect the conditions to be so wretched."

The healer eyed her, then nodded toward the far end of the dungeon. "We will treat the severely injured first." With a tsk, she took the lead.

Numb, Elizabet followed her, nae trusting herself to speak. As they made their way toward the back, several men from Wolfhaven Castle eyed her hard, and a new fear arose. Had they identified her? If so, please let them nae call out her name!

When she passed the falconer in his cell, recognition flashed in his gaze, followed by a scowl. Elizabet pressed a finger to her lips and gave a brief shake of her head.

The falconer nodded his understanding, his scowl of displeasure remaining.

However angry the falconer was at her being here, if she saved them, 'twas worth the risk. She glanced forward; the healer was near the end. She hurried to catch up, passing empty cells on occasion, cells that had once housed living, breathing men, mayhap even her brother.

The heavy wheezing of a man a bit farther down broke into her somber musings. Pain rolled from his every breath

She glanced past Deredere and froze. In the cell at the end of the corridor lay her brother.

Another tormented moan rolled from his lips. Giric jerked, then twisted as if fighting an invisible demon. A wool blanket that had once covered him lay tossed onto the cold stone floor.

"Giric!" Elizabet hurried to follow the healer into the cell.

The healer shook her head as she knelt beside her brother. " 'Tis a shame." With her eyes on Giric, she waved Elizabet forward.

Trembling, she set the basket on the stone floor. "Will he live?" she asked, wanting to reach out and soothe the man who was everything good in her life.

The elder shook her head as she withdrew several leather sacks and began measuring small amounts of powdered herbs. "I am unsure." Once finished, she secured each sack, then returned them to the basket. "He has been ill for days and with each that passes, his condition worsens."

Needing to touch him, Elizabet knelt by his shoulder. She took a rag and dampened it with some cool water from her leather pouch, then wiped his brow. *Live, damn you!*

Giric jerked against her touch. "Nay! Bloody Sassenach. To your right, Colyne!"

"Hold him," the healer ordered as she fought to pin his arms.

Desperation seized her. "Stop it!" Elizabet whispered in his ear, tears rolling down her face, stunned that in his delirium he'd mentioned Colyne MacKerran, the Earl of Strathcliff, who'd offered for her hand, but a man she didna love. Her brother shifted, and she focused on him. "I am here now."

At her voice Giric settled, and his brow wrinkled into a deep frown. He opened his eyes glazed with pain. "Elizabet?"

Mary's will, what had she done? She glanced at the healer, expecting the worst.

The elder gave a sympathetic tsk then released him, apparently satisfied her patient had calmed down. " 'Tis naught to worry about, lad. He has mumbled the lass's name on and off since his arrival."

"Do you know who she is?" Elizabet asked, fighting for calm.

The aged woman shrugged. "Nay."

That was too close. Nerves slid through her as she watched the healer unwrap his bandages and inspect his wounds. He had several deep cuts on his body, with a nasty gash along his left side.

"'Tis probably this wound on his side that did him in," Deredere said, nodding toward the neatly sewn skin discolored with angry yellows and red. "The injury will have to be drained and repacked daily or the infection will kill him for sure." After treating the wound the healer rubbed salve on his cuts, then coaxed Giric until he sipped the powdered herbs she had mixed with water.

His throat worked and his face twisted into a grimace when he swallowed.

The healer laid his head back on the straw. "There is little more we can do for now." She gestured to Elizabet. "Cover him up and we will tend to the others."

As much as she wished to remain by his side, for now she'd be thankful to have found her brother alive. "I will be back," she whispered into his ear.

Giric shifted, but this time he didna speak.

The rest of their morning treating the wounded passed quickly. The joy of finding so many of her men alive entangled with the fear that they would die before she could set them free.

Elizabet covered her nerves by asking the healer questions about treating different wounds as they tended to the men. With surprising patience the elder answered each one, explaining the different herbs she used along with the dosage for each.

As their rounds ended and the healer started to leave, Elizabet stole a quick glance down the far end of the dungeon toward Giric.

"Come lad, we are finished for the day."

She hesitated, wanting to return and see her brother one last time without drawing suspicion. "What about the man who is running a fever? Can you check on him again before we go?"

Sadness filled the healer's gaze, and she shrugged. "Aye, we can, but I doubt there is any more that can be done for him today. Time will decide his fate."

A knot worked in her throat as Elizabet followed the healer down the narrow hall. When they arrived, thankfully Giric was asleep. His raven hair, mangled by sweat, dirt, and blood, half shielded his face. Elizabet wanted to scream at the injustice of the situation, to bring him to a warm chamber and nurse him back to health.

"The castellan should be informed of his condition," Elizabet said.

The old woman shot her a pensive glance. "Aye, he has, and he asked me to personally tend to this prisoner on every visit, and after report his condition."

"He has?" Shame filled Elizabet. She should have expected as much from Nicholas.

A frown settled on the healer's brow as she glanced down at Giric then back up toward her. "Do you know him?"

Elizabet looked her square in the eye. "He is a Scot. 'Tis enough."

Understanding dawned in Deredere's eyes and they softened. "Aye." Her quiet burr thickened as she glanced toward the prisoner. "That he is." Sadness creased her weary face. "'Tis hard to see our men rot in these cells, but they fight and die for Scotland's freedom. Never forget that."

Nay, she never would. "He deserves better."

"They all do, lad. They all do." With a sigh the healer lifted her basket. "'Tis time to go."

Elizabet took one last long glance at her brother. *I will be back, Giric. And I will rescue you from this den of hell along with the others.*

CHAPTER 7

Fatigue washed over Nicholas as his mount cantered under the portcullis. As he headed toward the stables, he slowed to a walk and shoved back his mail hood and padded coif, welcoming the fresh summer breeze and the softness of its scent.

He mulled his impromptu visit to the healer to learn of Lord Terrick's condition. Her stark recount of his deteriorating state worried him. This day he would move his prisoner to the keep and place him under guard. If left within the cell, he would die.

As he halted at the entry of the stable, Thomas moved from the shadows to meet him.

The pleasure at his squire's promptness changed to caution at the lad's stilted actions.

Thomas walked to his steed's head, caught the halter without meeting his gaze, and waited for him to dismount.

So, his squire didn't like the setdown he'd received earlier this morning? He would learn that life's lessons often came with a price. Nicholas dismounted. "After you have cared for my horse, meet me on the practice field."

Without turning, Thomas nodded.

Upset or not, the lad would show him respect and learn that he must face the situations life dealt him head-on. "I will have an answer, and you will look at me when you do it."

Thomas's shoulders stiffened. He curled the reins tight in his slender hands, drew himself up to his full height, and turned.

Nicholas had expected to see anger or irritation carved into his expression, but the fragile pain, the swollen redness rimming his eyes, and the heart-wrenching loss filling his gaze threw him off guard. Without hesitation, he stepped toward his squire then halted, realizing his intent. He'd almost swept the lad into a hug to whisper words to soothe, to try to ease his obvious hurt.

His squire watched him unsure, his eyes too wide, his face too pale, and his anguish tangible, painfully so. For a brief moment need flashed in the emerald depths before fading to despair.

God's teeth, he was going insane! "Go and be quick about it," Nicholas snapped before he gave in and consoled the lad. On a curse, he dismissed the slash of need in Thomas's gaze—a trick of the light, a bedeviling of his mind. He'd but censored his squire. 'Twas not as if he'd beaten him with a stick.

And sometimes words hurt the most.

Guilt erased the hard edge of anger. Battered by self-doubts, he stared at his squire as he hurried away. None of this made any sense.

Nicholas struggled to pinpoint exactly what he'd said to the lad to instill such a grief-stricken reaction, but as if an illusion of its own, the answer eluded him. He gritted his teeth wanting to scream, but finding through it all that he wanted to help.

On a muttered curse, he strode to the armory and called himself every kind of a lack-witted fool. No doubt his brother, Hugh, would be amused by his confusion. Until a moment ago, he would've joined in as well.

As he entered the armory, Sir Jon looked over. "Everything is set for this eve's meeting as you requested."

Nicholas nodded. So caught up in the moment, he'd forgotten to inform his squire of the upcoming evening's events. "I will be pleased when it is over."

Sir Jon nodded. "'Twill not be a gathering for the faint of heart."

"Indeed." Nicholas glanced toward the dungeon. "Take several men and move Lord Terrick to an empty chamber on the second floor of the keep. Ensure it remains under guard."

"Aye, Sir Nicholas." Mail clanked as the knight strode out the door.

Though Lord Terrick's condition weighed heavy on his mind, Nicholas focused on the upcoming eve. Meeting with the Wardens of the Western Marches from both English and Scottish soil, along with other border officials, was a necessary evil. He'd been warned that many times their discussions turned into drunken, fist-crunching brawls, and often the wardens on both sides of the border were as guilty of reiving as those charged. This night he was determined to keep peace between them, or at least a semblance of order for the few hours they would remain within Ravenmoor Castle.

From their assembly he hoped to establish his quest for peace and unravel any further dealings of the previous castellan, illicit or otherwise.

He walked to where the weapons were stored. Tonight and its worries would come soon enough. Now, to find Thomas a sword. After skimming through the pitiful selection, making a mental note to send the battered lot to the blacksmith along with a request to forge more, he withdrew the best from the bunch.

The tarnished steel of the sword would be Thomas's task to polish and maintain. For now the sharpening of the blade could wait.

The weapon balanced well in his hand. Pleased, Nicholas moved the sword through a rapid succession of maneuvers, wielding the blade with quick, efficient sweeps. He selected a partially moth-eaten but serviceable gambeson and headed toward the lists.

The clang of swords echoed behind Elizabet as knights began to spar in pairs around her while she kept watch for the castellan to appear.

Inside, her stomach churned. She'd thought herself composed, prepared to face Sir Nicholas upon his return from his rounds. But when he'd ridden through the gates, her emotions had begun to shatter, inch by unnerving inch. Then he'd dismounted and gazed at her with sincere concern, and the last barrier of her resistance had crumbled. When he'd taken a step toward her, it'd required all of her willpower nae to throw herself into his arms.

The desperate need to be held, to draw from his endless strength, startled her, but her unexpected vulnerability toward Nicholas left her off guard.

Elizabet glanced in the shadowed nooks of the repaired walls, half-expecting to see fey eyes brimmed with mischief glittering at her plight.

Blades rang out with a solid clash paces away.

"Saint's curse!" the knight to her right called out.

She glanced over as the fighter danced away from the bite of the sword.

His stocky opponent feigned to the left and away from his opponent's blade, then attacked.

Sadness slid through her as the men continued their practice. She appreciated their skill and respect for one another, and ached for both in her own life.

"Thomas," Nicholas called.

She turned. The castellan walked toward her with a smooth, deadly grace. A man accustomed to the fight as well as the win. 'Twas easy to imagine him wielding his sword, the play of his muscles as he moved through a series of quick rapid thrusts, or the gleam of victory in his eyes at his conquest.

Desire for Nicholas pulsed through her. Shaken, she shoved the emotion aside. How appropriate for the castellan to choose this moment to enter, in the midst of challenge, with the meeting of steel echoing around them.

Nicholas halted before her. Steel-gray eyes searched hers, darkened, then became guarded. "You are ready then?"

Never for you. "Aye."

He handed her a sword and a gambeson, then gestured toward a vacant corner sprinkled with sparse patches of grass. "We will begin the lessons there."

After donning the worn, padded tunic, she followed. As she was used to her lighter crafted claymore, the English broadsword weighed heavy in her hands. 'Twould be a test to adjust to this heavier, bulkier weapon, but when had anything with him been anything but a challenge?

After explaining the basic maneuvers to Thomas, Nicholas stepped back and moved into a defensive stance. "Remember what I said." He lifted his broadsword waist high.

Determination glittered in his squire's eyes as he nodded and followed his lead.

Nicholas walked him through each maneuver, pleased by Thomas's quick grasp of his instructions and proficiency at handling his weapon.

"This time," Nicholas said, "try to block my advance." He swung.

Thomas lifted his blade to fend off his blow as instructed.

He stepped to the side and delivered another hard strike.

His squire made the proper countermove and deflected his blade once again.

"Good," Nicholas said, impressed by the lad's innate ability. "Again." They worked for the next half hour without pause.

Sweat slid down his squire's face as Thomas feigned and lunged toward him, becoming more aggressive.

Nicholas danced back and easily averted his attack. A quick study indeed. The lad was ready for the next lesson. "On the battlefield never let your opponent unsettle you. Every swing must be wielded with purpose, not passion. When emotions become involved, they can overrule common sense, then 'tis easy to make mistakes. Remember that."

Emerald sparks flashed in his eyes. "I am nae a fool."

No, far from it. At this point, Nicholas wasn't exactly sure what the lad was; thief or victim, or mayhap a combination of both.

Again the secrets the lad withheld taunted him as did the change in their relationship. Through their time spent together over the past sennight, an intimate bond had ignited between them as precious as rare. It'd become more than the teaching, but personal. Yet Thomas refused to trust him enough to confide his worries.

Nicholas neatly avoided his squire's charge when he feigned to the right, then swung a quick, sharp blow. Questions festered. "Who hurt you so that you close yourself off to anyone?"

Surprise darkened to anger in Thomas's eyes. He blocked Nicholas's thrust. With a grunt he twisted his blade and served one of his own. "'Tis my affair."

That damn wall his squire chose to erect around him. The scrape of steel shuddered around them with a ragged hiss. "I would help you if you would give me the chance."

Thomas's eyes flashed. "Keep your bloody sympathy. I do nae need it."

Irritation severed Nicholas's good intent. He caught his squire's swing, then advanced with a series of intricate thrusts, pushing the lad back.

Pride and anger caught in a ruddy swirl in Thomas's expression as he fought for each breath, meeting him swing for swing.

At his squire's continued defiance, his anger rose. "You do not need anyone but your bloody self, do you?"

"I do nae need a blasted Sasscnach!" The scream of their blades backed his decree, hard, unforgiving.

Nicholas repelled another swing and drove forward with his sword. The lad stumbled back, cornered, but in the confusion of emotions, he felt as trapped as the lad. Bloody hell! 'Twas supposed to be a lesson in arms, naught more.

He rotated his sword and caught the hilt of Thomas's blade. With a sharp jerk he flung the weapon to the ground, leaving his squire unarmed. Without hesitation he lifted the tip of his blade to Thomas's neck.

The lad stilled. His breath tumbled out in jerky breaths, but instead of fear, Thomas's ferocious spirit burned in his gaze.

Shaken, Nicholas removed the sword. The intensity of emotions this youth incited unnerved him. "If your focus slips, even for a moment, you will lose all you sought to gain and mayhap more." His fingers clenched tight upon the hilt of his blade. In dealing with Thomas, 'twould do well for him to remember that advice as well.

Elizabet touched her throat where Nicholas's blade had pressed. Though the weapon was heavy and awkward to use, it'd taken every shred of her will to withhold her full ability with the sword he'd given her; but a part of her wanted to see how well she would hold her own against Nicholas, more so with her own blade.

"Thomas."

Startled by the intensity that had unfolded between them, she met his gaze. Shame filled her at the pride on the castellan's face, admiration she'd nae earned. Even in this, the simple act of learning to protect oneself, she deceived him. It appeared in her effort to free her brother she would lose a piece of her pride as well.

The castellan nodded. "You did well for your first spar."

Heat swept up her cheeks. Unable to face him further, she turned away.

Silence spanned the void broken by the nearby clash of steel.

"We are done for the day," Nicholas said. "When you are ready to trust me, I will be here."

His slow intake of breath then sigh of frustration matched her own. The day to trust Nicholas with the truth would never come. She tried to gather herself, halt this ridiculous flow of dismal self-pity. Regardless of how much she was coming to care for him, her destiny was set. Whatever the cost she would free her brother.

"Your muscles will ache on the morrow." The slide of the castellan sheathing his sword whispered behind her. "Clean your blade,"

She faced him, as off balance by the rough edge of his voice as the hurt in his eyes.

"Do you know how to care for the weapon?" the castellan asked.

"Aye."

He nodded. "Then be off with you."

Shaken by the emotions he inspired, she hurried off, anxious to be away from him, aware that she cared too much.

"Thomas," Nicholas called as she reached the exit.

She stopped, her breathing rapid, her pulse racing. Time. She needed time alone to settle her nerves, but even that small token was nae to be. She turned.

"I have called a meeting of the Wardens of the Western Marches this eve, along with other officials along the border. Your blade is to be readied by then and worn at your side. See Sir Jon about a leather belt and sheath."

Elizabet nodded, nae trusting herself to speak. She turned and almost stumbled as she hurried away. It'd been easy to fool the English knights of Ravenmoor Castle and the few remaining local villagers of her identity, but what about the wardens and the other gentry who would arrive in a few hours?

Over the years, her father, a respected leader of this land, had played an integral part in the keeping of law and order throughout the marches. On many occasions she'd welcomed the Wardens of the Marches and border officials into their home. Dressed as a lad and playing the role of a squire, would she be recognized by them?

At the armory she gathered the sand needed to clean her sword. Elizabet settled into a solitary corner near the guard shack and began to scrub the neglected steel. What was she going to do? She couldna risk the chance of being identified, but Nicholas expected her to attend him throughout the meeting.

A small patch of the tarnished blade began to gleam beneath her ministrations. Worry for her brother fevered in his cell ate at her as she continued working in slow circles. It would all work out, she had to believe such. Regardless, at this point, there was no turning back.

Hours later, a pitcher of ale in her hands, Elizabet hurried around the corner of the great room.

"What out!" a deep authoritative voice boomed.

Too late, she barreled into a tall, sturdily built man.

Narrowed hazel eyes glittered with unsheathed malice when she dared to glance up. "You clumsy fool. Out of my way."

The stench of mead clung to her as she scrambled from his path. "I am so sorry, my lord!"

Mail rattled as he stormed past.

Elizabet closed her eyes as the rich brew dripped from her bangs to slide down her cheeks like golden tears. So lost in her own worries, she hadna even considered that the Earl of Dunsten would be in attendance. Thank goodness he'd nae recognized her.

Fighting for calm, she bent down to mop up the spilled mead, and slid a glance toward the dais where Nicholas and the other officials sat, their voices raised in heated debate.

Lord Dunsten stepped onto the raised platform, confidence as well as arrogance embedded in his stride.

Conversation halted.

Nicholas stood and turned toward the new arrival, his gaze assessing. "Lord Dunsten, I am Sir Nicholas, castellan of Ravenmoor Castle, I bid you welcome."

After a brief introduction, Lord Dunsten took a seat. Within minutes the men became engrossed in the discussions of border law.

With a relieved sigh, Elizabet finished mopping up the sticky mess, then moved to the shadows. She must keep out of Lord Dunsten's sight.

As she stood shielded by the murky light, Dunsten's entreaty to her father for a marriage contract echoed in her mind. Thank heaven Giric had intervened and swayed her father's decision. Though they had played as children while their fathers discussed concerns of Scotland's future, she didna love Dunsten. Aye, a foolish belief in this day, but the wish to marry for love throughout the years lingered.

Nor could she forget the rift between her brother and Dunsten spanned many years. At the age of six and ten years, Giric had gone on a hunt with Dunsten. Her brother had returned, anger carved upon his face. When asked, Giric refused to reveal what had passed between them, but from that day forth her brother and Dunsten had remained at odds.

Giric's insistence to their father to deny Dunsten's request for marriage had served to add another wedge of dissent between the now grown men, one that still thrived.

Elizabet took in the earl as he debated with the officials halfway across the room chamber. Was he aware Sir Nicholas held her brother imprisoned within his dungeon? A shiver stole through her. More than likely he was aware, news that had pleased him. A new fear arose. Would he use her brother's imprisonment to his advantage, charge him with false crimes, and rid himself of Giric for good?

A warden slammed his fist on the table and rose; another heated argument ensued.

Elizabet jumped. What was she thinking? She couldna hide. Nicholas had sent her to fetch another round of mead. With a prayer she could avoid Lord Dunsten's notice this eve, she turned and hurried to refill her pitcher.

* * *

Tension began to ebb between the powerful men seated at the table, and Nicholas paused, intrigued by his squire's cautious approach, curious as to his drenched state. He lifted his tankard and drained the last few drops.

Considering the two times during the heated discussions that swords had been drawn in an angry retort, and twice he'd diffused each confrontation, he was pleased with how well the evening had fared. It had taken all of his experience as a mediator to keep the men focused on the topic without bloodshed; not an easy feat when mixing Englishmen and Scots.

Thomas worked his way along the table, refilling cups with the golden brew, but all the while he kept his gaze averted, and his body remained tense.

Sinking back in his chair, Nicholas took a long drink of his ale. He covertly scanned the powerful wardens surrounding him. The lad's cautious manner assured him Thomas knew at least one of the influential leaders. Whoever it was, the man terrified his squire.

Thomas halted at his side. "Would you like more, Sir Nicholas?"

Nicholas met him square in the eyes and kept his voice low. "Which man is it?"

Color fled from his squire's face. "Which man is what?"

That the lad should fear someone this much infuriated him. "Who do you know that you are afraid of?" Nicholas asked in soft demand.

"Please," Thomas whispered, his gaze slanting briefly toward the powerful men seated at the table. "Let me serve you and be gone."

The desperation laced within the soft-spoken plea convinced Nicholas to end the subject—for now. With the volatility of the officials gathered around the table, he needed his wits about him. After the meeting was another matter. Nicholas waved his squire away, but searched for recognition in any man's face as Thomas passed.

Naught.

Frustrated, he sat back, strummed his fingers upon the edge of the table. Secrets, he despised them. With a grimace, he lifted his cup and took a long draught. For the moment he would celebrate his achievement, but on the morrow Thomas's secrets would end.

* * *

"*And the whoreson shall live no more,*" Nicholas's rich voice sang out in a deep, hearty bass, but in a key that would surely rival a wounded bear.

The fire in the hearth popped cheerfully, warming his immense chamber as Elizabet rolled her eyes at his drunken rendition of an English fighting song.

The bells of Matins pealed.

She glanced out the window. Stars glittered in the sky, but soon streaks of dawn would come. Regardless of the late hour, after she'd helped Nicholas stumble into the room, he had demanded a bath.

She scrubbed the damp linen on the bar of soap until it formed a thick lather as she eyed the castellan propped in the wooden tub with frustrated tolerance. Even drunk, why did he have to be so charming?

Nicholas kicked back and plunged into the next chorus with fervor, and water sloshed over the sides of the wooden tub to join a growing pool.

He opened his mouth, but before he sang another word, she clamped her washrag over his mouth, stifling the next off-key verse.

"Lad," he sputtered as he shoved away the offending linen. "'Tis no way to . . . I say 'tis no way to treat your kniiiight!" He shot her a fierce frown, but the slurred sentence punctuated by the hiccup stole the impact of his inebriated threat.

The smile she'd fought to suppress as she'd guided him up to his chamber this night stole to her lips. He was incorrigible, but in an enchanting manner. She sighed and again began to scrub his broad shoulders hewn by countless battles. How could she nae be charmed by this fierce warrior when he wallowed in such a defenseless drunken state?

He lolled his head back and closed his eyes as she continued to scrub, giving her ample opportunity to view him at leisure.

Running the soaped cloth over his well-muscled chest sheathed in a mass of silken curls, she braved sliding it down into the lukewarm water to wash his taut, flat belly. Honed muscle rippled beneath her touch, and excitement stole through her. How would it feel to be loved by this man, for his hands to skim over her flesh in a soft caress?

At her wayward thoughts, guilt filled her. She glanced up at Nicholas.

His eyes remained closed, and he lay limp against the wooden frame. On a mumble, a hearty snore fell from his lips.

Elizabet gave a soft laugh. So much for him noticing her interest. The warm fragrance of soapy water steamed between them as she knelt and rested her arms on the side of the tub.

Golden rays of candlelight flickered over his face in a soft caress, easing the hard lines.

How easy 'twould be to reach out and ruffle his sodden hair, to trace her fingers over his jaw, or to lean forward and steal a kiss.

Struggling to deal with all this man made her feel, she shoved to her feet. Why couldna he be the callous Englishman she'd expected? This position as his squire was temporary. She was a fool to think it could lead to anything more.

Nicholas would be furious to learn his squire was nae a deprived lad that life had treated with a callous hand, but a woman of stature who had used his empathy for her own goals. Nay, he must never find out. Such a discovery would put her life in jeopardy, worse it would end her chance of freeing her brother and people.

He gave a soft snore.

For the heartache he caused her, 'twould serve him well if she left him in the tub overnight. She grimaced. Like it or nae, at this moment he needed her. And like it or nae, she needed him as well.

Resigned to her task, she moved behind his head and worked her hands under his arms. His rich scent of male and soap teased her, and desire stormed her senses. Blast it! "Up you drunken beast."

He mumbled something about his sword as he rose an inch in her arms.

She tugged. He was as heavy as weighted armor! She let go.

With a splash, Nicholas slid back into the tub and gave a low snore.

With the front of her tunic soaked, she stood, placed her hands on her hips. If the situation wasna so hopeless, 'twould be funny. Should she go to the great hall and fetch his men to help her? Nay, after the meeting that had turned into a drinking fest, she would be hard-pressed to find a man less drunk than the castellan.

Well, the sodden beast would just have to help. She nudged his shoulder none too gently. "Wake up."

"Is my horse readied?" Nicholas slurred.

She'd give him a horse—a clonk over his head with the blasted shoe was more like it. " 'Tis time to go to bed." She gave him another nudge. "Get up. I canna lift you myself."

A sensual grin slid to lips. "Anicia?"

Jealousy sliced Elizabet, and she released him. What had she expected? She'd nae guarded her speech, and he'd heard a woman's voice. Her spirit sagged further. Who was Anicia? A friend? More like his mistress, a woman who'd tasted his lovemaking many times over.

"Where is my bloody sword?" Nicholas grumbled.

Disgusted by her own regret, she caught his shoulders and shook him hard. "Get up, Sir Nicholas. 'Tis late and you need to seek your bed."

His eyes flicked open. "To bed?" He wrinkled his brow then searched the chamber with a sluggish look. "Anicia?"

Her throat tightened. "Nay," she replied, deepening her voice. " 'Tis Thomas, your squire. You are dreaming." She tugged on his arm. "To your feet now. I canna carry you alone."

"Ah, Thomas lad." With her help, Nicholas struggled to his feet. Water sloshed over the sides of the tub as he fought for balance.

As he stepped out, Elizabet tightened her grip, steadying him as best as she could. Only by the grace of God did she aid him from the tub without him taking them both to the floor. The moment of victory faded when water streamed down her tunic as his naked body pressed against hers.

"Sir Nicholas, I—"

"No more rambling lad. To bed!"

The bed. She would nae think of that! Too aware of him, she tried to focus on her task and ignore the intimate press of his muscled body against hers. Well into his cups as he was, she doubted the castellan could even see the bed much less distinguish that she was nae a he.

A mixture of pleas and tugs brought him to the edge of his bed. Relieved to be able to escape his nearness, she released him and made to move away; but he swayed then floundered.

Flailing, he reached out and caught her shoulders.

"Nicholas—" Elizabet lost her balance and tumbled onto the mattress.

With a grunt, he landed on top.

Her breath left her in a rush. 'Twas a blasted plot! "Get off of me, you oaf." She shoved against his massive chest thick with water-slicked hair, trying to ignore how his body fit perfectly against hers and how his lips hovered but a breath away. "Nicholas!"

He didna budge.

Elizabet closed her eyes as his honed curves pressed against her with sensual heat. A fine mess! She tried to pry him off.

At her shove, Nicholas's eyes opened. Confusion filled his gaze as he stared at her. Then, passion darkened his eyes to a deep smoky gray and he grew hard.

Panic assaulted her as her body answered with a burst of need.

His gaze shifted to her lips.

Her body burned. How she wanted to kiss him. Mary, Mother of God, what was she thinking! "Nicholas!" Her words came out in a panicked rush as her body pulsed with desire.

A low, sultry laugh filled with intimate promise seduced her further. "Do not be afraid." He lowered his head. "'Twill be good, I promise."

And that was what she was afraid of. "Nich—"

His mouth muffled her plea as he captured her lips, silencing any further protest. She tried to resist, but his taste, the softness of his assault, and her own undeniable hunger stripped away further protest. And why nae enjoy this moment? He would be none the wiser, and this would be her only chance to ever get close to him as a woman.

With her conscience appeased, Elizabet fell into his kiss. Like a hot summer day he warmed her, teasing her with the beauty of it all. He nibbled her lower lip. On a moan he slid his tongue into her mouth.

As if the most natural response, she answered, tasting, teasing, giving back and demanding more. A low groan swirled deep in his throat as her body spun out of control.

His hands captured her face with infinite tenderness as he deepened the kiss.

"Nicholas," she murmured, lost to sensations.

He pressed kisses on her cheek, along the curve of her jaw, then worked at a slow, torturous pace down the column of her throat, halting every bit to glide his tongue across her sensitive flesh in a destroying assault. With a groan of appreciation, his hand cupped her breast, his finger stroking her nipple until it grew taut.

Though she'd never lain with a man, any shame fled at the rightness of the moment. "Nicholas."

His mouth curved in a lopsided grin, and he continued his sweet torment until she could only feel, respond to the waves of pleasure coursing through her. That he shifted, and she nay longer lay pinned beneath him, mattered little. All she could do was experience, want, beg for more.

"Nicholas, please . . ."

His hand slid down to her most private place and stroked her slick folds with mind-teasing expertise. "In time, Anicia."

She froze. Humiliation engulfed her and Elizabet rolled away and scrambled to her feet. What had she been thinking? Nay, she hadna a thought in her mind except being with him! Her body aching with need, she stared down at Nicholas.

He reached out for her, and confusion slid into his gaze. Then his lids flickered twice before they finally closed. He sighed a quiet, lonely sound and began to snore.

Tears burned her eyes as she made her way to her pallet, missing his touch, and shamefully, wanting him still. She'd been a fool to dare even a simple kiss. A rough laugh fell from her lips. Naught about that kiss had been simple.

Regardless of how much she wanted him, he was English, an enemy who held her brother within his dungeon, and a man she must keep at a distance.

CHAPTER 8

A dagger plunged through his skull. Nay, ’twas more like a mace. As his head pounded and nausea wrenched in his gut, with great care he brought the back of his hand to rest over his brow.

What a pathetic state.

On a groan, he drew in a slow breath, struggling for the next. The distant shrill of a morning bird shattered through the wash of pain.

God’s teeth!

Nicholas braved opening one eye, then the other. Firelight flickered over the room in a soft glow. Through the window, streaks of dawn caressed the sky, silver through gray, orange through black; but the throb of pain obliterated the beauty before him. He closed his eyes willing the hours, like his misery, to flee.

“Would you care for water?” Thomas asked, his voice a beacon in this storm of misery.

“My dagger,” he forced out, wincing at the cost. ’Twould be the only way to end this agony.

“I . . . Your dagger?”

If not for the pain the gesture would bring, he would have smiled at his squire’s confusion. “Fetch me the water.” His whispered words slammed through his head as his mind remained under siege.

The soft pad of footsteps moved away.

Blast it, but he was too old to endure this living hell. He opened his eyes and sat up. The room spun. Even the quiet glide of the sheets against his skin hurt.

As Thomas approached, he stole a covert glance toward him then dropped his inquiring gaze, but not before Nicholas caught the concern etched there.

His squire held out the wooden cup.

"My thanks." Nicholas curled the mug in his hands like a lifeline, then downed the contents. The bitter liquid slid down his throat, igniting a fresh wave of pain to assault his head. He tossed the cup; it bounced on the floor with a mind-screaming clatter. "God's teeth, what was in there?"

With an appraising glance, his squire retrieved the cup, clutched it to his stomach. "Herbs to aid thee."

Nicholas laid his palm over his brow and willed the pain away. "Herbs?"

"Iceland moss for your stomach and feverfew for your aches." Thomas refilled the mug and held it before him. "This time 'tis only water."

Nicholas debated accepting the brew, but the bitter aftertaste in his throat won over. He emptied the cup, thankful for the cool slide, then returned it to his squire.

The lad walked to a corner table where two small leather bags sat. Without looking back, he cinched the first sack then stowed the cup inside a nearby pack.

Unsure if he should be grateful to be so accurately read, he studied him for a moment. "You have done this before?"

Thomas shrugged but didn't turn. "I do what is necessary."

"And am I necessary?" Each word fell out with a measured calm. Whatever existed between them was a hell of a lot more than necessary. He wanted his squire's respect, and to make a difference in his life.

Thomas's fingers fumbled as he tied off the second sack. Once secure, he stowed the pouch. "I . . ."

Why was getting answers from him like pulling an ox from the mud? "Face me when you speak to me!" Pain rushed him with merciless force. Nicholas cradled his head in his hands. If he lived through this he would never imbibe to such limits again.

With a hesitant move, his squire turned. Firelight fluttered across his face, haunting his eyes and the apprehension swirling within.

Silence, broken only by the crackle of flames and the hush of the soft breeze, filled the chamber. Tension thrummed through Nicholas, matching the throb in his head. "Answer my question."

Regret slid through Thomas's gaze before he could shield the emotion. "By taking me on as your squire you have offered me hope when I had little."

He hesitated, unsure if his squire had answered the question. Rubbing his temple, Nicholas owed his confusion to the lingering haze of ale.

The meeting with the Wardens of the Western Marches last eve came to mind and Thomas's hesitancy when around the powerful Scots, along with his resolve to find answers to his questions as well. "Which man did you know last eve?"

Thomas cleared his throat. "You will be wanting something to eat."

Blast it. "Do you think I would let anyone harm you?"

His squire hesitated. "Nay."

"Then why do you evade my questions, give me half-answers, or keep the truth from me at every turn?"

"I think you are a fair man."

Then he understood the lad's reserve, and had missed the obvious from the start. "And you did not want me to be fair, did you?"

Flames curled and drifted up in the hearth. Thomas released a slow, deep breath, then shook his head. "Nay." His hands clenched tight. "And you have no right to be!"

"Why?"

"Because you are English," he said, his voice raising a pitch with frantic desperation. "Because the Sassenach take without care and leave naught but devastation." Thomas's breath hitched. "And because 'twould be easier that way." His voice broke. "Then I could hate you."

He was stunned by the ferocity of his squire's charge, and his anger dissolved. Compassion filled Nicholas. Pain like this took years to foster. What had Thomas seen, experienced? He shuddered to think. "Who hurt you?"

Expression guarded, his squire took a step back. "This isna about hurt."

"Is it not?" A residual pounding pulsed in his head as Nicholas grabbed his braies and jerked them on. He pushed to his feet, ignoring his body's protests. "Last night when you served the ale, 'twas all you could do to avoid the men around my table."

The lad swallowed hard.

Nicholas stepped closer. "Why?"

"Please do nae do this."

His squire's harsh whisper halted Nicholas, but the flash of tears had him taking another step forward. To hell with propriety. He embraced Thomas and gave in to his own need to offer succor, to be there for the lad when it appeared everyone else had walked away.

The lad struggled in his arms, then his slender frame shuddered and he sagged against him.

Hot tears spilled against Nicholas's chest, but he held him close, understanding all too well the need for release, to empty oneself of the shame and humiliation, and having someone there who cared enough to make a difference.

After his father's death, he'd dealt with the sadness, but his legacy of shame as well. Now, with Thomas in his arms falling apart, the old hurt spiraled through him, the pain of abandonment, and the knowledge that his father was a coward.

Nicholas closed his eyes, stunned by the roll of emotion.

Like a warm caress, Thomas's sobs faded into tattered breaths upon his skin.

A sense of peace invaded Nicholas as he held his squire, as if a need fulfilled. His throat tightened, caught by the power of emotion rushing him, by the rightness of it, of wanting the moment to go on forever.

The hazy image of a woman entwined in his arms last night confused him. The erotic sensations even more. Flashes of heat, bodies wrapped in an intimate press, and the taste of her kiss teased him. Nicholas struggled to form a clear image of the woman's face.

Failed.

The bells of Prime tolled. A guard yelled to another. Laughter, then muffled voices, invaded the silence.

Thomas lay nestled within the circle of his arms, relaxed against his half-naked frame; and God help him, it felt so right. Staggered by the unnatural course of his thoughts, Nicholas caught the lad by his shoulders and held him away. He was going mad. There was no other answer.

Nicholas cleared his throat. "'Tis time to tend to the duties of the keep." And he needed to bloody get out of here!

Emerald eyes too wide, too sad, and tinged with burgeoning trust lifted to his with distress. Thomas sniffed. "I canna even do this right can I?"

God's teeth. It seemed that neither could he. Nicholas worked up a tender smile not wanting to frighten his squire. "I would say you are doing everything fine." He released him and took a step back, fighting to come to his senses, searching for answers to his unexplainable draw to this lad, answers that wouldn't come.

The familiar stubbornness worked its way back into Thomas's gaze much to Nicholas's relief. Someone needed to retain their grasp on sanity in this moment of madness.

A lone tear slid down the lad's cheek. He wiped it away with an angry slash. "Weak men cry."

As much as Nicholas wished to, he couldn't look away. The fierce pride of the lad held him. "No. Tears are only shed by those brave enough to love."

Thomas eyed him in silence.

"I need to don my garb," Nicholas said, unsure at which point he'd lost control as well as his mind. "The Wardens of the Western Marches will be awaiting my presence as well as the others."

His squire stepped back. "Aye, Sir Nicholas."

That cool mask shifted back onto the lad's face, and Nicholas wanted to shake him, to erase the indifference Thomas seemed to erect between them with ease when he barely held himself in check. Frustrated, he strode to the hearth, knelt, and threw another log on the fire.

* * *

Elizabet jumped as the wood clattered into the flames, shaken by the intimacy that had passed between her and Nicholas. This definitely wasna good. She hurried to gather the castellan's clothes. "Here." She handed him the hose, shirt, and tunic.

His face littered with confusion, he donned the garb.

Consumed by guilt, she turned to retrieve his boots. What a fool! How could she have allowed him to embrace her or stayed within his arms? Wanted more? Wanted him still?

Why do I not just tell him that I am a woman and end my misery?

By the saints she was a lackwit. After her stolen kisses last night, which he'd thankfully nae recalled, she should have applauded his misery from too much drink and left him to flounder with the resultant pain.

But she couldna watch him suffer. She glanced toward him, then looked away, wanting him and damning him more. Why did he have to be so blasted endearing!

"'Tis getting late." Elizabet knelt at his feet and shoved on his boots, trying nae to admire his well-muscled legs or his teasing scent of male with a hint of soap. Her blood warmed at the nearness, all too familiar with the feel of his body against hers. She glanced up, stilled.

He watched her with a cautious expression, as if not trusting himself.

And why shouldn't he? She had felt it, the thrill, the flash of desire when their gazes met. And from his panicked reaction when she'd looked at him moments ago in his arms, he'd experienced the same.

Mary's will. If she believed herself a convoluted mess of emotions, he must think himself more so. She had botched this from the start.

Nicholas stood, walked to the hearth where the flames danced before him with a mocking twist, shoved his hands upon his hips.

She forced herself to keep busy, setting the pack containing the herbs out of sight before he realized that lads rarely knew about healing. Another muddleheaded move.

"Was there a woman in here with me last night?"

The sack of herbs trembled in her hands. Oh God, he'd remembered! She shoved the sacks into the pack before they spilled. Calm. She must remain calm. "Sir Nicholas?"

He exhaled as if to continue then paused, mumbling something under his breath about a bloody dream. The castellan shook his head. "Never mind."

Mary, Mother of God, that was too close!

Dropping his hands to his side, Nicholas turned. A frown creased his brow as his eyes scanned hers assessing, undermining her crumbling bravado.

She stilled. What now?

"Which of the men below do you know?"

She gave a mental groan. Why had she believed he'd forgo that line of questioning? Elizabet shrugged. "They are all familiar to me."

He arched a brow. "All?"

Pinpricks skittered across her spine, and she gave a slow nod. "The Wardens of the Marches are known to all who live within their boundaries."

He muttered a soft curse. "I have not figured out who is the bigger fool, you for not trusting me, or me for trying to earn your trust."

"How could I nae trust you?" she said, finding it the truth. His every action bespoke a man to be admired, a man to count on. A man she wanted with her every breath.

"Give me something about the men below, Thomas."

Need churned within his heartfelt demand. At the very least, he deserved an answer. She moved toward the bed and began to make it, needing a release for her restlessness. "On occasion I have seen them. They are powerful men, leaders of their people." She faced him. "Though their duty calls for them to uphold the law, most ride beneath the night and raid across the borders. Or worse, steal from their kinsmen without remorse—as did Sir Renaud."

Sir Nicholas's eyes narrowed. "You knew the previous castellan?"

Relieved by the change of topic, she nodded. "Of him, to be exact." She tugged the sheets up, fighting to steady the fury that always accompanied thoughts of Sir Renaud. Once the sheets were drawn tight, she pulled the wool blanket on top, smoothing out the rumples with her hand.

"Of him?" Nicholas asked.

An icy calm settled over her as she straightened. "The previous castellan was an evil man. He reived as many of the other leaders do, but for him 'twas nae enough. 'Tis rumored Sir Renaud even stole from his own king by smuggling goods." She shook her head. "A more ruthless hand I have never heard of."

Nicholas remained silent.

She tried to stem the rush of anger, but 'twas too late. Sir Renaud was responsible for the uprising along the border, the deception to his king, and the murder of her father and many others. 'Twas time Sir Nicholas knew the truth.

"Worse," she continued, outrage fueling her words. "He blamed the Scots in his treachery against the crown and used their deaths as justification for his own barbaric acts. After murdering them in their beds, Sir Renauld claimed he'd chased them after catching them on his land. Or, he would charge the Scots with transporting illegal goods." A harsh laugh fell from her lips. "But he did nae halt there. He burned the Scots' homes, claimed their land as his own—"

"All with King Edward's backing," Nicholas broke in, his words tainted with indignance.

She halted, surprised he understood, then nae surprised at all. He was a rare man in this harsh world. "Aye."

Nicholas's eyes darkened to a dangerous cast. "And with the king behind his claims, none would challenge the right of it."

She nodded, pleased and distressed by his insight.

"King Edward never knew of Sir Renaud's crimes," Nicholas said, his voice gentling. "I swear it. He seeks peace. He would not condone the acts you have described."

She snorted her disbelief. "Your king laid siege and captured Ravenmoor Castle, once held by the Scots. 'Tis an act of war."

"Nay, 'tis an action of our times."

'Twas true the land upon the borders was often raided and claimed by the other country, but losing a piece of Scotland to English hands, even the most remote loch, was an unbearable thought.

"And what of your king's seizure of the Isle of Man? Or his negotiations in the Treaty of Birgham? Admit it. Your king doesna seek peace, but wants Scotland beneath his rule." She angled her jaw. "At least be honest enough to admit that."

He lifted a skeptical brow. "You are surprisingly well educated on political matters for a homeless Scot," he said, his voice too soft.

Heat flared on her face as she scrambled for an explanation. "If your country was threatened with war, at risk of being overtaken by another, would you nae listen as nobles discussed your country's fate?"

"Aye." Though his quiet response agreed, the wedge of doubt in his expression remained.

She stepped toward the door. "The men will be waiting below."

"So they will." He strapped on his broadsword, watching her all the while.

Elizabet moved closer toward the exit, tasting freedom.

"Wait."

Heart pounding, she paused.

"You have given me answers, though not the ones I wish to hear. But we both know that, do we not?" He shook his head as she opened her mouth to speak. "Rest assured, Thomas, in the end I will know."

Nicholas strode past her to the door, confidence exuding in his every step. When he opened the hewn entry, he turned to face her. Gray eyes narrowed. "I do not lose."

Icy chills rippled through her. "This isna a game."

"No, that it is not." He watched her a moment more. "I expect you downstairs posthaste. Be there or I am coming back for you." He stepped out, pulled the door shut with a firm snap.

Out of the fire and into the flames; Lachllan's words echoed through her mind, and loneliness for her mentor engulfed her. Except the steward was miles away.

Whatever happened now depended on her.

And in the next few hours somehow she had to manage to keep any of the Scots below from recognizing her.

Hours later, anxiety filled Elizabet as she hurried up the turret to the dungeon followed by the healer. At the top, she held up the basket to show the guard.

He nodded, allowing them to pass.

At least something had gone right this day. When the leaders had stayed until late morning, she had wondered if Nicholas would still complete his rounds or send his men to do the task without him. Thankfully he had delayed his knights' departure until his guests had departed. Now he was miles away, but his words from this morning haunted her.

Nay, a man like him didna lose.

She fought to quell her rising sense of doom. Time was running out. Only by mentioning Sir Renaud had she sidetracked Nicholas from more personal questions, questions she could never answer. But the time was coming when she couldna avoid the inevitable.

Both knew it.

Elizabet turned her focus to the task. As before, even with the use of lye soap and plenty of water to clean the dungeon, the stench of bodies and death assaulted her. She stanched the rise of nausea, needing her wits to tend to Giric. Had the fever passed? Would he recognize her this day? How was she going to free him along with the other Scots locked within these walls? Patience. She had nae come this far to give up.

"Lad," the healer called.

She turned. "Aye?"

"We will begin here." Deredere pointed to the cell on her right.

On edge, Elizabet glanced toward Giric's cell at the end of the narrow corridor. "Yesterday we began with those who needed aid the worst."

"He is gone."

Fighting to remain calm, she clutched onto a nearby bar. "Gone?"

"Aye, they carried him out yesterday."

The healer's words echoed around her.

Her world tilted. She clawed for each breath, for sanity, for reason through this impenetrable grief.

"Lad, are you well?"

The buzzing grew louder. Coldness filled her, a chill so bitter she doubted if she would ever recover. Giric was everything, and since her mother's death, the only person who had truly loved her—ever.

Now he was dead.

CHAPTER 9

Tears burning her eyes, Elizabet clutched the cell's thick-framed door. *Giric is dead!*

A soft yet firm hand touched her shoulder. "Lad?" The healer's voice echoed from far away.

Engulfed in the dungeon's dank surroundings, she lifted her head and met the old woman's concerned gaze. "I—I am fine. A touch dizzy for a moment."

Deredere's mouth tightened, then she waved her forward.

Tears glazed her eyes as she followed the healer. Everything had changed yet naught was different. Her men remained locked within the dungeon, Scots she would free.

A long while later, with all the people tended, the healer headed toward the exit.

With a heavy heart, Elizabet shoved the dungeon door shut, then followed her down the stairs. As she stepped outside, sunlight glittered in the pristine sky, steel clashed in the distance as knights trained in the practice field, the smithy plied his hammer on glowing red steel, and men worked on the new structures Nicholas had ordered built. 'Twas another day as if naught had changed.

Except Giric was dead.

Deredere frowned. "You look a might peaked, lad."

She felt like death, sure she appeared little better. "I am . . ." Fine? Nay. She would nae offer the obvious lie again. "I need rest is all."

Understanding shone in the healer's eyes. "'Tis nae an easy task to bind wounds knowing very well the men could easily die by the morrow."

Tears threatened and she could only nod.

The healer took the basket from her arms. "Get along with you then," she said, her voice softening. "I will take care of the last prisoner myself."

A lone tear trailed a path along her cheek as Elizabet stared at her, lost in a numb haze. The pruned face blurred. Her throat constricted in a rough knot.

The healer headed toward the keep.

The last prisoner? Elizabet scrubbed the tears from her face and ran after the elder. She caught her arm, almost throwing the woman off balance. "The last prisoner?"

"Aye." Deredere frowned as she studied her. "The man who was running the fever." She shook her head. "'Tis a sorry business."

Giric is alive!

"Sir Nicholas stopped by my hut," the elder continued, ignorant of the myriad of emotions pouring through her. "When I informed him of the prisoner's worsening condition, he ordered the Scot moved to a chamber inside the keep."

Elizabet wanted to weep with joy. Nicholas hadna let her down. She should have known that he wouldna tolerate a prisoner wasting away with nay even the hope to live. Joy faded beneath the weight of reality. Giric wasna any prisoner, but a noble, a man of importance. The castellan must have learned of her brother's name and title, which is why he wanted to ensure he lived. Why? Did he believe Giric would aid him in bringing peace along the border?

As if now was the time to be worrying about such? Her brother was alive. She would worry about the rest later.

Wizened eyes watched her carefully. "What is the prisoner to you, lad?"

Everything, she wanted to shout. She stared at her straight in the eye. "A man I admire and respect."

The elder's aged mouth settled into a grimace. "Well, come along then. No sense in us standing out here for everyone to gawk at."

Sunlight brushed over her face as Elizabet followed. Mayhap the warmth of its rays would touch her soul after all.

At the second floor, Elizabet spotted a knight standing before a door halfway down the corridor. Uneasy, she followed the healer. Nicholas had forbidden her from entering the dungeon, but he'd nae said anything about a room within the keep.

The healer halted before the chamber.

The guard's eyes leveled on Elizabet.

"I am assisting the healer," she blurted, prayed he'd allow her entry.

The guard lifted a questioning brow.

"I do nae have all day," the healer said with impatience.

Elizabet could have kissed her.

With a grimace, the guard stepped to the side and opened the door. "After the fever broke the prisoner regained consciousness for a short while, then he fell asleep."

"A good sign." The healer walked into the chamber.

As the door shut behind them, Elizabet sighed with relief. "Thank you."

Deredere gave her a wink. "I had a friend once whom I did whatever it took to see. Come on, lad. We have a Scot who needs us."

Thick curtains canopied over the large bed centered against the wall. Tied back, they framed the tall man lying within.

Giric!

She forced herself to walk to the bed as the healer halted and set her basket on a nearby table.

With a soft groan, her brother's eyes flickered open. He stared at her a moment then frowned as if confused.

Clear. His eyes void of the fever that had almost taken his life. Elizabet swallowed hard. Thank God!

"Here." The elder held out a damp cloth, ignorant to the emotions pouring through Elizabet. "Wipe his brow while I tend to him."

Her entire body trembled as Elizabet moved to Giric's side. With care, she began wiping his brow.

Without warning Giric's hand clamped over her wrist, then his fingers trembled and his hand fell to the bed and his eyes fluttered closed.

"I think he recognized you as well," Deredere said with a smile.

Indeed Giric had. Before her brother had passed out, she'd caught the recognition, and a flicker of outrage.

"I am pleased to see his fever is gone."

"'Tis a blessing," Elizabet agreed. Between sneaking out from under Lachllan's parental gaze and trying to keep Nicholas's suspicions at bay, she'd forgotten about having to face Giric's reaction to her attempt to free him.

As if his anger was anything new? When she'd rescued her brother from the bog when he was ten and fifteen summers, he hadna approved her presence then, but she had pulled him out had she nae? Mayhap the fact that she had put the burr under his mount's saddle had been a factor to his getting stuck between two rotting logs, but who was remembering that anyway? 'Twas a youthful prank, one long past.

She took in Giric, shaken by the frailty and his pale skin. But this was different. He needed her. And with their father dead, she needed him.

Gently she again pressed the cool cloth along her brother's brow.

He grimaced.

The healer dug out several pouches of herbs. "After battling his fever for the past sennight, he will be weak. He has swallowed little more than a bit of broth each day." She moved to Elizabet's side. "I will give him a bit of white willow bark to ease the pain, but 'twill be food and rest that put him back on his feet." She set a small leather sack on the table, away from the others. "'Tis chamomile. It will aid his sleep after he has eaten."

Elizabet nodded, familiar with both. As of late, with her people's attacks on Ravenmoor, both herbs were a staple in her own castle.

The healer mixed the herbs.

Giric's eyes flickered opened, slid toward the healer, then focused on Elizabet. He frowned.

"You have been sick," the healer said in a soft voice as she gave Giric the mixture.

He grimaced, swallowed.

"Here is some water," Elizabet said using her pseudomale voice before he could speak.

Ice-blue eyes narrowed.

Before he worked up the energy to use her name, she gently put the cup to his lips. "Drink." She couldna risk him exposing her true identity.

He made a choking sound.

"Do nae be drowning him there, lad."

Chagrined, she pulled the cup away. "I—I am sorry."

At the healer's use of the term *lad,* Giric's eyes darkened with suspicion.

A light gust of wind swirled into the hearth, filled with the scent of heather and smoke. She could almost hear the echo of fey laughter.

"A few sips, nae more," the healer added, ignorant of her dilemma. She turned to her basket and searched through the sacks of herbs and ceramic pots of ground herbs.

Elizabet pressed her finger to her lips and shook her head at Giric in warning. She'd rarely seen her brother this angry. Mary help her once they were alone.

With a groan he turned toward the healer. "Wh-where am I?" His rough whisper tore at Elizabet's heart.

"You are at Ravenmoor Castle," Deredere replied. "I am the healer and have tended you since you were brought here." She gestured toward Elizabet. "The lad is helping me, his name is Thomas."

After slanting Elizabet a hard glare, he glanced back at the elder. "How long have I been here?"

"Over a fortnight." The elder woman gave a nod. "You have had a fever. For several days I didna know if you were going to live. Now, I say your chances are excellent." She extended her palm, which held a small pile of herbs. "Swallow them as well. They will ease your pain."

After downing the herbs, he accepted the cup from Elizabet than drank. "What now?" he asked as he handed her the empty container.

"Upon his return," the elder replied, "I reckon the castellan would be wanting a word with you."

Anger flashed in Giric's eyes. "Sir Renaud?"

"Nay," Elizabet answered, thankful the previous castellan lay dead. "Sir Nicholas."

Giric pinned her with a hard glare.

"Sir Renaud died nae too long after your imprisonment. Sir Nicholas arrived more than a fortnight ago." She paused, steadying her voice. "The new castellan is a fair man."

He lifted a brow at that, but before he could question her further, the healer lifted her basket of herbs. "Nay more questions. You need to rest."

Elizabet darted a quick look toward her brother. "Aye, he is tired and overwrought." *And furious and waiting to get me alone.*

"Go the kitchens and bring him some broth." Deredere pointed toward where she had set the small jar of herbs. "If I am gone before you return, after he has eaten, give him a cup of chamomile tea."

She nodded, thankful for the chance of a few moments alone with Giric. Outside she paused before the guard. "The healer bid me to fetch broth for the prisoner."

The knight nodded.

Through a high window, sunlight streamed in golden ribbons upon the floor, a blunt reminder of the passage of time. Nicholas should finish his rounds soon. Desperate for at least a few minutes alone with her brother before his return, once out of sight on the turret steps, she ran.

In the kitchen, Elizabet silently cursed the cook who'd bid her to wait while she'd prepared an extra meal for the guard. She was losing precious time! Only a short while remained before she must go to the stables to await Nicholas's return, like a well-trained squire would.

As she approached the guard balancing the meals in her hands, his watching her with unfeigned skepticism far from eased her nerves. She handed over the extra fare.

He eyed the chunk of roasted venison swimming in broth with great anticipation. "I will accompany you inside," he said, setting the bowl on the floor. "Though sick, the man is dangerous."

"The healer—"

"Has left." He opened the door and gestured for her to go ahead of him.

This time when she entered, Giric watched her. His gaze flicked warily to the guard then back to her.

"I have brought you some broth," she said, her voice a bit breathy, nae even beginning to match the turmoil churning inside. "'Twas made fresh this morning." Sweet Mary but she sounded the lackwit. And she'd best stop rambling.

The guard gave a grunt of irritation.

Elizabet sat on the edge of the bed, giving neither Giric nor the guard a chance to stop her. "He is weak as a babe. I should be fine." She held the steaming bowl to his mouth. "Just a sip now. 'Tis a wee bit hot."

The scent of meat, onions, and herbs rose in a steamy mist between them. With trembling hands, he cupped the bowl and tipped it higher.

At the hungry growl from the guard's stomach, she glanced back, praying she appeared calmer than she felt. "I will see that he eats. After, I will give him the herbs the healer left." She gestured to where the secured sacks sat, thankful for the excuse.

The guard crossed his arms over his chest. "The man is a murderer."

Nay more than the English who laid siege to Ravenmoor Castle, she wanted to scream. "Whatever drove him to his actions, for the moment he can barely eat, much less wield a sword."

Giric coughed, and she retrieved the bowl from his trembling hands. Sweat had broken out across his brow from his effort. She helped him to take another sip. Elizabet glanced back at the guard. "Please eat. If I need your aid, I will call."

The knight glanced toward the door where his meal had begun to cool. He grimaced as if mulling over the wisdom of such a move. "I am leaving the door open. If I hear anything, I am coming in."

She nodded, then sighed with relief as he stepped into the corridor.

"Saint's breath! Your explanation had best be good!"

At Giric's fierce whisper she jumped. "I—"

He shoved the bowl into her hand. Warm broth sloshed over the side and trickled down her fingers. "And your hair." His eyes raked over her. "You have cut it off!"

She set the bowl on the table and started to rise, but he caught her wrist. "I want an explanation—now!"

"I—I didna know if you were alive or dead." Her voice broke. A tremor slid through her body, then another. "One way or the other, I had to know."

"But a lad?"

"'Twas the only way."

"The only way?" He arched a brow, a familiar gesture he made when he was determined to get to the bottom of things.

She handed him the bowl and again sat by him on the side of the bed. "I will explain while you eat."

He hesitated then took a sip, then another.

"I took the position as the castellan's squire."

Broth spewed out as he choked. "Wh-what!"

Shuffled steps scraped outside the door.

They both froze.

"Is he threatening you?" the guard demanded as he moved into the entry, his sword readied in his hands.

"Nay," she replied. "His wounds are bothering him, and I bumped one by mistake."

The sentry grunted, sheathed his blade, and returned to his meal.

Giric wiped his chin as she knelt by his side. "Be quiet," she whispered. "I need to explain."

"Does our father—"

"He is dead."

Sorrow filled Giric's eyes, and silence fell between them.

The cadence of men, the daily routine outside the window, filled the somber void.

"When?" he asked.

Grief swept her. "He was dead when I arrived."

"Caught in a fever," he said, sadness raw in his voice, "I was nae sure if he had died, or if 'twas a delusion."

The image of her father's body in the guard's arms came to mind, but she shoved it aside. She couldna dwell on the horrific sight. "'Tis too late for him, but nae for you and the others."

Giric looked around the room as if for the first time realizing where he was. A frown darkened his brow. "Where am I?"

"In Ravenmoor's keep. On the second floor to be exact." She paused. "The other men who were captured from Wolfhaven Castle are still locked within the dungeon."

He cursed. "Why was I brought here?"

"My guess is that because you are a prisoner of importance, and with your being feverish, Sir Nicholas didna want to risk your death."

"It makes sense." He eyed her. "And where are you staying?"

She hesitated, dreading this moment. "As the lord's squire, I . . . I sleep within his chamber."

"In his chamber?" Red slashed his cheeks. "Are you bloody mad?"

"Shhhhh! Lackwit, as his squire, where else would I sleep?" She shook her head as he started to speak, then glanced toward the door, relieved to find the entry empty. Elizabet rounded on him. "I have a pallet by the hearth. Nor does he know that I am a woman."

"And he is nae going to find out. You are to leave here now! I will nae have you remain and risk your life." A muscle worked in his jaw. "And when I get hold of Lachllan, he will nae be hearing the end of it."

"Do nae blame him," she rushed out. "He forbade me to go. I allowed him to believe I agreed, then left him a note of my intent and snuck out in the wee hours of dawn."

Giric caught the front of her tunic and hauled her to within an inch of his face. "I will nae have you here another moment longer. 'Tis lunacy! Your—"

Horns sounded.

Mary, Mother of God! Elizabet jerked from his grasp. "'Tis Nicholas! Nay say a word. Please!"

"Elizabet—"

"Giric. Trust me. I must go."

He glowered at her, but time had run out. With a quick hug, she hurried from the door and slowed to a walk as she passed the guard. Once out of sight, she raced down the turret. The last thing she needed was to raise Nicholas's doubts or suspicions.

The rattle of chains spurned her on as she exited the keep. Her heart pounded as she flew across the courtyard toward the stable.

Dust swirled through the gates, preceding the mounted knights.

"Sir Nicholas arrives," a guard announced.

Hoofbeats pounded on the drawbridge and echoed like a battering ram in her mind.

Nay, she was only halfway across. He couldn't see her now! Elizabet bolted toward the stable.

CHAPTER 10

Dust swirled around Nicholas as he drew up before Thomas stepping from the stables. A ruddy hue slashed his squire's cheeks. He dismounted, handed the reins to the lad. "You look a bit flushed. Is something wrong?"

Thomas took the reins. "It has been a busy morning, Sir Nicholas," he replied, breathless. "I hurried through the last of my chores, wanting to be here for your arrival."

He smiled. "You did well."

"Sir Nicholas," a knight called, striding toward him.

"Aye?" he replied.

"Lord Terrick is awake and his fever has broken."

"'Tis good news indeed." Nicholas pulled off a gauntlet. "My thanks."

With a nod, the knight headed toward the keep.

Now, to begin building trust with Lord Terrick. With the hatred he must have after watching his father die in the cell, 'twould be a monumental task indeed, but one he was determined to achieve. Nicholas glanced toward Thomas. "Stable my mount. After, you will accompany me."

His squire's face paled. "I—I have several chores that need tending."

Nicholas worked the second gauntlet free, curious at Thomas's reluctance to see the prisoner. Did he know this man? During his interview with the earl, he would watch his squire for any telltale signs. 'Twas most likely the dubious title of the criminal that had shaken the youth. And why not? Lord Terrick's reputation as a fierce warrior preceded him. "As my squire is it not your duty to serve me?"

"Aye, 'tis, but—"

"Thomas—" He shoved back the mail hood and padded coif, appreciating the cool breeze over his skin, then waved him toward the stable. "Go and be quick about it."

Dread shrouding his expression, Thomas led his mount away.

A short while later, knights greeted Nicholas as he entered the great hall along with the scents of spices and roasting venison. Hounds nosed the floor eager to find a scrap of remaining food, and a woman swept away stale rushes and replaced them with fresh dried flowers.

With his squire on his heels, Nicholas strode past, pleased by the changes in Ravenmoor Castle since his arrival, and the fact that his daily rounds along his border now delivered naught but brisk, invigorating rides. A peace he hoped would continue.

He started up the curved stone steps and his thoughts turned to his prisoner. Thank God the man had lived. The Wardens of the Western Marches' reports confirmed Lord Terrick's staunch following among the Scots. With his father's death and newly acquired title, he now held a prestigious position. The man would make a powerful friend or a deadly enemy. His goal during this meeting was to ensure the first.

As he approached the prisoner's chamber, the guard snapped to attention. "Sir Nicholas."

"Is Lord Terrick awake?" Nicholas asked as he glanced toward the open door.

"And fed," the guard replied, then glanced toward his squire with a frown. "But then you would be—"

A groan echoed from the chamber.

Nicholas waved off the guard. "I will check on him." He entered and found Lord Terrick struggling to sit up in the bed, his face white, his body trembling. The gasp behind him reminded him his squire was at his heels. "Thomas, remain here."

His squire edged closer. "I can—"

God's teeth! Nicholas whirled, not needing a show of bravery here. "Obey me."

Thomas's face blanched. His eyes cut toward the prisoner with a nervous edge, and he took a step back. "Aye."

Blast it, why did it seem that everything he did with the lad turned into an event? Would naught ever come easy between them? On a muttered curse, Nicholas strode to the bed. Two paces away, he halted, taking in the warrior before him. "Lord Terrick."

Ice-blue eyes, hard and unforgiving, scrutinized him with a feral intent.

Only a fool would underestimate this man. Even pale and weak, he was a formidable opponent. "I am Sir Nicholas Beringar, castellan of Ravenmoor Castle."

Lord Terrick cast a damning glance toward his squire, then back to him. Their eyes locked. The room seemed to hum with unbridled energy; the force that surrounded the man would consume the weak.

Dangerous.

The description fit him well. A deep sense of pride also pulsed within him.

Nicholas silently acknowledged and respected both qualities in Lord Terrick, neither would he back down. He, too, was a man who held his own, regardless the cost.

At Thomas's nervous inhale, protectiveness swept Nicholas. A leader of his people or not, by his own oath, neither this man nor any other would bring harm to those in his care. "I ordered you brought within Ravenmoor's keep to recover."

Lord Terrick studied him a long moment. "And my men?" His soft question rumbled with demand.

"They remain in the dungeon awaiting my judgment."

The noble's eyes narrowed in challenge. "Sir Renaud would have slain them."

"I am not Sir Renaud."

The earl folded his arms across his chest mirroring Nicholas's action. Though weak, his hard gaze never wavered. "That you are nae, but you still speak the king's English, heel to Longshank's command."

At Lord Terrick's slang reference to King Edward's height, Nicholas understood—the silent gauntlet had been thrown: Prove to me that you are different. And why wouldn't this man distrust him, question his every move? After Sir Renaud's tyranny, 'twould be easy for this Scot to despise those who supported England's king.

"In the next few days," Nicholas said, "I will speak with each prisoner and judge them fairly."

The earl's brow raised, his gaze filled with skepticism. "You would take the word of a Scot?"

His respect for the noble rose a notch. Lord Terrick's questions were for his people, not of his fate. "I am a man who judges from the facts and upholds the truth." 'Twas easy to see why people would follow this noble, if necessary, to their deaths. Lord Terrick would inspire more than respect, but their loyalty as well, another reason why he needed to gain his trust. Though the Wardens of the Marches enforced the laws, men like Lord Terrick made the rules. "I have met with the Wardens of the Western Marches. I seek peace between our lands."

A muscle worked in the noble's jaw. "Then release me and my men."

"You laid siege upon Ravenmoor Castle, the king's possession. 'Twas an act of war upon the crown."

A ruddy hue slashed up his cheeks as the earl shoved himself up straighter. "Ravenmoor is a Scottish castle."

Nicholas narrowed his gaze. "Was."

The Scot opened his mouth to retort, then released a slow, controlled breath. "Aye," he agreed, his tone anything but acquiescing defeat. Tension sang between them. His hand moved to his side and clenched as if wrapping itself around the hilt of a sword. "And your king would be taking the whole of Scotland if he bloody could."

"My responsibility is to bring peace to our borders," Nicholas said, bringing the discussion back to his objective. The actions of King Edward and his intent toward Scotland were beyond his control. He would focus on what was within his authority. "I have reports of stealing along our boundaries."

"Reiving is a staple along the border," Lord Terrick said without apology.

Nicholas eyed him hard. "And murder?"

The Scot's eyes blazed. "If there was murdering about, 'twas Sir Renaud who headed the lot."

He remembered Thomas's same accusation. Nicholas gave a slow nod. "As others have claimed, along with reports of the previous castellan's smuggling. I am determined to uncover the truth—on both accounts."

Tired lines etched the earl's brow. "So what do you want with me?"

"Your cooperation."

Lord Terrick grunted. "How do I know that if I give it, you willna kill me regardless?"

"Because I give you my word as a knight." Nicholas uncrossed his arms and laid his hand upon the hilt of his sword. "If I find Sir Renaud has committed the crimes levied against him, I will include it in my report to the king."

"And my men?"

"They will be released."

Lord Terrick glanced toward his squire. His eyes darkened then turned back on him. "You have given me your word as a knight. In that I trust your actions will reflect those as inscribed within the code of chivalry."

An uncomfortable feeling slid through Nicholas. He sensed an underlying anger radiating from this man, as well as a deeper meaning to the earl's question. It felt personal. Why? He'd never met the man before. "I have given you my word. The decision to accept is yours."

"I will aid you in your quest, for 'tis mine as well. But if you betray me," he said in cold warning, "there willna be a place far enough from me to hide. I will find you. And when I do, 'twill be my own hand that ends your life. On that you have *my* word."

Nicholas walked to the bed and glared down at the noble. "My word does not bend like the willow."

"Nor mine," Lord Terrick said, dauntless.

Seconds passed.

Each eyed the other.

Nicholas had to admire this man; his values paralleled his own. He extended his hand.

The earl hesitated, then clasped it. Despite his weakened state, his grip was firm.

Releasing his hand, Nicholas stepped back. "Lord Terrick, I will return once you have rested."

The earl nodded. "And 'tis Terrick to you."

Relief edged through him. "Terrick." Nicholas turned and caught his squire's gaze upon him with something akin to relief. " 'Tis time to leave, Thomas."

"Aye, Sir Nicholas." His squire darted from the room.

Nicholas sighed as he watched the lad flee. This was not working out as he'd hoped, but the lad had only been with him but a short while. What did he expect that by now he'd have the lad's complete trust? 'Twas a foolish thought. Blast it! He was a sorry lot. Disgusted with himself, he strode from the chamber after his squire.

Elizabet hurried down the corridor without a backward glance. Thank goodness Nicholas's confrontation with Giric had gone so well. With both men of strong will, she'd feared the worst.

"He seems a fair man," Nicholas said as he caught up to her at the turret steps.

She started at his voice. "Aye, but nae as intimidating as they say." His laughter caught her off guard. Surprised, she halted and turned.

Torchlight illuminated him as he towered over her. "Lad," he said, his smile punctuated by irresistible dimples, and his mouth curved into an enchanting grin. "I could hear your knees shaking the entire time we were in the chamber."

Heat stroked her cheeks. "My knees didna clatter once!"

Her ardent denial only fueled his laughter.

Caught by how foolish she must sound, she joined in. Her eyes filled with happy tears, she met his gaze.

Torchlight softened the sculptured planes of his face with its golden touch, casting shadows of light that faded into gray as if embracing them in their own private world. The humor of moments ago echoed along the spiraled walls fading into awareness, and the moment shifted.

Desire nearly dropped Elizabet to her knees. Her breath caught, and her laughter faded. The beat of her heart thundered in her ears. Her fingers trembled as she yearned to reach out and stroke the planes of his strong face. And God help her, to lean forward and again taste his lips.

Desire flickered in his eyes, then horror.

What had she done! On a cry she whirled and bolted down the stairs.

His footsteps slapped on the steps behind her. "Thomas!"

Nicholas's confused plea made her feel worse. She ran faster and stumbled. Pain shot through her as she slammed against the wall. She reached for the stone and tried to catch herself before she toppled down the stairs.

Nicholas grabbed her arm and turned her to face him. "God's teeth! What were you thinking?" His voice lowered to a shaken whisper. "You could have killed yourself."

And ended both of us this misery. She pushed at his chest; her soft fingers connected with hard muscle. How she wanted him! "I am sorry, I . . ."

He muttered an oath under his breath and set her away. Without meeting her eyes, he knelt before her. "Where does it hurt?"

In my heart. "My leg." Shame washed through her as she pointed toward her knee.

He laid his hand upon the joint and ran his fingers carefully over the area. "I feel naught broken, 'tis likely a bruise."

"I shouldna have run. 'Twas foolish."

A deep sigh rumbled in his chest. He looked up, his eyes filled with guilt. "Thomas, I . . ."

Pain ripped through her. This couldna go on. Nicholas was a good man. He didna deserve the strife she was putting him through. She must tell him the truth. "Please, do nae say anything or apologize. If someone is to blame, 'tis me." *For more than you could ever begin to know.*

The scrape of footsteps echoed from below.

Someone was coming up. Embarrassed, ashamed, and realizing the enormity of what she'd almost done, Elizabet pushed to her feet.

A knight rounded the corner and paused. He glanced from her to the castellan. "Sir Nicholas," he said, eyeing them both with concern. "I heard the lad yell. Has he broken a bone?"

"He tripped," Nicholas replied. "Thankfully 'tis naught but a bruise."

The knight nodded, his face grim. "It can be dangerous travel as the stairway is not well lit."

Dangerous in more ways than he knew, Elizabet silently agreed. She'd almost compromised all she'd sought to gain. Until Giric was free from Ravenmoor Castle, he wasna truly safe. "I will use greater care." In silence, she headed down the turret.

The great hall was a buzz of activity as she entered. Several families had moved back into the castle during the last week, the slow trickle she was confident due to word of Nicholas's intent to rebuild Ravenmoor as well as bring peace along the border. From his discussion with Giric, a peace that would hopefully last.

"Thomas, fetch me a trencher and some ale," Nicholas said.

"Aye." She hurried away, sure after the flash of desire she'd witnessed in his gaze, he questioned his morals. The attraction between them was undeniable. For a man like Nicholas that fact would be a burden unto itself.

But with her brother agreeing to assist Nicholas to uncover the truth, surely only a short while should remain before Giric was freed and she could leave and shed her guise. The unrest along the borders would end, and a measure of peace would fall upon their lands.

And she would never see Nicholas again.

Shaken, she halted at the entry to the kitchen and glanced back. She should be happy, thrilled at the prospect, but emptiness filled her heart.

Nicholas made his way to the dais, his steps slow, his expression intense.

As if she didn't understand his confusion? The bond that had grown between them was as unexpected as unwelcome. She'd never meant to want him, but from the moment she'd entered Ravenmoor Castle, 'twould seem destiny had carved its own path.

And when she left, it would hurt him, sever the tentative trust he believed they'd reached. A relationship under any other circumstances she would cherish. How would Nicholas feel if he learned the truth?

Betrayed.

And he would hate her.

How could he do anything but? At every turn he'd given her his trust. And he'd nae only offered her a position within the castle, but believing him a lad with an abused past, he had taken the extra step and tried to become more than a mentor, but a friend.

From the short time in his company, if nothing else, she'd learned he valued honesty. And she'd repaid him with deceit. When she'd first agreed to be his squire, how could she have known of the attraction between them?

Moving to the corner of the kitchen, avoiding the women working to prepare this night's fare, she grabbed a goblet and filled it with wine.

What did it matter now? The deed was done. 'Twas too late to change anything now.

Unless Nicholas discovered the truth.

CHAPTER 11

The savory aroma of roasted venison and onions filled the air as Nicholas drained the cup of mulled wine. The spiced liquid slid down his throat in a warm glide. At his side his squire shifted, and guilt sliced through him. On a silent curse, he set his goblet on the table, shoved his trencher away. As if he could bloody eat? On the stairs he'd meant to tease Thomas, but at some point their easy banter had turned into something more.

With each passing day he sensed the change between them. At first, he'd owed the easy manner growing between them to camaraderie, to a bonding between men. But after today's events on the stairs . . . Nicholas closed his eyes and exhaled. For that brief moment on the steps, what had existed between them fit no description he would willingly give.

"More wine?" Thomas asked.

Nicholas opened his eyes, wary and at odds with himself. He nodded.

Without meeting his gaze, Thomas filled the goblet, then stepped away.

Nicholas lifted the cup, drained it. Whatever bond was growing between them must stop. 'Twould destroy the trust he sought to nurture. Mayhap 'twould be best if he sent Thomas to his brother's to finish his apprenticeship.

Damn this entire situation. And damn him. He'd taken in the lad to offer him a chance. So what in Hades was happening to him? When his squire had stumbled in the stairwell, he'd feared for his life, but when he'd held Thomas in his arms . . . God's teeth. 'Twas the second time in days when with Thomas, he'd been overcome by this unexplainable need.

A pounding started in the back of his head, promising to grow to an unbearable throb. God's teeth, 'twas a convoluted mess.

Lord Terrick's question of his adherence to the code of chivalry echoed in his mind. Mayhap the noble had discerned his attraction toward Thomas, actions that indeed betrayed those inscribed within the very code he'd pledged to withhold. For the most important oath of a knight forbid him from ever bringing harm to those beneath his protection.

He swallowed hard, his decision made. This night he would pen a missive to his brother, Hugh, and request that he sponsor the lad. Within a month Thomas would be gone, a move best for all involved.

"Sir Nicholas," a knight called from the entry of the great hall.

He glanced up, and the movement sent a stab of pain through his head. Served him well for the drink he'd imbibed last night.

"The steward from Wolfhaven Castle, Lachllan MacDouglas, has arrived and requests to speak with you. He awaits you in the courtyard."

With their earl held within his castle, Nicholas had expected the steward's arrival. 'Twould seem word of his intent to seek peace along the borders was being passed. The meeting with the Wardens of the Western Marches had served its purpose. Now, to ensure that with the groundwork laid, he could nurture it to provide peace in the days to come.

"My thanks." Nicholas turned toward Thomas.

At his glance, the lad's face paled, and he took a step back.

Blast it! This was his fault. He shoved to his feet. "Come." Nicholas strode past, needing to escape the confines of the keep. The last thing he wanted was for Thomas to cower at his presence, but after his untoward actions in the turret, what had he expected?

* * *

Sunlight peeked through the cloud-filled sky as Elizabet followed Nicholas across the courtyard. From the darkening clouds to the west, a storm was moving in. As if she didna have her own tempest brewing?

She should have expected Lachllan's appearance. Caught between her goal to find Giric and trying to keep her growing feelings toward Nicholas at bay, she'd set aside her steward's forbidding her to come here. From the anger in her mentor's weathered blue gaze as he stood with several knights from her castle and watched her approach, how could she, even for a moment, have dismissed his fury?

Nicholas halted before her steward.

Anxious, she stopped beside the castellan, opposite to where Lachllan stood.

"Sir Nicholas Beringar," the steward said, his gaze hard and unyielding. "I am Lachllan MacDouglas, steward of Wolfhaven Castle."

Expression grim, Nicholas nodded. "I expected you. I regret to inform you that your lord died within the dungeon before I was notified of his presence."

Only the slight waver of the steward's breath betrayed his unyielding stature. "And his son?"

"He lives," Nicholas replied.

Relief flickered across the steward's face. "Will I be allowed to see him?"

The castellan paused as if weighing his request, and Elizabet held her breath, praying that he would.

"Indeed." The castellan glanced at her. "Thomas, see if Lord Terrick is awake."

"Aye, Sir Nicholas." Elizabet stole one last look at her mentor before she ran toward the keep. She took the castle steps two at a time, trying to ignore her emotions as she passed the curve in the turret where Nicholas had held her a short while before. At the second floor, she hurried toward the chamber.

At her approach, the guard blocked her path.

"Sir Nicholas requests that I am to check if Lord Terrick is awake," she rushed out, "as he has a visitor."

The guard stepped aside.

Wind tumbled through the window as she entered the chamber, the air slightly chilled and filled with the taste of rain. One last sliver of sunlight flickered through the chamber then faded. The murky light seeping into the room enhanced the somber ambiance of this dreary setting.

As she crossed to his bed, she found Giric's eyes closed and his breathing even. A shiver ran through her at how close she'd come to losing him. "Sleep well, Giric." She turned toward the door. Lachllan would be far from pleased that he would have to wait to see her brother, but 'twas little to accept when, without proper care, he could have died.

"Elizabet."

At Giric's voice, she turned. "Lachllan has arrived and wants to speak with you."

He searched her face. Anger warred with his obvious fatigue. "You must leave Ravenmoor Castle."

"I *need* to inform Sir Nicholas you are awake."

His gaze narrowed. "If you do nae leave the castle this day, I am going to have Lachllan charge you with thieving and haul you back to Wolfhaven Castle."

Panic swept her. "You wouldna dare."

"God's teeth, Elizabet, why are you being so stubborn? With each moment you remain on English soil, you are putting your life in danger."

"Because," she replied, her voice softening, "you need me."

His jaw tightened. "You heard the castellan," he whispered, his tone harsh. "When he discovers the truth about Sir Renaud, I will be free. There is nay reason for you to remain."

"What of our men locked within his dungeon? And what if the castellan doesna release you?"

At the latter he arched a brow. "What in God's name is that supposed to mean?"

The last thing she wanted was to make him worry further. "Giric, I must go. Nicholas is expecting me."

"Nicholas?"

At the hard burr edging his voice she cringed. Mary's will, she'd used the castellan's familiar name! Understanding registered in her brother's eyes as she backed up a step and she wished she could recall her words.

"What is he to you?" Ice culled his words.

"The knight whom I serve." Her voice trembled but thankfully didna break.

Anger frosted his gaze. "'Tis not what I asked and you bloody know it."

"Please."

The anger on his face crumbled to disbelief. "Merciful God, you care for him."

"Aye." She swallowed hard, the price of needing a man like Nicholas higher than she'd ever imagined. "Giric, he is an honorable man." Elizabeth held up her hand as her brother opened his mouth to speak. "Say nay more. I must go." Heart pounding, she turned and fled.

As she stepped from the keep, wind, ripe with the scent of rain, swirled around her. She glanced up. Thick, blackened clouds churned overhead. In the distance, lightning cut through the ominous sky. Seconds later, thunder rumbled as if a catapult fired. *Please let this nae be an omen.* With a shiver, she headed toward the men.

Nicholas nodded in agreement at the steward's last comment, and noted MacDouglas's glance toward his squire at his approach. A hint of recognition along with anger flashed in the steward's eyes before it disappeared. So he knew the lad.

Thomas halted at his side.

He turned to his squire. "Is Lord Terrick awake?"

"Aye," Thomas replied, breathless. His shot a nervous look toward the steward then back to Nicholas. "Though he is a bit sleepy from the herbs the healer gave him."

"My thanks." Nicholas nodded to the steward. "Your men will remain here, and you will accompany me to his chamber."

Lachllan nodded and followed him as he headed toward the keep.

A short while later Nicholas leaned back against the cool, stone wall near the window as Lord Terrick and the steward spoke. Throughout the men's exchange he also kept watch of his squire who lingered near the door as if he wished to bolt. In addition, though covert, he noted not only Lachllan's covert glances toward the lad, but Terrick's as well.

Unease rippled through him. He glanced toward his squire, and found Thomas watching him.

Guilt flashed in Thomas's eyes, and he looked away.

Blast it, what in bloody Hades was going on? His discussion two days past with Thomas reared its ugly head. He'd known the lad withheld something from him, but with the Wardens of the Western Marches in residence, he'd been sidetracked. With them gone, naught would interrupt him. This night, once alone in his chamber, he would find out!

Lachllan's muffled cough pulled him from his brooding. He turned to the find the steward watching him with curiosity. As much as he longed to ask him or Terrick if they knew the lad, the answers he sought would come from their source—his squire.

Nicholas pushed away from the wall and walked to the steward. "I will escort you out," he stated, leaving no room for question.

Thomas's eyes widened as he passed.

He remained silent. Let his squire worry, he would learn this night that secrets brought their own consequence.

Fat, cool splotches of rain slapped Nicholas as he led the steward from the keep. "You are welcome to remain until the storm passes," he said, noting his squire stiffen at the offer.

Lachllan drew up the hood over his head. "My thanks, Sir Nicholas. 'Tis growing late, and best if I leave now."

He nodded, understanding the man's reserve. Until he released the earl, a true bond of peace between them would not exist.

Lightning raced across the sky and thunder shattered in its wake as they crossed the courtyard toward Terrick's knights. As they reached the stable, a horn sounded at the gates.

"Lord Dunsten's banner is on the horizon," a guard called, his message tattered within a gust of wind.

'Twould appear his day would be wrought with meetings from the Scots. Nicholas nodded to the steward. "I look forward to our meeting again. Mayhap on the next visit, 'twill be to release Lord Terrick."

Weathered blue eyes leveled on him. " 'Tis my hope as well."

The clatter of hooves echoed from the drawbridge.

Curious as to the reason for the Earl of Dunststen's visit, Nicholas faced the portcullis.

Lord Dunsten and a small band of men cantered into view. Inside the courtyard, the powerful earl and his men slowed their mounts to a walk, then drew to a halt before Nicholas. "Sir Nicholas." He glanced toward the steward. Hazel eyes narrowed. "MacDouglas."

The steward's weathered gaze grew cautious, tinged with dislike. "Lord Dunsten."

Lightning split the sky and thunder exploded with a vicious crack.

Intrigued, Nicholas watched the tense interaction. In a country on the brink of war where every Scot counted in their need to unite, what would cause such dissent between the two Scots? If given a choice, from their mutual distrust, he would deduct the cause as personal. Yet another puzzle to solve. For now he would deal with the ones within his grasp.

Lachllan turned toward Nicholas. "Until next time, Sir Nicholas." He mounted, then cantered from the castle, his men riding in his wake.

After a quick glance into the blackened sky to check on the approaching storm, Nicholas focused his attention on the earl. "What brings you to Ravenmoor Castle on such an adverse day?"

The earl scowled. "Several of my cattle were stolen early this morning. We tracked the reivers onto Ravenmoor land. In a show of good will, I would gain permission before conducting a search."

Furious that reivers would dare seek shelter on his soil, Nicholas nodded. "I will ride with you." He nodded to his squire. "Thomas, tell Sir Jon to gather five men to ride with me, then prepare my mount."

"Aye, Sir Nicholas." His squire hurried away.

The earl followed the squire's progress for a moment then took in the churning sky. He grimaced. "Sir Nicholas, there is nay need for you to go out in this weather. It promises to be a nasty storm."

"If the thieves are on Ravenmoor land," Nicholas stated, "they are my responsibility."

"'Twould be my own way as well," Dunsten agreed. His horse snorted and shifted nervously. "Your assistance will be welcome. 'Tis time the reiving ended."

"Indeed," Nicholas replied, unsure why the man's agreement to his own principles left him unsettled.

As they rode from the gates of Ravenmoor the heavens opened. The long hours of riding over his land yielded naught except miles of mud, biting rain, and lashing wind. Cold soaked him to the bone.

At the top of the next hillock, Nicholas drew his mount to a halt and scanned the narrow valley. A river ran through the glen and widened near the center where it spilled into a lake. Shrub edged the pond with a stand of trees on one edge that led up to a large rowan tree shading the northern edge.

He continued his search over the lush green as the scent of wet leather and earth filled the air. Though the thunder had ceased several hours ago, the chilling rain continued to fall in the fleeting light. Before it grew too dark, they needed to start home.

Lord Dunsten guided his mount toward him in the soft turf. "With the heavy rains, any tracks that we could have trailed have been wiped away."

"'Tis my belief as well." He'd hoped to catch the thieves this day. 'Twould have stressed to those along the border his determination to end the struggles between them and bring peace. "Let us return to Ravenmoor Castle. I would offer you a hot meal and a warm bed for the night."

"My thanks, Sir Nicholas." Lord Dunsten studied him a moment. "The king chose wisely when he installed you as the castle's castellan."

Nicholas stiffened, finding his comment far from holding praise. "My efforts to bring peace are those any knight loyal to King Edward would undertake."

The earl raised a lazy brow, but his eyes remained as sharp as a hawk's. "Mayhap. But some would pursue a path more to their own reward."

The hairs on the back of his neck prickled. "You speak of Sir Renaud?"

The noble shrugged. "How well does anyone truly know another?"

Nor, 'twould seem, would he reveal his relationship with the previous castellan. "Were you aware of any unlawful acts instigated by Sir Renaud?"

He ran his hand along his mount's withers. "I doubt King Edward is interested in a few misdeeds by one of his castellans or the reported death of a Scot, however achieved. His true interest is in gaining Scotland, regardless of the cost."

"My king seeks peace and unity between our countries," Nicholas stated.

A threadbare smile tainted with scorn touched Lord Dunsten's lips. "If you wish to believe so."

"And what do you believe?" he asked, curious to discover what spawned such contempt toward his king. Regardless of the noble's words, Nicholas doubted Lord Dunsten's loyalty lay with anyone but himself.

The earl's eyes hardened. "I believe that each man has his price," he said, his words calculated. "What is yours?"

How dare he try to buy him like a whore! Nicholas curled his hand around the hilt of his sword. "My loyalty is not bought and sold, but earned."

Lord Dunsten laughed as if a bard had spun a jest. Though his eyes twinkled with mirth, mercilessness glittered beneath. "Sir Nicholas, you are a rare find in this callous time. Mayhap you will indeed achieve the peace Sir Renaud failed to obtain."

His cynical response stroked Nicholas's temper. "There are still those who believe and fight for what is right." That he had invited the earl to Ravenmoor for the night ate at him like maggots to a wound, but propriety forbade him to withdraw his offer. "The night is almost upon us. We must return to Ravenmoor Castle."

Not waiting for an answer, Nicholas wheeled his mount and galloped for home, more than ready for the long and trying day to be at an end. Before the night ended, he would know his squire's secrets.

The bowls slipped from Elizabet's hands, spilling uneaten stew onto the battered kitchen table. Blast it. Ever since Nicholas's return and his subsequent announcement that Lord Dunsten would remain the night, her hard-won control had shattered.

As if worrying about the upcoming confrontation between her and Nicholas wasna enough? Somehow she'd managed to evade Dunsten, but there would be nay avoiding Nicholas. With the exception of exposing that she was a woman, she would tell the castellan the truth about knowing those from Wolfhaven Castle, or as much as possible.

The ache in her heart grew. As hard as it was to dwell upon the fact, their days together were numbered. If naught else, when she left Ravenmoor, at least she would do so with a measure of pride.

The weight of her worries smothered her. If only for a few minutes, she needed to escape. After wiping up the splattered broth from the floor and picking up the bowls, she tugged on her cape and slipped outside. Closing the door, she walked to the left of the steps and slipped into the shadows. With a weary exhale, Elizabet leaned against the chiseled stone.

Stars dotted the sky, as clear as bright. A full moon ascended on the horizon bathing the treetops in a silvery light. After the thunderstorms this day, the peace of the moment touched her.

"You play your role well."

At Dunsten's cold words she whirled. Dread filled her as she stared at the morbid satisfaction etched in his expression. "I—"

"Elizabet," he drawled, a thin smile curving his lips. "You do me a disservice to think you could fool me. Though I admit, I didna recognize you on my first visit." He took a step toward her. The moonlight carved his face, partially shielded by the shadows, into a macabre blend of hard angles.

She stepped back, Dunsten's oath of revenge on her brother after he interceded in his bid for Elizabet's hand echoing in her mind. What was his true purpose here? A man like Dunsten did naught without a reason. "What do you want?"

With an apathetic sigh he studied the full moon rising in the east. Glancing toward her, his face softened, and he reached out and brushed his thumb against her cheek. "'Tis a lover's moon," he said with a rich silkiness.

She jerked from his touch, startled by his unexpected advance. "What do you want? You know everyone here thinks I am a lad."

His slow smile unnerved her further. "An intriguing situation, but then, you always seem to implicate yourself in, how shall we say, less than desirable circumstances."

The bastard. "Like being here with you?"

The tenderness in his eyes curdled to anger. "'Tis nae the way to treat the man you are to wed."

The crisp night air slithered across her flesh as bile rose in her throat. "I would never marry you!"

His ruthless gaze traveled up her body, from the tip of her deer-skin boots to her cropped locks, before they locked on her eyes.

A shiver rippled through her.

"I do nae see where you have much choice." The outline of his well-muscled form adorned with sword and dagger exposed a sinister portrayal of exactly how lethal his threat could be. "To begin with, Lady Elizabet, I could inform Sir Nicholas of your duplicity."

"I . . ." Panic swept her. Nicholas couldna find out she was a woman. 'Twas hard enough preparing to leave without having to face the castellan's hatred as well. That would come soon enough.

"What would he think if he found out you are naught but a fraud?" he continued, voicing her worst fear. "He is an honorable man who values the truth." He leaned closer. "As I am sure you are well aware."

"I but tend to his horse, carve his meat, and other mundane chores," she said with a nonchalance she didna feel. "I doubt his interest in a lad, or a woman for that fact, would cause him great concern."

His soft laughter crawled up her spine as if a dull pin dragged. "For most 'twould nae matter if they were tended to by a gout-ridden spinster. But Sir Nicholas is nae most, is he? He is a man who values integrity."

Her heart thundered. "I know nae what you are trying to say."

"Aye you do. I am nae blind," he hissed. "I saw the way your eyes followed him during the meal when you believed nay one watched. 'Tis a fancy you hold for him. And I have nay doubt of his anger if he were to learn of your treachery."

She opened her mouth to deny it, then closed it. Everything he'd said was true. Nicholas appealed to her more than he should, because of his honor and desire to do what was right. And when he learned of her deception, he would be furious.

Lord Dunsten nodded as if pleased by her silence. "Then, there is your brother."

"Giric—"

"Is locked inside Sir Nicholas's dungeon, and your father is dead." He stepped forward and pressed his body tight against hers, effectively trapping her. "And the only thing keeping your brother alive is that Sir Nicholas believes Sir Renaud is involved with illicit dealings, and provoked your brother and family's attack."

She tried to escape, but he caught her chin with his hand. "'Tis the truth!" But even as she said the words, she realized his implication. Repulsed, she glared at him. "But you would frame him, would you nae, twist facts to make my brother appear as if a murderer?"

"I will do whatever it takes to have you," he said with slow menace. "This time nae your brother, or any other, will interfere with my plans to marry you."

The air grew thin, hard to breathe. If she'd worried about the danger the earl's being here posed before, now she understood how much of a threat he could be. If given the opportunity, he would turn Nicholas against her, and then wrongfully manipulate circumstances to ensure Giric's death. She couldna allow either. Until her brother was set free, she must remain at Ravenmoor Castle to protect him.

"I willna marry you." Her reply sounded feeble to her own ears, but somehow she would find a way to outwit him.

"Oh but you will." With obnoxious confidence, Lord Dunsten reached out and lifted a cut lock. "Or Sir Nicholas will hate you and your dear brother will be dead."

Pain shot through her as he jerked her forward; his lips hovered above hers. Bile rose in her throat. "Release me!"

"I will give you a fortnight to give me the answer I wish," he said with deadly calm. "You are nae a fool, Elizabet. If nae for Sir Nicholas's sake, we both know you will do anything to save Giric." He claimed her lips in a savage assault.

Furious, she fought him, but he overpowered her. After he'd bruised her lips in a punishing kiss, he released her.

She stumbled back and wiped her mouth with the back of her hand.

"A fortnight." He turned on his heel and strode into the keep. With a jerk, he slammed the door closed behind him.

Dread crept through Elizabet as she leaned against the cold stone. She stared unseeing into the moon-filled night. A fortnight. It gave her little time, but somehow it would have to be enough. She would never marry Dunsten.

The bells of Compline tolled, and her heart sank. Nicholas. She still had to face him, and their confrontation would be anything but pleasant.

Steadying herself she turned and approached the door. At least for the moment Nicholas's anger was confined to believing she hid but a few paltry secrets from him.

God forbid if he discovered the truth.

CHAPTER 12

Dunsten's threat echoed in Elizabet's mind as she halted before Nicholas's chamber. With a calming breath she entered, then pushed the door shut. The forged latch clicked into place like an executioner's blade. The scent of smoke tainted the chamber, and the fire blazing within the hearth doing little to warm the chill invading her.

"Thomas."

With a start she turned.

The castellan stood by the window in an easy stance, but she caught the fury raging in his eyes. "Sir Nicholas?" Her breathless whisper carved the silence with an abrasive edge.

"Pour me a cup of wine."

The icy quiet of his words unnerved her further. Her hands trembled as reached for the bottle. The ruby liquid sloshed over the side as she filled the goblet. She glanced over.

Nicholas was staring out the window into the night.

With a hard swallow, she returned the bottle to the small table.

At the soft click of the glass upon wood, he remained facing the darkened skies.

Nicholas's controlled stance unnerved her more than if he stalked the room in a caustic rage. His bearing represented the stalwart man she'd come to know, a man who knew his purpose with unnerving clarity. And this night as he stood with the quiet intensity of a warrior preparing for a siege, 'twas nae a castle he sought to conquer, but her secrets.

She brought him the wine. "Here, Sir Nicholas."

In silence, he took the goblet. His muscles rippled with a sleek grace as he lifted the cup, underscoring her original assessment of him being a formidable enemy when she'd first encountered him from the bough of the rowan tree.

Distant voices of the guards echoed from the bailey. A wolf howled in the distance, a rough, lonely sound. The castellan continued to stare into the night.

Why didna he say something? Nicholas turned, and his gaze bore into hers.

Dread filled her. The many untruths she'd spun had brought her to this shameful moment. And he detested lies. If she exposed her true identity now, even if she revealed her reasons, she'd deceived him and he would hate her. The deed was done. She would stand by her original goal, to free her brother and men. Once they were released, she would leave. Then, Thomas, the lad Nicholas had come to know, would vanish forever.

The pounding at the back of Nicholas's neck grew as he scoured Thomas's face, reading the lad's indecision as well as the anguish. His own state of mind was little better. After the disturbing conversation with Lord Dunsten this afternoon, the last thing he wished for was another confrontation this day, but the time had come for secrets to end.

"Tell me the truth," Nicholas said.

Distress flashed in Thomas's emerald-green eyes.

Nicholas laid his hand upon the roughened stone of the sill. "You know Lachllan, the steward of Wolfhaven Castle?"

After a brief hesitation, Thomas nodded.

"And Lord Terrick?"

"Aye." His answer fell out in a quiet hush, hinting at more than a passing acquaintance.

Secrets, his mind echoed. Nicholas curled his hand into a fist. "How?" The wood on the fire shifted. Hot embers rebelled with a loud snap.

His squire drew a deep breath, slowly exhaled. "I used to live there."

Of all the answers he'd expected, the lad living in Wolfhaven Castle was not one of them. He'd suspected Thomas of reiving their cattle and being caught, then punished. As a criminal, 'twould have explained the lad's nervousness around the men and the Wardens of the Western Marches as well.

His squire looked away. "I tend to be a bit headstrong." Thomas slanted a nervous look toward Nicholas, and a blush crept up his cheeks. "To be a bit set in my ways."

Set in his ways? An understatement. In the short duration Thomas had lived beneath his care, his strong will had laid siege to every aspect of Nicholas's well-controlled life.

"At times my stubbornness gained the attention of the steward, and too often, the lord's son, Giric."

With ease he could envision Lord Terrick pushed to the brink by this wisp of a lad. In only a few days, how often had he experienced the same frustration?

"Once, in a fit of temper, I snuck a burr under Giric's saddle." A flicker of a smile touched his lips, then faded. "He was angry as a boar, and I canna blame him, but at times he is as pigheaded as they come." He shrugged and his thin frame drooped. Any glint of rebellion vanished. " 'Twas but one of my many exploits."

"And Lord Terrick tolerated this?"

Guilt spread over his face. "I didna stay around to find out."

"So you ran?"

"Aye."

Afraid a powerful and respected man like Lord Terrick would seek him out, and with nowhere to go, Thomas had turned to a life of reiving. Until the lad had tried to rob him.

Nicholas grimaced. The leather of his sheath creaked as he set his hand upon his blade. Steel, cool and firm, lay against his fingers; a sword designed to defend as well as protect. His temper began to ebb. His squire's admission answered many questions, and explained the haunted eyes and the fear, but it also emphasized the lad's need to learn to make wise decisions.

"'Tis better to face your mistakes then flee from them," Nicholas said. "Wiser still to think before you act irrationally." Which is why when this was settled he would send Thomas away. The lad needed guidance, but not from him.

Irritation flickered on his squire's face. "Think you I didna try? As often as I am wise, I am a fool. For as my own mother stated"—his voice broke—"'tis my heart that rules my actions."

Passion. It emanated from the lad in waves. Terrified by the longing Thomas inspired, Nicholas refocused on their discussion. "Where is your mother?" His squire's face paled, and he wished he could recall his harsh words. "Is she dead?"

"Aye," Thomas whispered, the words forlorn.

"And your father as well?"

Thomas nodded and looked away.

A sense of hopelessness for the lad infused him. Blast it. "Is there anyone kin or friend you can ask for help?"

His squire turned, his eyes dry, filled with anger. "If I had another option, do you nae think I would have chosen it?" He brushed back a lock of hair that had fallen onto his cheek and his emerald eyes grew fragile. "In but days you offered me pride, hope, and respect, more than my da offered me my entire life. For that I thank you. Neither do I expect you to understand what I needed. You never were supposed to." A sad smile touched his mouth. "But you did."

The tension between them shifted, became personal. Nicholas silently cursed.

"As I said before, I didna want to like you, but now I do, too much," Thomas finished in a harsh rasp, the regret of his words tangible as if torn from his heart.

Nicholas swallowed hard and stared out the window. The full moon spilled across the moors in a surreal glow. A dense mist hung over the land as enchanting and as alluring as Thomas.

His emotions crumbled and he clung to one, the overwhelming urge to protect. "There is much you need to learn, but 'tis not my expertise that would serve you best. On the morrow I am sending a missive to my brother, the Earl of Carridon, to request he continue your training." He didn't turn at the lad's sharp intake, but stared unseeing across the rugged terrain. Though he'd anticipated the lad's distress, it still hurt. "Once I receive confirmation, you will depart. I expect you to depart within a fortnight for his home, Raedwulf Castle, which is located on the northeast border of England. My brother will ensure that you are given shelter and continue your training."

"Why?"

At his squire's pained whisper, Nicholas turned, hurting inside at the devastation on Thomas's face and wanting him with his every breath. He remained silent. Let the lad believe his reasons were based on the secrets he'd kept from him. "Considering the circumstance," Nicholas finally answered, " 'tis for the best."

The self-condemnation in Nicholas's voice tore Elizabet apart. Though his mind saw a lad, his body sensed the woman. If only she could explain, but she'd already said too much. And his noble act to want to protect her from himself only endeared him to her more. "If 'tis your wish."

" 'Tis."

With a heavy heart, she walked across the room to make her pallet.

The soft scuff of the castellan's boots echoed into the silence as he moved up behind her.

She remained still, afraid if she faced him she'd admit everything.

Tense silence hung between them, then he released a frustrated sigh. "I have an errand to see to. Do not wait up for me."

A lump grew in her throat. "Aye."

"Thomas . . . I never meant to hurt you."

Silence.

Several moments later, wood scraped as he pulled the door shut behind him.

Hurt? A pale feeling compared to love. Overwhelmed by emotion, Elizabet knelt on the cold stone. She wrapped her arms around her stomach and sobbed, tears falling until they refused to come. Soon she would leave. When she had disappeared he would be angry, but with the passage of time he would forget her. But never would she forget him.

A few days remained to spend by his side, time she would forever cherish. And in that time, she would figure out a way to free her men. Then, she would go. 'Twas best to let it end this way.

The candle sputtered at Nicholas's side, casting long shadows into the small chamber as he penned the missive to his brother. Finished, he set the quill aside and lifted the parchment. Sipping his wine, he reread the letter asking for Hugh's assistance. A simple message. Although the request was anything but.

Laying the yellowed parchment upon the desk, he rolled it tight, then sealed it with heated wax. Before the wax cooled, he pressed the face of his ring into the thickening gel, then set the missive aside.

Exhaustion washed over him. He should rest, but he hesitated at the idea of returning to his chamber and Thomas. He rubbed his eyes, wishing the missive was long sent and his squire was already ensconced within his brother's care; then his life would return to normal and he would again have peace.

As if he bloody believed that!

Nicholas shoved back his chair, stood, and paced the small confines. He doubted distance, much less time, would smother his growing feelings toward the lad. And with his emotions tangled, 'twould be foolish to return to his room.

Muttering an oath he sat at the desk, withdrew the castle's ledger, and flipped past his own neat entries to Sir Renaud's narrow scribbles. If he could not attain rest or sanity of mind, he could at least search for proof of the previous castellan's smuggling.

The scent of tallow filled the small chamber as he scanned page after page. Grit grew in his eyes and the poorly blurred notations swam before him. Nicholas glanced at the half-burned taper then back to the many unread pages left to review.

Thus far, all he'd found was documentation of the accounts of the castle's daily expenditures, the wine drunk, bread eaten, oats fed to the horses, along with a long list of other used goods.

The final entry on the page before him recorded a visit by Lord Dunsten. Along with the number of his household staff, including horses that traveled with him, the inscription ended with an onerous remark, of how *it was the last day of feeding the heathen lot.*

Intrigued, especially in light of Lord Dunsten's subtle proposition to him, he marked the location of this entry then moved on to the next page.

A strand of raven black hair lay caught within the crevice.

With an irritated sigh he pulled the silken wisp free and brushed it away. For a moment, like a fairy's wing, it became illuminated by the flame's golden glow. Then it slowly spiraled to the floor.

What was he bloody thinking? With a curse, Nicholas returned his attention to the ledger as pleased by the thoroughness of the entries as he was frustrated. With painstaking attention, he scanned page after page. As he reached to rub his brow, the candle sputtered. He glanced over.

A thumb's width of wax remained.

Except for the personal comments on Lord Dunsten's stay, he had found naught more. A nagging feeling persisted, insisting that he'd missed something significant.

As he sat back, an ache built in his head. Nicholas rubbed his eyes. He needed sleep. Though only a few hours of the night remained, he would try to rest.

With a sigh, he closed the thick, leather-bound book, slid it into the drawer, then pushed it closed.

Wood scraped, then the ledger stuck two-thirds the way in.

Blast it! He jerked open the drawer, straightened the book, then shoved it closed. This time the drawer slid neatly into place.

Cramped muscles screamed as he stood. He flexed his fingers and stretched his back, more than ready for bed. Lifting the near-gutted taper, he departed.

The faint odor of cooked meat and spilled ale greeted him as he stepped into the great hall. The snores of knights bedded down for the night echoed around him. Hounds lay amongst the rushes, and several raised their heads as he passed.

With quiet steps, Nicholas headed up the turret. Once he'd rested he would review the ledger again and try to discover what he had missed. At the moment his brain was too fogged for logic.

Jagged rows of early morning sunlight slanted across the curtain wall as Nicholas rode into the keep with the king's courier at his side. He scanned the darkened entry to the stable and frowned, his lack of sleep having already left him on edge. He didn't need to be chasing down his squire as well.

Another lad stepped from the stable and nodded. "Sir Nicholas."

"Where is Thomas?"

"He is in the dungeon, my lord."

A muscle ticked in his jaw as Nicholas glanced toward the turret. He remembered the night the lad had all but passed out when they had carried the bodies from the dank confines. And now, against his explicit orders, he dared to return. "Why?"

"To aid the healer as he does every day," he added, his voice hesitant. "Did you wish me to fetch him?"

Stunned he stared at him. "Every day?"

The lad shot a nervous gaze toward the dungeon, then back to Sir Nicholas. His face paled and he nodded. "Aye. Once you depart for rounds he . . ." He cleared his throat. "I—I thought you knew."

God's teeth, once he was finished with the king's man, he would know why his squire had disobeyed him! Nicholas dismounted and handed the reins to the lad.

The courier followed suit.

Nicholas held out the reins. "Take both horses to the stable and tend to them."

With a wide-eyed nod, the lad led the horses away.

Nicholas turned to the courier, keeping his simmering temper in check. "Follow me."

The king's man kept pace as they headed toward the keep.

With each step, Nicholas mulled his squire's deception. After breaking his fast with Lord Dunsten and once the earl had left, he'd departed for his daily rounds. He'd looked forward to the morning's ride, hoping to rid himself of some of his pent-up anxiety after the frustrations of yesterday.

But when he'd spotted the king's courier in the forest, any hope of relief had ended. He'd sent his men on to finish their rounds. With the messenger in tow, he'd returned to the Ravenmoor Castle, sentenced to remain within the walls after all. To make matters worse, upon his return he'd expected to find Thomas readied to tend to his mount. Instead he'd learned his squire had his own agenda.

The dungeon!

Anger rumbled in his chest. After he'd strictly forbidden him from going there. Nicholas fumed as he strode with the courier to the keep, but as the anger faded, understanding bloomed.

Hadn't Thomas said he'd lived at Wolfhaven Castle? He would know those in the dungeon, and 'twould be the lad's way to aid, to nurture. From the first he'd seen it. Not only did his squire perform his duties with great care, but often after he'd finished his chores, he aided others in completing theirs.

Though he didn't want the lad exposed to the horrors of the dungeon, his squire obviously believed it necessary for him to fulfill his duty.

Like it or not, Thomas would learn to obey him or the knight whom he served when given an order.

After he'd left the king's man in the great room with a cup of ale, bread, and a trencher of meat, Nicholas strode toward the castellan's office. Once he shut the door behind them, he broke the blood-red seal and viewed the king's missive.

News that negotiations between the Scottish parliament and King Edward in choosing a new Scottish king pleased him, but the tone of the missive drew his concern.

Ever since Queen Eleanor's death, the king's temperament had worsened. On his few visits to Westminster Abbey he'd witnessed the great affection between them, a closeness he wished within his own marriage when he took a wife.

On his sovereign's journey to Scotland, the queen's illness then sudden death had dealt the king a stunning blow, a wound from which he'd yet to recover. Whispers abounded that without the queen's intercession the king's inherent cruel streak would rage unchecked, spread like wildfire through the realm.

Well aware of his king's volatile temper, Nicholas prayed King Edward could overcome his grief in his dealings with Scotland. Anger would serve to kindle already volatile negotiations between their countries.

Nicholas penned his reply, giving the status of the castle's progress, information as to his concerns about Sir Renaud's inappropriate behavior toward the castle's occupants and the Scots along the border, and his possible involvement with smuggling. Once finished, he rolled the missive and sealed it with wax, again pressing his ring into the cooling liquid.

A short while later Nicholas stood near the stable before the king's man. He handed the missive to the courier. "May God ride at your side."

"To you as well, Sir Nicholas." The messenger tucked the missive safely away, mounted, and kicked his steed into a canter. Hoofbeats echoed as he rode from the castle.

A light breeze scented with peat and a hint of heather swept in from the moors as Nicholas watched the man depart. When the courier had disappeared from sight, he focused on a much more immediate concern.

His squire.

On a muttered curse, he strode toward the dungeon. After last night's discussion and everything they'd gone through, he'd believed they'd exposed all of the lad's secrets.

Obviously not.

As he stepped inside the turret, mildew and the faint stench of death usurped the sweet fragrance of the moors. The solid slap of his boots echoed around him as he climbed the spiral, carved steps, debating his censure.

The knight guarding the entry opened the door, then came to attention as Nicholas topped the steps. "Sir Nicholas."

"Sir Jon." Nicholas stepped past, scoured the narrowed, torch-lit corridor between the cells. No sign of Thomas. The muscles in his shoulders relaxed. "I came to speak with my squire. I see he has left."

"Aye, Sir Nicholas. A short while ago. He went to tend Lord Terrick in the keep." The guard pointed toward a cell near the end of the dungeon. "The healer is still here mending a wound within if you wish to speak with her."

"Thomas went alone?" Anger trickled into his voice.

His knight cleared his throat. "He did."

Was the lad addled? Though Thomas admitted knowing Terrick, the earl was still his prisoner, and a dangerous warrior at that. "Sir Nicholas, the lad has worked side by side with the healer and tended the prisoners for the past several days," his knight explained. "At first

I hesitated to leave your squire's side as he tended the wounded, but he insisted that because he is a Scot he would be safe. After seeing how the prisoners have taken to the lad, I believe him."

"Unless I give orders otherwise," Nicholas said, his each word crisp, "my squire is not to be left alone with the prisoners again, especially Lord Terrick. Is that clear?"

"Yes, Sir Nicholas."

Scot or otherwise, how dare Thomas risk his life due to his foolish pride? He whirled and stormed down the steps. His blood still pounding hot, moments later, he entered the corridor on the second floor.

At his approach, the guard snapped to attention.

Nicholas shook his head when the guard made to speak. He stepped before the open doorway. Standing beside the prisoner, his squire was bathing the man's face with a tender hand. The blasted fool. If the Scottish lord wished, he could snap the lad's neck in a trice.

Anger burning, Nicholas stepped inside. "Thomas!"

His squire whirled. All color drained from his face.

CHAPTER 13

Mary, Mother of God, what was Nicholas doing here?

The castellan took a menacing step forward. "Out!"

Heart pounding, Elizabet fought for calm. "Sir Nicholas, I was but—"

"Another word and I will haul you outside, and by God you will rue the day!"

Elizabet dared one last glance at Giric, warning him with a subtle gesture to remain quiet, then hurried out. She held her breath as she rushed past the castellan. Why hadna the guard announced his arrival? Or, so immersed in tending to her brother had she missed that as well? As if it mattered now. After last night's confrontation between them, this was the last thing she needed.

"Thomas," the castellan boomed.

Halfway down the corridor, she turned.

Nicholas's gray eyes narrowed. "To my chamber."

"Let me expla—"

"Now!"

With leaden steps, she followed him as he stormed past.

The door to his chamber swung open with an ominous creek as he shoved it. "In."

She hurried past.

The door slammed.

Fear pounding through her, Elizabeth whirled and came a hair's width from colliding with his immense frame. Mary help her! Nicholas towered above her, and his body rippled with battle-honed muscles—every ounce the warrior. With a hard swallow, she took a step back.

"You deliberately disobeyed me!" With sleek speed and grace, he closed the distance.

Torchlight brandished yellow paths of light exposing the fury carved on his face.

"I—I had to."

His brow raised in a dangerous slant. "What you *had* to do was to follow my orders. I entrusted you to be my squire, to serve me with unyielding loyalty. Instead, you challenge me on every front."

She wanted to rebel, but he spoke the truth. "You do nae understand," she said in a rough whisper.

"I understand all too well," he said through clenched teeth. "I was a lackwit to trust you—ever." He leaned inches from her face. "And more so to even care if you are foolish enough to endanger your life by tending the prisoners without the aid of a guard!"

"They willna hurt me."

"Blast it," he boomed. "Lord Terrick is a dangerous man. My prisoner, for God's sake!"

She stiffened. "He is a Scot!"

He muttered an oath and stared at her as if fairies danced around her head. "A Scot who could end your life with a flick of his hand."

Elizabeth lifted her chin. "He wouldna harm me."

Fury blazed in his eyes. "You do not know that for certain, but that is not the issue. You are. Blast it!" He prowled the confines of the chamber.

With his each step, her foreboding grew. Never had she seen Nicholas this upset. What was he going to do?

He halted near the window, skewered her with his gaze. Regret flashed in his eyes.

Panic swept her. He was going to release her as his squire. Nay. She couldna lose this lifeline to her brother, especially with Dunsten intent on killing Giric. Her body trembling, she stepped forward.

"Please. Let me stay." Her heartfelt plea echoed between them. Though her every instinct warned her to keep her distance, she took another step closer. "I know these people. They touched my life." She searched his gaze, desperate for him to understand. "I couldna leave them to die or to go without knowing whether or nae they lived. Though my leaving Wolfhaven Castle was nae the way I would wish, 'twas done out of necessity. Please, I beseech you, allow me to remain."

Nicholas stared at his squire, furious at himself for even listening. But Thomas's loyalty toward his people moved him, more so because after having been banned from the prisoners, he went there to care for them, even at the risk of being caught.

A dangerous decision he knew too well. When he'd stood up for Dougal all those years ago, hadn't he risked censure from his peers as well as losing his position within the monastery? He could have sat by while Dougal had received the beating for his outburst, but like Thomas, when the life of someone he cared about lay in peril, he couldn't stand silently by and do naught. He studied the lad whose guilt lay only in his sincere desire to help.

Blast it! If any of Thomas's actions had been for a selfish cause, 'twould have been easy to cast him from the castle without hesitation. But the lad's every deed was for the sake of others, never himself.

For the first time in his life, Nicholas was at an impasse. By rights he should dismiss the lad for his disobedience, but how could he send him away? Though their causes were different, the reasoning, to protect those they cared about, was the same.

"Sir Nicholas?" Thomas laid his hand upon Nicholas's forearm.

He stared at the slender fingers wrapped over his arm, the gesture intimate. Sweat broke out on his forehead.

"I know you are angry and have every right to be so, but please, do nae send me away. Give me this one chance." Desperation tainted his words. "In the future, if I displease you in any manner, I will pack my things and leave without protest. And I will nae bother you again. Ever."

Compassion collided with the anger of being misled. Admiration warred with the fact this lad was a reiver. Blast it, he was going insane!

Nicholas released a taut sigh unsure how to handle this complex situation. At some point in his time spent with Thomas, he'd lost his objectivity in how to deal with the lad. 'Twould be best once he was within his brother's care.

Guilt at his growing personal feelings toward Thomas eroded his last reservations. "You may tend the wounded Scots, but with a guard nearby."

Relief tumbled over Thomas's face. "My thanks."

Nicholas stared at his squire's hand, then jerked his arm away. "Do not thank me," he snapped, ashamed of the warmth the lad's touch left. "Naught has changed. Once I hear from my brother, you will depart. Remember that."

Hurt darkened his squire's emerald eyes. With an unsteady breath, he nodded then walked to the door.

The bells of Terce tolled as Nicholas studied Thomas's stoic departure, wanting to remain unmoved. He gave a silent curse, damning the entire situation, wishing the lad was already with Hugh, and damning the day when Thomas would leave.

A hard knock sounded at the door.

Thomas reached for the handle, glanced back.

Nicholas nodded, and his squire opened the door.

Sir Jon hurried inside, glanced briefly at Thomas before facing Nicholas. "The lad Malcolm has fallen into the well!"

"Is he alive?" Nicholas demanded as he stepped forward.

"He is," the knight replied, "but from his cries, he will not hold out much longer."

He bolted past Thomas and the knight. As Nicholas shoved open the door of the keep, he spotted the crowd gathering around the brick enclosure. He strode toward the throng. "Move back!"

The knights and Scots huddled around the well parted.

Nicholas reached the edge of the layered rock, peered down the narrow shaft. Blackness greeted him. "Malcolm!"

A whimper rose from the inky depths.

Sunlight warmed his face as Nicholas turned to Sir Jon. "How long has he been down there?"

"Not too long," his knight replied.

"Find another rope," Nicholas ordered. Moments later a rough twist of braided hemp was passed to him.

"Sir Nicholas," Sir Jon said. "We have already tried to lower a line to him. He will not grab it."

"The lad is in shock." Leaning over, Nicholas fed the braided cord down the narrow shaft until the faint splash of water alerted him the line had hit the surface. "Malcolm, grab the rope." His deep voice echoed to a muted call, and he prayed the lad would respond to his authority.

Seconds passed.

The cool, fresh scent of the spring blended with stale rock and moss as Nicholas moved his hand in a circle over the well to trail the rope back and forth, confident that at some point it touched the lad. "Malcolm."

"I—I canna." Exhaustion swirled heavy in the boy's weak reply.

God's teeth. This wasn't going to work. Either Malcolm was too scared or weak to try. "Hang on. Someone is coming to help you." He stepped back and turned. Whoever went down the shaft had to be small. His gaze swept over the men. That immediately ruled out of the remainder of his knights. Neither did he see anyone from the Scots whom he'd consider.

Thomas's small frame, wedged between his warriors.

Nicholas waved the lad forward.

His squire's oval face grew chalky white and he didn't move.

"Come here," Nicholas snapped, irritated by his hesitation. Didn't he realize that every moment counted? "You are the only one small enough to go down into the well. Come here—now!"

His squire stared at the circle of stone. Fear, clear and stark, darkened his eyes.

"Thomas?" In an instant he realized his problems extended beyond the lad in the well, but he brought his focus back to one. For the moment, Malcolm needed saving.

Small shuddered gasps fell from Thomas's lips, each one raw and desperate.

Nicholas handed the rope to Sir Jon. "Move everyone back," he said, all the while never taking his gaze from his squire.

The lad's eyes widened at his approach. Then he stepped back.

"Thomas," Nicholas said as he closed, keeping his voice soft. "Malcolm is trapped in the well. You are the only one who can fit inside and is strong enough to save him."

His lower lip trembled. "I—I do nae think I can."

He advanced another step. This time his squire didn't pull back; a small victory. "You can."

The lad's body shuddered. "There must be another way. If we can—"

"No!" He'd wanted to avoid pressuring him, but no time to debate the issue remained. Like it or not, he would go. Nicholas clasped Thomas's shoulders, shoulders too small to bear this burden, a lad too young to wear the scares he bore. "I am going to wrap the rope around you," he said in a cool, firm voice. "Then you will be lowered."

"I—"

"Once you reach the water," he continued, giving his squire no room to argue, "tug on the line. Is that clear?"

"Aye—Nay." The fear in his eyes avalanched to panic. "I—"

"God's teeth! If you do not go down there, Malcolm will die."

Thomas emotionally withdrew, the clarity harsh, cold in his eyes, but he nodded. "I will go," he whispered, his voice dull.

Nicholas led him to the opening before his squire had second thoughts. After securing the rope around his waist and double-checking the knot, he lifted Thomas to the ledge of the well.

His squire's boots scraped as he slid them over the edge, then he grasped either side of the stone circle.

"Ready?" So slight was the lad's response, he almost missed it. "When you reach Malcolm, tug on the rope." Slowly he lowered Thomas into the void. After a moment blackness engulfed him.

A dog barked in the distance, a bird cried overhead as if on a normal day, when it was anything but.

Inch by inch Nicholas lowered the rope, haunted by Thomas's ragged, fading breaths as he lowered him further down the well. Each second seemed an hour. Sweat beaded his brow as he continued to feed line into the black hole.

"Thomas?" Nicholas yelled when he could no longer hear his panicked breaths.

Silence.

Blast it! Had his squire passed out from terror? "Thomas?"

"I—I am here," came the shuddered reply.

"Thomas is on his way down to help you, Malcolm," Nicholas called, damning himself for having had to force his squire. If there'd been any other way . . .

The splash of water echoed up.

Nicholas kept a tight hold on the line as he wrapped the end twice on a nearby post to keep the line taut.

He waited for Thomas to signal.

Long moments passed.

Nerves edged through Nicholas. "Thomas."

Water splashed, then a tug.

"My squire has reached Malcolm," he yelled, the sigh of relief of the crowd matching his own. As much as he wanted to call down and ask if Thomas was all right, he remained silent. By the tormented state when he'd lowered his squire into the well, the lad was far from fine. Regardless of what had traumatized Thomas in his past so that he feared narrow spaces, at this moment the lad was living his own personal hell. Nicholas grimaced. Whatever the state of his squire when he emerged, he would deal with him once both were safe.

Another tug, though weak, jerked on the line.

"Bring them up," Nicholas called.

In unison, he and several other men pulled on the rope. The line steadily moved through their efforts.

Another hand's length.

Two.

Shadows fluttered.

Thomas's head came into view, then Malcolm's, who clung to him for his very life.

"Pull!" Nicholas urged.

Another tug, then hands reached down, clasped onto the youth, and hauled Malcolm over the rim. Water poured from his drenched body as blankets were wrapped around his tiny, shivering frame.

"Let me have the lad," a woman called as she worked her way through the throng. Once she'd gathered him in her arms, she hurried toward the keep.

Nicholas caught Thomas under his right shoulder as Sir Jon grasped him under the left. Together they pulled him up and over. As they set him on his feet, a man stepped forward and wrapped a blanket around Thomas's shoulders, but his squire only stood there, his eyes dull, his body trembling.

"I will take care of him," Nicholas said, untying the dripping rope around his waist.

Sodden and shivering, his squire stood before him, his eyes wide and empty.

"You did it," Nicholas said, watching for any response.

Naught.

Fear streaked through him as he rubbed Thomas's hands. They felt like ice. With a quiet curse, he drew the blanket tighter around the lad as guilt festered. He knelt before him, stared at him straight in the eyes, eyes the color of iced emeralds. "I am sorry."

Blue lips chattered as he stared straight ahead.

"You are wet and need a change," Nicholas continued as helplessness stole over him. His gut jerked. He'd never intended this.

Thomas didn't move, nor answer, but stood there shaking.

"God's teeth!" Nicholas swept the lad into his arms. "Sir Jon, send a man to fetch the healer."

"Aye, Sir Nicholas."

Thomas trembled in his arms.

With distance-eating strides, Nicholas headed toward the keep. He yelled out orders for a hot bath and food as he crossed the great hall, then half-ran up the stairs. Once inside his chamber, he set Thomas down intent on changing his clothes and getting him dry.

He rubbed the blanket with brisk movements over his shoulder and arms. "We are in my chamber now," he said, keeping his voice soft. "You are going to be fine." As Nicholas started to remove his squire's shirt, with a gasp, the lad shoved his hand away and stepped back.

White-knuckled fingers clutched the front of his shirt with a wild edge. "Stay away!"

"You are wet," Nicholas said, relieved by Thomas's reaction. At least he had one.

A tremor ran through Thomas, then another. "I—I am fi-fine."

Blasted stubborn! "You are not fine, you are shaking like a leaf, you can barely talk, and you are scared to death." He wanted to reach out and shake him, but he wanted to draw him near and comfort him more.

A knock sounded at the door.

"Stay!" Nicholas walked over and opened the door, then moved aside to allow the men carrying the buckets of hot water inside.

Water steamed from the tub as the last man emptied his bucket.

"Thank you," Nicholas said, accepting the platter of sliced meat, bread, and cheese from another man before closing the door behind him as he left.

Thomas stood where he'd left him moments ago, watching him, the hint of fear still clinging to his gaze, and water dripping from his tunic and trews onto the floor.

"A hot bath and a change of clothes will help."

His squire's shoulders slumped. "I—I am sorry. You needed me to help, but I . . ."

"Thomas, 'tis over."

"I have to explain my fear of dark, confined spaces," Thomas whispered, an ache in his voice. "At least in part."

Moved by his squire's caring, he nodded. "Take a hot bath first. You can tell me after you eat."

"Please, I need to tell you now, before I lose my courage."

He sighed, understanding the lad's pride demanded an explanation.

Shrouded in the blanket, Thomas shuddered. "When I was younger, I became lost in a tunnel. I—I do nae know how many hours I tried to find my way back. Then, my candle burned out." His eyes grew dark, afraid. "It was black. Everywhere." He shuddered. "It was so dark."

The crisp snap of the fire shattered the silence, and his squire's eyes began to glaze as he once again slid toward shock.

Nicholas caught the lad by the shoulders. "Thomas," he said, refusing to lose him again.

The first sob came, then the next. "I—I am sorry."

"Do not be," he said, drawing the lad against his chest, stunned by the ability his squire had to touch him to such an intense degree, and more so by his strong need to give in return. When the sobs eroded to tears, Nicholas released him, then gave Thomas an encouraging smile. "Take a bath, then eat. After you will rest."

"Th-thank you."

The humbleness of his squire's words moved him. "You are welcome."

Thomas glanced at the tub, and a light blush suffused his cheeks.

"You will have your privacy," Nicholas assured him.

"My thanks."

His squire's face softened, became alluring, almost sensual.

The moment shifted. Need slammed into his gut. With a muffled curse, Nicholas departed the chamber, cursing himself the entire way. The sooner Thomas left for his brother's, the better.

Inspired by the beauty of the day, Nicholas urged his horse faster, needing to erase his growing feelings for Thomas. Hoofbeats thrummed upon the fertile earth as his steed raced across the glen. Pansies, poppies, purple thistle, and foxglove swayed as he raced past, their sweet scent and explosion of color doing little to lighten his mood.

The dense turf gave way to moss and rock as he guided his mount past timeworn boulders then up the steep, rocky incline toward the edge of the cliff.

Cool, salty air greeted him as he reached the ragged plateau. He drew his mount to a halt and closed his eyes, savoring the serene moment. His decision to escape the confines and pressures of his position, even for a brief time, had been the correct one.

On a rough exhale, he gazed over the harsh, unforgiving land. A land where for hundreds of years men had fought for their beliefs, endured hardships for their people, and through it all loved with a fierce abandon.

Pride filled him. Since his arrival he'd accepted the challenges of this land and of the people hewn from its soil. Inroads to build a foundation of peace with the bordering Scots had taken shape. Now, a fragile peace had settled over *The Debatable Land.* A peace allowing him much-needed time to focus on Ravenmoor Castle.

No longer did the remaining Scots eye him with malice, but with a guarded sense of trust. With a firm but fair hand, in time the last inhibitions of the residents would flee. Then he would have fulfilled his duties to his king.

Nicholas stroked his gelding's neck, then guided him down the rocky path and back onto the thick grasses of the glen. He urged him into a gallop, and they raced as one across the rolling expanse of green.

A light sheen of sweat coated his horse as he reined him to a halt at the end of the valley. Wind sifted past, rich with the taste of summer, warmed by the abundance of sun.

He sat back in his saddle, absorbing the golden rays, but an issue he must resolve haunted his peace of mind—the sentencing of Lord Terrick.

Nicholas frowned. He'd reviewed the previous earl's ledger filled with heinous charges against the Scot: murder, reiving, and plotting against the crown, to name but a few. After meeting with the earl once he'd regained his health, he, too, believed him dangerous, but the notorious villain crafted within the bindings of the ledger didn't characterize the noble locked within his dungeon.

He rubbed his jaw. When he'd asked, Terrick's claim that his retaliation and subsequent attack on Ravenmoor Castle were spawned by the injustices served to the Scottish people by Sir Renaud were confirmed by the Wardens of the Western March. As well, Lord Terrick had stated he'd heard rumors of Sir Renaud's raping and pillaging for his own gain, but he'd never caught the man in the act.

The governing officer's charge substantiated Lord Terrick's suspicions that Sir Renaud had acted without the king's knowledge or best interest at heart. In fact, given the vile acts the previous castellan had committed, death by the hand of a Scot had been a fitting reward for the scoundrel.

But, had the previous castellan smuggled goods and sold them for his own gain, then sent false reports to the crown as well? The ledger, though inscribed with personal comments, indicated no such actions.

He wrapped the reins around his hand. What if there was another ledger? Would Sir Renaud have been so brazen to document his treachery? From all he'd learned, the man would. If indeed a second, personal ledger existed, 'twould be the undeniable proof he needed. Then he could connect Sir Renaud with his illicit dealings, release Lord Terrick and clear his name, and end the last of the discord between the borders.

He was convinced that the recent uprisings, though agitated by the unrest arising from the state of affairs between England and Scotland, were due to the atrocities committed by Sir Renaud.

Neither would he keep Terrick locked up much longer when he believed the man had been wronged and just in his subsequent siege upon Ravenmoor Castle.

Shadows engulfed him. Nicholas glanced up.

Thick, billowing clouds dark with rain slowly filled the sky.

A storm was moving in. 'Twas best if he returned to the castle. With a nudge, he guided his horse down the steep incline. At the base, he headed west, the most direct route home. Foxglove, bog myrtle, and heather lined the bog as he skirted the edge, the rich scent of decaying foliage intermixed with that of imminent rain.

Nicholas kicked his mount into a canter and left the moors. As he crested the hillock, a river unfolded in the valley before him, graced with a stand of trees all but hiding an enlarged pool. With the incoming downpour, the river would swell and the tranquil waters would grow into a raging torrent. Long before it rose to such treacherous depths, he would be safe within Ravenmoor.

The thrum of hooves biting through soft turf accompanied him as he rode. At the bottom of the glen, he guided his horse to circle the stand of trees.

A horse whinnied.

Anger slid through him as he drew his mount to a halt. Had the reivers who'd stolen Lord Dunsten's cattle returned? If so, they would rue this day. He scoured the area.

Within the small grove trees, and nearest to the stream, stood a huge, twisted rowan tree enclosed by a hedgerow of brambles. Blast it, in the dense thicket, he could see naught. Regardless, he would catch whoever it was. Nicholas withdrew his broadsword and urged his mount forward.

The first drop of rain splattered on his cheek.

Careful to keep quiet, he guided his steed through the outlying trees. As he neared the water, a blackbird fluttered amongst the branches of the gnarled rowan tree, heavy with clusters of red berries. At the edge of the thick shrubs he spied a horse tied to the lower limb. Closer inspection disclosed no traces of any other riders.

The intruder was alone.

Where was the rider? By God he'd find out. Dismounting, he shoved the thick, prickly brambles aside.

A woman's sweet voice echoed through the stillness.

Blast it! What maiden would be daft enough to be out here alone, much less with an advancing storm? The thickheaded woman. Torn between propriety and her welfare, he chose the latter. He walked around the base of the rowan tree and searched the sweep of water. Near the shore, a beautiful woman swam through the chilled water with ease, laughing, diving, and then floating on her back.

He groaned as her pert breasts glistened, water beading on their rosy tips. Heat speared through him like a well-honed lance. With a soft curse, Nicholas sheathed his sword and stepped back trying to clear his lust-fogged brain.

A swath of white through the branches caught his attention.

He stilled.

On the edge of a broken limb, a familiar white tunic hung beside a conspicuous pair of trews.

The hair on the back of his neck prickled.

The playful slosh of water shattered his musings.

Stunned, he glanced from the garments given by his own hand to his squire, to the woman frolicking in the water naked.

The tap of rain upon the leaves around him increased to a steady patter. Thunder rumbled in the distance. Wind gusted through the thicket and brambles scraped across his face.

A woman.

Nicholas clenched his fist on a sturdy twig then jerked back as a thorn pricked his flesh. A small drop of blood beaded on his thumb. The color of lust. The color of lies. With an angry swipe against his trews, he wiped it away.

Thomas! 'Twas bloody not even her name!

All this time he'd believed his squire to be a wayward lad, mistreated by society, shunned from love. Gullible, he'd taken him—*her* under his wing.

The events since Thomas's arrival replayed in his mind. His squire's adamant refusal to bathe with the other knights, the extreme caution he'd used to avoid being around people, and his guarded words.

And she was beautiful. So why in God's name hadn't he recognized her as a woman?

Because he'd expected to see a lad and had looked for none other.

And yet, from the start his body had discerned what his eyes had failed to see. The hot rush of desire he'd battled to keep in check over and again had been as natural as the fury searing him now.

His ire shoved up a notch.

The many nights they'd lain in his chamber discussing his dreams and his desires, and all the while a slow but sure bond had grown between them. Had their closeness been a lie as well?

He glared at the woman frolicking in the water with innocent abandon. 'Twould serve her well if he hauled her to shore and demanded answers, kissed her senseless as he'd yearned to do since the first.

Nicholas shoved another bramble aside, and halted as her reason for accepting the position at Ravenmoor slammed into his gut.

Terrick.

The strand of raven black hair he'd found caught within the pages of the ledger, her nervousness when accompanying him to the earl's chamber, and her tender hand wiping the same brow but a day later. Was there no end to his blindness in dealing with this woman?

Jealousy clawed through him with biting green fury. The pain was immediate, searing. She'd used him, deceived him at every turn, for another man. He shoved his way through the dense thicket.

The deception would end now!

CHAPTER 14

Water rushed over Elizabet's skin as she surfaced, then spilled around her in a soft rush. She lay back as the water slid down with a cool tickle between her breasts. This was so relaxing. She should have slipped away before.

"Thomas!"

At Nicholas's furious voice, fear slammed through her. Pulse racing, she turned toward shore.

Hands on his hips, wind clawing through his hair as lightning streaked across the storm-churned sky in the background, Nicholas stood on the bank as if an enraged god. But judging from the anger carved on his face, he was very, very human.

Mary, Mother of God!

With her clothes clenched tight in his fist, he held them out toward her in a vicious shake. "Come here!" His angry shout melded with a clap of thunder.

Icy rain pricked against her skin like arrows, but Elizabet didna move. Couldna. If she tried to escape he would catch her.

A second passed.

Then another.

The water blackened around her. Waves crested with white rose from the depths, but she held, feeling safer stranded shoulder deep in the churn of storm-fed water than in the throes of Nicholas's outrage.

With a curse he tossed her clothes aside, trudged in. Water sloshed in a ragged spray as he closed, with his each step rising higher.

He couldna catch her! She dove, but the churn of waves pushed her back. A hand shot out, hauled her forward, another caught her other arm.

Waves slapped her flesh as he held her before him. His eyes raked down her nakedness filled with heat, clouded with lust.

Warmth whipped through her. Was she a lackwit? He was furious, how could she want him? Except, shamefully, she did.

His gaze lifted, speared hers in a ruthless hold. "You thought I would not catch you?"

As if she could deny the truth? Elizabet nodded.

"And how long had you planned to remain here," he demanded, the pain of her duplicity laced within his demand. "Until *he* was freed?"

So he'd learned that Giric was her brother. Aching that she'd betrayed his trust given in good faith, she swallowed hard. "Aye."

"And when *he* left, you were going to walk away?"

Tears burned her eyes. "You were never supposed to find out."

Disgust raced over his face like the lightning streaking through the sky. "Damn you, 'tis not a game."

Pain numbed her heart. "I never meant to hurt you."

His hands on her shoulders tightened, then he loosened his grip. "You lied to me! Used me every step of the way. And for what? Your lover!"

Lover? Stunned, she stared at him in disbelief. How could he think . . . What had given him the idea that she and Giric were lovers? Then she understood. Ignorant of her blood bond, he'd believed that only a woman in love would have dared play the part of his squire in an attempt to help her lover escape.

Her elation at figuring out the riddle deflated. It changed naught. Her father's caustic claim that nay man would ever want her as his wife echoed in her mind, that she was naught but a burden in his life, words he'd repeated many times over. Did she think her life with Nicholas would be different? Sadness extinguished any glimmer of hope. Given time, she would disappoint him as she had her father. 'Twas best if he believed she belonged to another, then his desire for her would end here. And, 'twould save them both further pain.

"I—I never told you an untruth." The wind whipped away her shattered plea.

"An untruth?" He raked his eyes over her face then down to the outline of her breasts exposed as each wave of the churn of storm-blackened water passed. "And is he worth risking your life for?"

She opened her mouth. "He—"

Nicholas caught her mouth in a blistering kiss.

Elizabet shoved her hands against his chest, but he slanted his mouth and took the kiss deeper. His taste consumed her, and her last defense crumbled. Desire pouring through her, she savored his taste, a raw passion that too soon would end.

Nicholas's body trembled with desire as the beautiful woman in his arms kissed him back. God how he wanted her! He caught her face in a tender embrace and nipped gently on her lower lip.

A moan shuddered through her.

His blood ran hot, and his anger of moments ago slammed to need. Lost to the moment, he pressed his mouth against her cheek, her jaw, then trailed kisses down the silken length of her neck.

She tilted her head back, exposing the slender column.

The splash of rain tasted sweet against her skin, and his body shuddered. On a moan, he captured her breast, then suckled the tender velvet tip.

She gasped. "Nicholas."

At her throaty plea he looked up.

Wind tugged at her sodden hair, tossing the wet strands in sharp angles to frame emerald eyes dark with desire. The temptress, the seductress. And by God, his! This moment, Lord Terrick and the bond they shared would be severed.

He claimed her mouth, demanding, taking, thrilled when her heated kisses matched his own. Wanting to touch her every inch, to make love to her until she screamed her release, he slid his hand along the curve of her back in a possessive slant, pulling her against him in an intimate press.

He wanted her here.

Now.

And when he sheathed himself within her slick warmth, she would think only of him.

Panic raced through her eyes, and she tried to pull away.

His body pounded with unspent desire, and he held her tight.

She twisted in his arms. "Nay, I—I canna. This is wrong!"

Anger speared him in a savage slash. "Because of him?"

"Yes . . ." She shook her head and her hands clenched into fists upon his chest. "Nay."

As if he wasn't confused enough? "Do you love him?"

"Nicholas—"

"Do you!"

"Aye." Her words fell out in a rough tumble, thick with regret.

He released her, wanting her still. Damn her to Hades! He stormed to the shore, snatched her clothes from the bank.

Water sloshed in a frantic chop behind him as she followed.

He glared at her. He was a fool!

Naked, she halted.

With a curse, he tossed her garments to her. "Cover yourself."

The beautiful woman caught them and held them against her nakedness, but the clothes hung in disarray, shielding only one breast and exposing the downy juncture with painful clarity.

"When I make love with you," Nicholas rasped, "you will not think of Terrick, but me." He drew another ragged breath, fighting to maintain control. "Let me assure you, though I have left you untouched, we are far from through!"

Her eyes clouded with distress. "But I—"

"Get dressed."

He strode toward the thicket with the whip of wind and rain slashing against him.

"Where are you going?" she called, fear crawling through her voice.

He kept walking. Once he settled things between him and Lord Terrick, then he would finish with her.

* * *

"Nicholas!" Elizabet's heart pounded as he kept walking. She had to stop him! Shaking, she slogged through the blackened water, then dragged on the sodden clothes as the rain cut an icy path against her skin. "Wait!"

Without turning back, the castellan strode past the rowan tree and disappeared into the thicket.

With the howl of wind, he couldna hear her! She scrambled up the bank as the muffled beat of hooves echoed. Nay! Fear raced through her as she ran through the shield of leaves. "Nicholas!" She broke into the clearing.

In the downpour, she caught his outline fading in the sweep of rain.

Giric! Nicholas would kill him! She must stop him! Heart pounding, she ran to the base of the rowan tree. Her legs threatened to give as she tugged on her boots. She could accept Nicholas's anger. Throughout her life she had disappointed those whom she loved, especially her father. She'd grown up beneath his brutal eye, never being able to be good enough, to earn his praise.

Nicholas believed he cared for her. For now, everything was fresh in his mind, a mix of emotions he'd nae dissected. In the end, with the passage of time, he would he find himself wishing he'd let her go. Her heart wrenched at the latter. 'Twas better if he shunned her, exiled her from his life. Except she hadna counted on him turning his anger on Giric.

After she tugged on the other boot, she mounted and dug her heels into her steed's side. Mud flew from his hooves as he galloped across the moor, but her thoughts already raced ahead, and she prayed for her brother's life.

Rain pelted Nicholas as he rode hard toward Ravenmoor Castle. Lightning cut through the blackened sky, wind howled, melded with the rumble of thunder, but he pressed on.

Terrick.

Terrick.

Terrick.

The cadence of his horse's hooves slammed out his name. Each beat of his blood pounded with unleashed fury.

Ravenmoor Castle's walls rose before him, clawing toward the heavens like talons of stone. The bells of None pealed as the guard's distant call announced his arrival.

He glared into the churning clouds, daring the heavens to interfere. A man who prided himself for his strict self-control, the rage burning through his veins shook him to the core. He understood his anger at finding out his squire was a woman, the breaking of his trust, but as he rode toward home, the sense of betrayal took its toll.

Hooves clattered upon timber as he cantered across the drawbridge. The pointed spears of the portcullis hung in a foreboding arch over his head.

He entered the courtyard and headed toward the stable. The empty outline of the timber portrayed the deception. Nay, his squire would not meet him this day. After his abrupt departure, terrified for her lover, no doubt she was racing back.

He drew to a halt, dismounted.

Malcolm rushed out from the stable.

Nicholas handed him the reins. "When my squire returns, tell him to await me in my chamber."

At his hard tone, the lad gave a wary nod. "Aye, Sir Nicholas."

Memories of the enchantress slicing through the river seared his mind, evoked unbidden thoughts of lust as he strode toward the keep. The taste of her lips, the feel of her pressed intimately against him tempting, teasing, seducing with the skill of a courtesan.

He struggled to block his erotic musings, not wanting them. Failed. Blast it! How dare she enter his home and betray his trust for another man.

Lightning severed the blackened sky as he reached the keep. He stormed through the great hall, took the carved stone steps two at a time.

The guard outside of Lord Terrick's chamber nodded at his approach, then stepped aside.

Fury hazing his mind, Nicholas entered the room, slammed the door shut. What he had to say to the earl was personal.

Lord Terrick, standing by the window, whirled.

Thunder shook the heavens as Nicholas glared at the ice-blue eyes, eyes of the man who'd known all along of the deception, and was the reason for this living hell. The urge to unsheathe his sword and slay his rival slammed in his gut. Never had he been played for such a fool.

Through the open window, lightning illuminated the sky. Thunder crashed in its wake, and the stench of heat, wood, and anger permeated the room.

Leather slapped against stone as he strode toward Terrick.

Instead of fear, the earl stood firm.

Most men would've shrunk back at his charge, but Terrick wasn't most. Nicholas's admiration for the noble grew. This man commanded respect, honor, and devotion, proven by his lover's efforts to free him at the risk of her life.

He halted a hand's length away. "I know Thomas is a woman."

Ebony hair framed his sharp, unforgiving features as Terrick watched him with incredible calm; the only visible reaction, a slight darkening in eyes.

Nicholas wrapped his hand around the hilt of his sword. His fingers trembled with the need to usurp justice in this unforgiving situation. But the noble remained unarmed. He dropped his hand.

Silence.

"I came upon her bathing in the river—naked." He waited for his reaction, pleased as the man's lips thinned. "A delicate and appealing form," he added to appease his wounded pride.

The noble's eyes narrowed. "Leave the lass out of it."

Nicholas cocked an arrogant brow. After his last few weeks of personal torment, Terrick could go to the devil. He would deal with her as he chose fit. "Who is she?"

The hard set of his jaw underlined his determination to withhold the information, but the angst in Terrick's face violated his plight.

Tension sung between them, alive, breathing.

A faint clatter of hooves cantering over the drawbridge shattered the taut silence.

Wind whipped through his hair as Terrick glanced out the window. His pale face blanched. "Bedamned." He turned back and eyed Nicholas, his gaze feral.

'Twould seem the object of their discussion had returned. Nicholas muttered an oath at the man's stubbornness, matching that of the woman below. As a prisoner in his castle, his options were nonexistent, yet Lord Terrick remained defiant. Wouldn't he react the same if the positions were reversed? He squashed the thought. There was no room in this quarter for pity.

Terrick curled and uncurled his hand. He glanced from Nicholas's sword to his face.

Nicholas wrapped his hand around the hilt of the blade in quiet assurance. He was in control of the fate of the woman, of this prisoner, and he would leave naught to chance.

The noble cursed again, then stalked the confines like a caged wolf. When he reached the hearth for the second time, he glared at Nicholas.

"She is my life." His hard-won admission, rough with emotion, fell between them like a gauntlet thrown in challenge.

"I will not hurt her," Nicholas offered, respecting the man for his honesty, and understanding how a woman like her could incite such ferocious devotion. He felt the same.

Terrick clasped his hand upon the mortar and stone. He shoved away. "Damn her!" He crossed the room and halted before Nicholas, his eyes ablaze. "I warned her to leave, but nay. Pigheaded she is!"

Intrigued as jealous by his passionate display, Nicholas watched with guarded reserve, his body taut, his blade readied. Her devotion toward this man was enviable. A sense of loss as the cold reality of how much he stood to lose came to the fore. She belonged to this man, body and soul.

The thought of Terrick taking what he'd sampled a brief while ago incited Nicholas further. He wanted her. Whatever it took, he would make her his. Enough with the games! He held the upper hand and both knew it. "I will know who she is!"

At his terse command, his prisoner's eyes darkened with a threat. "Elizabet, my sister."

His raw words echoed between them, but Nicholas honed in on only one. "Sister?"

As if grudging to admit the relation, Terrick nodded.

Nicholas had prepared himself to deal with the earl's admission that the woman was his lover, but not his kin. "Why would she . . ."

He stared at the noble in shocked disbelief. "She came to set you free?" Even as he asked, the irrationality of the question hit him. Since when had rational thought ever entered into his squire's frame of mind?

Frustration flashed in Terrick's eyes. "Aye, 'tis lunacy," he replied, his burr thick with annoyance. "I told her to leave, but nay. She wouldna hear of it." He cursed then skewered Nicholas with a hard look; the sickness that had claimed him for days haunting his eyes. "And by God's wrath, if you have harmed one hair on her head, you will regret it."

Harm her? Locked within his castle, the absurdity of his prisoner's threat should have humored him, brought a measure of levity to this tense situation. Instead he found the Scot's vigilance to protect his sister matched his own. What was it about this woman that could inspire such fierce devotion as quickly as the urge to throttle her?

His anger fell away. Empathy for the man and for the hopelessness of this entire situation weighed heavy on his shoulders. Both sought to protect a woman whose goal was to protect those she loved.

As unusual a means to an end, it appeared that one slip of a woman had found common ground to bridge the gap, and a reason to form an alliance and bring peace to their lands, when logic had made but scant inroads.

Nicholas gave a wry grimace remembering his soul-searching discussions with Thomas in the wee hours of the morning; his squire's confessions of her father's death. Harm her? He could never do such.

Nicholas let her name roll on his tongue as if tasting a fine wine. He found it fitting to the spirited and challenging woman he'd come to know. "I care too much for your sister to hurt her in any way." He sighed, bound to Elizabet as much as Terrick. "What do we do now?"

The noble eyed him with blatant skepticism. "We?"

"Yes, we." Though he'd not found the evidence to clear Terrick, from what he'd learned, he believed the noble innocent of the crimes lodged against him by the previous castellan. He glanced toward the door. "Guard."

The knight strode into the chamber. "Sir Nicholas."

"If my squire returns, he is not to be allowed access to this chamber under any condition. Is that clear?" Though he'd left orders for his squire to await him in his chamber, in her frazzled state of mind, he had sincere doubts of Elizabet's compliance.

"Aye, Sir Nicholas."

"Leave us."

The guard departed.

As the door shut, Terrick eyed him with caution.

Nicholas poured them each a goblet of wine then held the cup out, pleased when the Scot stepped forward and accepted it. He took a long drink. "I have decided to set you free."

"Why?"

Nicholas set down his goblet. "Because I believe you are innocent. And I need your help to prove it." The steady beat of rain outside echoed in the tense silence. "I found several log entries of Sir Renaud's activities within his ledger, but they are incomplete. They could be the tie-in I need to prove his involvement with smuggling. Until I have confirmation, they are useless."

"And how can I help?" Terrick asked, his voice laced with suspicion.

"I suspect there is another ledger hidden within the keep," Nicholas admitted, "but I have yet to find it. If you are well enough to ride, I have a few leads across the border that I need looked into. Due to my position as castellan, I cannot travel the distance required. Besides, even if I rode into Scotland, I doubt the villagers would willingly betray one of their own."

"One of their own?"

Nicholas nodded. "Several entries, each at the beginning of the month, note Lord Dunsten arrived at Ravenmoor."

Lord Terrick grimaced. "He is a foul lot."

"'Twas my impression as well," Nicholas agreed, pleased both shared the same feelings toward the noble. "There is little to go on, but if you could discover any connection of conspiracy between them, 'tis more than I have now."

He set his goblet down. "What about Elizabet?"

A situation he planned to deal with this very day. "Your sister will be safe here with me."

Terrick's eyes flashed. "She is to return to Wolfhaven Castle."

Bedamned. "I have knights to protect her. To allow her outside Ravenmoor Castle, even with a guard, is taking an unnecessary risk."

The earl hesitated. A scowl darkened his face but concern lingered as well.

"She will be safe here," Nicholas assured him. "I give you my word."

"Blasted Sassenach," he growled. Terrick paced the chamber, every few minutes turning to shoot Nicholas another distrustful glare.

"If I had wanted to harm her, or have her for that matter," Nicholas stated with quiet calm, "why would I offer you or your men freedom or a chance to clear your name?"

The Scot halted. "I will leave her, but harm her in any manner, and I swear 'twill be my blade that ends your miserable life."

"I would expect no less." Nicholas picked up his cup, took a sip of wine. "Can you ride?"

"Aye," the Scot spat. "I am more than able to, but I willna say the same for my sister when I am through with her."

Though the earl's words prophesied ill, he doubted Terrick would lay more than harsh words upon Elizabet.

Less than an hour later and with the bottle of wine drained, Nicholas leaned back against the wall watching the Scot, pleased by their progress. Terrick would ride across the border to find solid proof that Sir Renaud and Lord Dunsten had conspired to haul illegal goods into England. His suspicions were that whatever the pair had brought in under the cover of night was shipped from France. In the meantime, he would try to find the second ledger while keeping Elizabet safe at Ravenmoor Castle. Tasks that would take immense time and patience, especially the latter.

After returning the Scot his sword, cape, dagger, and a basket of food, Nicholas escorted him from the keep through a secret passage.

A mount, saddled and readied, stood at the edge of the forest. Once they discussed any last-minute concerns, the earl extended his hand.

Nicholas took it.

"Take care of my sister."

"If necessary, with my life."

Lord Terrick held his gaze, then mounted. Distant lightning severed the sky as he rode into the trees, his shadowed form lost within the dense stand of silver birch and elm.

Pleased, Nicholas headed back. A shiver raced across his skin as he walked toward the castle, his clothes still damp from his earlier venture, and his boots squishing with each step, but his blood ran hot. The moment of reckoning with Elizabet had arrived.

Upon entering the castle, he headed toward the guardhouse. After informing Sir Jon the earl had departed, Nicholas issued him to pass orders to the men to keep his squire ignorant of Lord Terrick's release. With this task done, he strode toward the keep.

Mud splattered from his boots as he closed, and sunlight broke through the cloud-smeared sky. Its warmth caressed his face like a lover's touch. He glanced at his window, toward his destination.

Toward Elizabet.

A twinge of guilt slid through him. Should he keep her ignorant of her brother's release? If she learned of Terrick's departure, could he trust her not to flee? No, he couldn't take the risk, and she needed to learn that she couldn't always make decisions and follow them on a whim.

At thoughts of her reiving to gather coin for her brother's release, any remorse at what he was about to do fled. Any of her victims could have turned on her, and her selfless acts could have cost Elizabet her life.

Like it or not she would remain here, innocent of her brother's departure. Except his plans for her stay were anything but pure.

CHAPTER 15

Elizabet paced Nicholas's chamber. From the many times she'd crossed the floor, a track should be worn by now. Where was he? And what of Giric?

The fire she'd built in an attempt to kill time popped cheerfully in the hearth. She glanced toward the window. Between the breaks in the clouds, sunshine flooded the land. She grimaced, finding little relief from the passing storm, nor of the glorious day unfolding. After her confrontation with Nicholas, how could she relax?

On edge, she glanced at the door. Blast him. The castellan was keeping her waiting on purpose. Aye, he had a right to be angry, but she must discover her brother's fate! Should she try to slip inside Giric's room? How could she nae? If she remained here she would go insane!

Before she pondered her decision overlong, she fled the room and ran down the corridor toward the turret. When Elizabet reached the second floor, she rounded the corner into the corridor, halted.

The entry to where her brother was staying stood open.

Unguarded.

Giric! She bolted down the corridor and flew into the room.

The scent of wood and herbs filled the chamber, embers glowed in the hearth. Everything was the same as when she'd left a short while before. Except her brother was nae here!

Where was he? Please God, let him be alive! Tears rolled down her cheeks as she searched for any clue of a struggle. The covers of the bed were rumpled attesting to Giric's recent presence, but naught lay in disarray, no blood smeared the floor, or any other indication of a fight. Where was he?

Heart pounding, she ran to the window and scoured the bailey.

Beneath the swath of broken sunlight, knights trained in the list, two women were hauling water from the well, and three small lads chased a loose pig.

No sign of Giric.

Or Nicholas.

There must be some sign of what happened in the chamber. She wiped the tears from her eyes, scoured the chamber. On the bedside table stood two goblets. Hope ignited. In her panic, she'd nae noticed them before. Hurrying over she lifted both cups, sniffed. The scent of wine lingered. What had she expected, one to have the faint tang of poison?

Elizabet gave an exasperated sigh. She was going crazy! Naught was amiss here except for the fact that her brother was gone. In Nicholas's anger, he'd moved Giric. The question was to where?

As if she didna expect retribution? After their explosive kiss in the turbulent churn of water, a kiss that could have easily led to more, she'd witnessed a silent declaration in his eyes—she was his.

Outrage should have shot through her at his silent claim. Instead, loving him, thrills of pleasure had whipped through her. Yet, now he had her lover, or so he believed.

Terrified for her brother's life, she ran from the chamber. She had to find them before Nicholas did something rash, like kill Giric.

Nicholas scrubbed his damp hair with a dry cloth, tossed the linen onto the bed, then walked to stand beside the hearth. Much appreciated warmth from the flames flickered against his skin.

He narrowed his gaze at the door. Elizabet would come. And with her frantic yells as he'd ridden away, he could well imagine the state she'd worked herself into, an anxiousness he would mold into passion.

Though undercurrents of anger simmered in his blood, Nicholas raised the goblet of mulled wine in a silent salute—to her dauntless spirit, and her fierce loyalty. The warm liquid slid down his throat in a gentle glide, as soft as a lover's kiss, as alluring as the woman who'd seduced his every defense.

The rush of steps echoed outside his door.

Nicholas leaned back against the stone of the hearth.

The door flew open. Elizabet ran inside, skidded to a halt. Eyes wide with fear met his.

He took in her slender form, accentuated with the lush curves of a woman. How could he have ever mistaken her for a lad?

"Where is he?" she rushed out.

Her forlorn expression tempted Nicholas to admit the truth, but another part of him, the part that had anguished for weeks, withheld any explanation.

"Please." She trembled as she took a step toward him. "I must know what you have done with him."

He took a drink of wine, swallowed. "He is alive."

Her shoulders sagged with relief. "My thanks."

"Did you think I had set off in a jealous rage and killed him?"

The flush on her cheeks confirmed his suspicions, but the reality of his answer stunned him. What would he have done to the man if indeed he had been her lover? He would like to believe that he would have made the prudent decision, but with what Elizabet made him feel, he couldn't be sure. Never had anyone laid siege to his heart with such fierce abandon.

His heart?

Stunned, he stared at her indisbelief. The emotional turmoil of the past weeks, the reason for his confusion, and for his private upheaval became perfectly clear.

God's teeth, he loved her.

No wonder he'd all but gone insane! Under normal circumstances he would have recognized the signs and would have pursued the natural course in courting her. Except, naught had been normal between them from the start.

And what did she feel for him? From her heated response at the water, she wanted him as well. But did her desire equal love? Needing to know, he set the goblet aside and stepped toward her.

The intensity of Nicholas's gaze shook her confidence, and Elizabet took a step back. So caught up in trying to find Giric, she'd nae considered the ramifications of being alone with a man in his chamber.

Nae just any man, but a man to whom his word was everything, a man whose trust she'd used, and a man whom she loved with all of her heart but could never have.

Nicholas's eyes roamed over her body, devouring, igniting need wherever they lingered, then his gaze lifted to hers.

Heat consumed her. Each breath was a feat unto itself. Elizabet struggled to bring her mutinous emotions in check. Except, how could she love him and push him away? As if considering the circumstance she had another choice? "Giric is—"

"Not the issue."

Nerves shooting through her, she backed up; the sturdy door halted her retreat.

Nicholas advanced another step. "We are. You—I. No one else."

She shuddered, more than aware of that fact, but needing to discover her brother's whereabouts. "Have you locked him in the dungeon?"

He closed the distance and placed a hand on the door on either side of her head, trapping her. His warm breath fell across her cheek, slid down her face to caress her lips.

Tension sizzled between them.

Heat ignited within. How she wanted him. "Where is he?"

Nicholas searched her face and his eyes softened. "Terrick and I came to an . . . agreement." He gave a frustrated sigh. "I had not planned on telling you, and God knows you do not deserve to be let off so easy, but I released him."

Giric was free! Elation swept her, then she paused. "And the others imprisoned?"

"Once they are well enough to travel, they will be released."

Relief spiraled through her and she almost wept. "My thanks."

His face hovered inches from hers. Steel-gray eyes pulsed with desire.

With her fears for her brother and people extinguished, the last of her resistance fell away. After everything she'd done, the humiliation she'd subjected him to, then for him to release her brother and men unharmed, how could she nae love him, or want him with her every breath?

Her father's constant rejections that she'd endured throughout her life splintered her thoughts. How many years had she tried to win his love, a token of his affection, and her each attempt to please him disappointing him further? And Giric, he loved her. Of that she had no doubt. But how many times throughout the years had she incited her brother's temper and disappointed him as well?

Reality smothered her desire. With her headstrong ways, 'twould be a matter of time before she served the same to Nicholas, and she'd already disappointed him enough.

She refused to hurt him further.

As if any of this mattered? With the threat for her brother and people over, she must leave.

Nicholas cupped her chin, startling her from her thoughts. The pad of his thumb skimmed over her lips, rough against soft, tempting against forbidden.

She gasped at the intimacy, aware she must go.

"Tell me what you feel. What you want."

His whispered words devoured her in a quiet hush, and her heart thrilled. Yet, even her fondest wish would be denied. "Nicholas, I—I canna."

His eyes softened as if he could see straight to her soul, and his sultry smile devastated her further. He lowered his head and his mouth grazed over hers in a quiet assault. "Make love with me, Elizabet."

Heat slid through her. "You do nae understand." Mary Mother of God, he thought Giric was her lover!

His powerful hands joined in the torturous seduction, gliding along her shoulders then down her arms to capture her hands. He lifted her right hand, palm up to his mouth. "Then deny me." Watching her, he kissed the sensitive skin, then moved to press his lips against the tip of each finger. "Tell me this is a lie."

Elizabet opened her mouth to speak, to deny him the intimacy that would join them, yet destroy them in the end. Words failed her.

Threading his fingers through hers, he clasped them together in a gentle embrace. Lifting her hands, he secured them against the door, palm to palm.

The air around them pulsed. Her head grew light, her body molten. She struggled to explain, ashamed when she could nae find the words, more so that she would wish that this moment would last forever. She dropped her gaze and shook her head.

He caught her chin and lifted it until their eyes met. "From the first moment there was something about you, an unexplainable need," Nicholas rasped. "All I wanted was to protect you. Yet, with each day, I wanted something more. Now, aware you are a woman, I realize I wanted this." His mouth covered hers, lazily roaming with a predatory grace designed to destroy.

When her body's trembling grew, when his kiss deepened until she gave in to her needs and was kissing him back, he broke the kiss.

Fierce hunger darkened his eyes. "I thought I was going insane."

Guilt swept her. "I never meant to confuse you."

"I know." He took her lips, teasing, taking, and seducing her with his every touch. "Open for me."

She couldna do this to him. Didna he understand? Had she nae hurt him enough? But with her heart ready to burst, she gave in to her foolish need and welcomed him, gasping with pleasure as his tongue entwined with her own. At some point he'd released her hands, but exactly when she wasna sure. All she knew is that now, with her fingers woven through his hair and drawing him closer, she was kissing him back, and wanted this man with all of her heart.

As his body tangled with desperate need, and her ragged breaths matched his, Nicholas tried to slow the pace, but as Elizabet writhed beneath his touch, her innocent assault destroyed his every defense. That she wanted him, that he could have her now, here, was obvious. But after everything between them, if they made love, with her an innocent, the choice would be hers.

Through sheer will, he broke the kiss.

Confusion glazed her emerald eyes as her lips, swollen from his kisses, parted in silent question.

He searched her face, fighting to ignore his body's demands. What mattered now was her. "I—I want to make love with you," he said on an unsteady breath. "But 'twill be because you want me, too."

In answer, she pressed her body against his. "I want you with my every breath."

Humbled by her precious gift, Nicholas swept her into his arms and carried her to his bed. Firelight danced in Elizabet's eyes as he laid her before him, woman and temptress. "I want to touch you, all of you."

With a nervous smile, she lifted her hand and smoothed her fingers along his jaw. "I want to touch you as well."

Her throaty words left him trembling, wanting to please her, to show her with his hands what he felt in his heart. "'Tis safest if you let me."

Elizabet's throat worked, then she nodded.

With reverence he combed his fingers through her raven hair, savoring the silken strands, all the while marveling at the woman before him. "You are beautiful." The blush sweeping up her cheeks enhanced her erotic appeal, then her eyes darkened and her lips parted in soft invitation. On a groan he knelt over her and caught her mouth in a tender kiss.

She tasted of wine and need, of gentleness and a desperation that matched his own. His hard-won control slid another inch.

"Nicholas," she whispered as she wrapped her fingers around his neck and drew him closer, her kiss urgent.

On a shaky breath, he removed her tunic followed by her linen shirt. The swell of her breasts curved proudly before him. "You are beautiful." Eager to taste, he wove lazy circles until his tongue reached the ruby nub.

With a moan she arched against him.

Need thrummed through him as he moved with painful slowness, drawing out both their pleasures.

A light breeze of summer, rich with the scent of flowers, wove around them as he edged down to the flat of her stomach, nibbling a sultry path. Then he knelt and slipped the last of her garments free.

Golden light from the hearth shimmered across her body as he skimmed his hands over her breasts then down the slender curves of her waist to the wedge of downy curls. He marveled at her innocent pleasure, humbled by the completeness of her giving. How had he believed that he could exist without her? He was a fool. Any doubts Elizabet held about this nae being right, about ever wanting to leave him, he would erase now.

She gasped as he slid his hand to cup her, then her eyes darkened with pleasure.

Wanting more, he slid his finger inside her slick warmth and kissed her inner thigh, tasting, teasing as he slowly moved up. Elizabet arched under him, her urgent gasps fueling him as he focused on his erotic task. His body ached, but he would wait for his own pleasure. In this as all things, her needs would come first.

She arched as his mouth reached her apex, and he dipped his tongue inside to taste.

A shiver swept over Elizabet, then another. Her body began to convulse. Nicholas slid his tongue deeper, and she fell over the edge. A rainbow of reds, yellows, and whites exploded in her mind as she fought for control.

Lost.

Then her body was floating, drifting back to reality. The thrill of her release pulsed through her as Nicholas trailed kisses up her flesh, touching, tasting, as if he could never have enough. Tears filled her eyes at the depth of this man, the beauty of his soul, and this gift he'd given her. How could she have thought to deny him?

"You are amazing," he whispered as his lips skimmed over her sweat-slicked body, again stroking the fire inside. When he again took her mouth, she returned his demand, her taste and his melding in a sultry blend.

A shudder raced through her, then another. "Please," she begged, empowered by his actions, curious to learn more. She arched against him and his hardness wedged against her slick wetness. She stilled.

"I will never hurt you," Nicholas whispered, his eyes dark with promise, his voice filled with tenderness.

And she understood. With him it would always be her choice. Warmth filled her. "I know."

"Elizabet." Her name came out in a needy sigh, erasing her doubts. He nibbled along her lower lip and pressed his length a degree deeper into her slick warmth. He drew back. On a bold thrust, he slid deep, stilled.

The expected pain never came.

Worry darkened his gaze. "Are you feeling well?"

She gave him a tender smile. "Aye."

"This time, 'twill be for us both."

With slow strokes he filled her, and her body melted, burned beneath his every drive. She gasped at the rightness of it, the feel. Engulfed by the sensual bliss, she matched his every move. The world raced around her in a violent frenzy. Heaven and earth collided as the first wave of her release wrapped around her in a dizzying assault. She gasped his name as the next rush consumed her.

Their eyes locked.

"Elizabet!" He thrust deep.

Tremors racked her body as his warmth spilled into her, and again her body spun out of control.

Slowly, ever so slowly, she drifted back. Sated, she watched his breathing become steady, his pupils focus, but beneath it all was love.

With a tender smile, Nicholas rolled to the side, and drew her into his embrace.

"I love you." The words slipped free before she had a chance to recall them.

His eyes darkened with tenderness.

And she saw it, the return of her love. Oh God, what had she done? Before he could return the declaration she never should have disclosed, she pressed her mouth against his.

On a groan he pulled her against him until their bodies merged as one. His tender kiss became urgent, seducing. Thankful to have detoured the catastrophe his pledge would have evoked, she released her inhibitions and savored what fate would deny.

* * *

The first rays of sunlight streamed into the window, gliding across Elizabet's body like a lover's touch. She sighed, then became aware of the arm draped possessively over her waist, and the very male hand cupping her breast.

Throughout the night, the hours they'd made love, the intensity, the tenderness of his passion, stole her breath. Passion, she'd tasted it, would forever hold in her dreams. Lips nuzzled against her neck and a slow smile curved her lips.

"Mmmmm . . ." He nibbled her ear. "I thought 'twas but a wish, but none could be as enchanting as you."

She turned toward him, the love shining in his eyes matching her own. A desperate need seared her, and her hand trembled as she smoothed her fingers across his cheek then along the rough stubble of his jaw. "Make love to me, Nicholas." On a thick groan, he drew her to him. He pressed soft kisses against her neck as he cupped her breast. "After last night, you will be sore. 'Tis best if we wait."

Need, powerful, demanding, ripped through her. "Now, take me, please."

"Never would I hurt you."

Tenderness filled her. "You willna."

In a swift move, he rolled on top of her. His eyes holding hers, he sank deep.

She arched against him, and his slow strokes drove her insane. On a cry, she climaxed, and he spilled into her, claimed her mouth and swallowed her cries of pleasure.

Their bodies slicked with sweat, and their breaths ragged from exertion, she let the tremors roll through her. They were one, bonded by the heart, by a forbidden love. Though only one night, she would hold this memory forever. How could she consider more?

Coldness swept her at the memories of her father's bitter words of his nae wanting her. How many times had she foolishly tried to earn his praise, only to be curtly dismissed? Hurt couldna begin to describe the torment, the daring to try to earn his love only to be shunned over and again. And her people locked within Ravenmoor Castle's dungeon. How many had died, including her father, before she could intervene? Then, 'twas Nicholas's fairness, nae her, that let them live.

Giric was right. She should have left. Her being here had changed naught, and she'd failed again.

Elizabet swallowed hard. However much she loved Nicholas, she was nae worthy of such a man. 'Twas best if she leave. He would find another woman, one who wasna damaged, one who could love him in return as he deserved.

The bells of Lauds tolled, melding with the call of the birds on this summer morning.

She wished this moment could last forever, but it was already too late. He had his duties, and her own path lay before her.

A life without him.

"I must get up," Nicholas said without conviction.

And she must leave. To remain would be the greatest of mistakes.

He pressed a soft kiss upon her lips, a kiss filled with the promise of many more. Though sated but tender, her body responded with a fierce urgency.

Ignorant of her emotional strife, he pulled away and stood with a lazy stretch. Sunlight shimmered across his muscled frame, the body of a highly trained knight, the body of her lover, and the body that had pleasured her many times throughout the night.

His soft chuckle made her glance up.

"Do not look at me like that," he half-growled as he began to harden.

Sadness filled her at how easy it was to be with Nicholas, at the possibilities ahead of them. What was she thinking? He believed he loved her, but he knew her naught. Making love didna equate to a lifetime of happiness. Time would expose her weaknesses, those her father so readily pointed out. Before that happened, she would be gone. But, she had this night, one she would cherish.

"Like what?" She gave a provocative stretch, well aware of the lust-filled battle he fought to control, pleased it was she who incited it.

He strode to the tub. With a grumble he sat in the water, cursed its coolness.

Loving how comfortable he made her feel to be with him, she moved from the bed and walked to stand behind him. "Let me scrub you." She reached for the soap, and he caught her hand. The silky lather oozed between their fingers.

His eyes, already darkening with promise, held hers. Surprise then realization spread over his face. " 'Twas you that night!"

"What?" she questioned with exaggerated innocence, aware of the night he referred to. How could she ever forget? 'Twas their first kiss.

"The night I was drunk. I believed that I had kissed a woman and 'twas—" At her delighted laugh, he drew her to him, his punishment tender and sweet. Water sloshed between them like a velvet caress, the combination of soap and man lethal.

Enjoying playing the intimacy of this moment, she splayed her fingers over his chest, reveling in the texture, firm against the downy soft hair. She slipped beneath the water's edge.

His eyes narrowed as he caught a lock of hair and drew her slowly to him. "Be careful, or I will plunder your body without remorse."

In answer, she cupped him.

On a hiss, he hauled her against him.

The slap of water merged with the sound of their hurried breaths. He pinned her against the inner tub and ravaged her.

"I promised your brother to protect you," Nicholas murmured between kisses. "Yet I cannot even protect you against myself."

Like ice thrown over her she turned in his arms and stared at him in shocked disbelief. "My brother?"

CHAPTER 16

Water sloshed between them in the tub as Elizabet glared at Nicholas, her emotions a mix of anger and hurt. "You knew Giric was my brother and didna tell me!"

Nicholas muttered a soft oath. "Aye, but 'twas minor compared to the secret you hid from me. Blast it, I have damned myself for my growing feelings over Thomas! Do you think I found pleasure in that?"

Guilt swept her. She'd watched him suffer. "Nay, but hurting you was nae my intent." But she had.

A muscle worked in his jaw. "Terrick is fortunate his relation to you was kin. Otherwise, I might not have been so forgiving."

Happiness trickled through her at his jealousy, then faded. What they now shared made the parting worse.

She must leave.

Now.

A cold emptiness filled her as she started to stand.

He caught her shoulders in a gentle embrace. "What is wrong?"

A heart-wrenching ache wrapped around her soul. Each moment she remained would make it that much harder to leave. "Release me."

His brow furrowed. "Tell me."

Loving him, if she didna go now she would fall apart. Tears burning her throat, water sloshed as she pushed at his hands upon her shoulders; they held.

"Blast it, you are going nowhere."

At his commanding tone she stared at him in disbelief. The weakening of moments ago gave way to irritation. "Is that an order?"

"I promised your brother I would watch over you until he returned."

"And that included bedding me?"

Laughter twinkled in his eyes as he caressed her chin with the tip of his finger. "An added benefit, I assure you."

She poked her finger in his chest. "This isna a game."

"No, 'tis not," Nicholas replied, his voice thick with emotion. "Lady Elizabet Armstrong, I am desperately in love with you." He drew her to him in the tub and claimed her mouth in a slow, seductive kiss.

His each touch was magic and she wanted more, wanted forever. Except, he didna understand, it couldna be.

Expression somber, he lifted his head. "My pledge to protect you was as much for me as your brother." He shook his head as she made to speak. "You will listen to me. Illegal goods are being smuggled into England, goods that have already cost too many people their lives. Besides the previous castellan, I am unsure who else is involved." He exhaled. "Your brother has ridden to Scotland to find information on several leads. I refuse to jeopardize your life by allowing you to return to Wolfhaven Castle. Until I am sure 'tis safe, you will remain with me."

Elizabet battled the conflicting emotions, but she clung to the scraps of irritation, needing the anchor in the sea of desire. "So you and Giric decided what is best for me. Just like that?"

He arched a curious brow. "And what would you do if I let you leave?"

Lord Dunsten's threat slashed through her in a chilling rush. "You do nae understand. Giric—Dunsten—"

"Slow down." He skimmed his hands up her arms to rest upon her shoulders. "What does this have to do with Lord Dunsten?"

Nerves trembled and her throat grew dry. "He wants Giric dead." She moved into his embrace, needing Nicholas's support.

"Explain."

She searched his face. "Ever since we were children, Giric and Lord Dunsten have been rivals. I am nae sure what made them enemies. My brother would never explain. What I do know is that at the age of ten and six, my brother returned from hunting with Lord Dunsten and swore their friendship was over." She paused, remembering her brother's face filled with angst when he'd told her. "Later, Dunsten approached my father and requested my hand in marriage. Regardless that I didna wish to marry the earl, my father was pleased by the match as he felt Lord Dunsten would be a strong ally. Except Giric intervened. I am nae sure what my brother said to my father in private, but after the meeting, he denied the earl's request. Furious, Lord Dunsten departed, but nae before he swore Giric would regret his interference." Nausea swept her as she remembered Dunsten's touch days before at Ravenmoor Castle. "When the earl cornered me outside the castle during his last visit, he said—"

"What!"

"I couldna tell you then. You thought I was a lad. I planned on avoiding him until . . ."

Steel-gray eyes narrowed. "You vanished."

She nodded, ashamed at her admission, saddened that now, even after he knew the truth, naught had changed. She still must go.

Tenderness interlaced the anger in his eyes as he cupped her chin and scoured her face. "Did he hurt you?"

"Nay, but after Lord Dunsten kissed me—"

"He kissed you!"

"Aye—"

His eyes blackened with rage. "That he dared touch you, threaten you, by God he will regret both!"

"Nicholas." Water slid down her arm and dripped into the tub as she took his hand. "'Tis nae my welfare that concerns me. He is a powerful lord, and I fear for Giric's life. Dunsten told me that if I didna marry him, he would expose me for being a fraud. I—I couldna take the risk. Please, you must warn Giric."

He gave her hand a gentle squeeze. "Lord Dunsten does not know your brother is free."

Foreboding crept up her spine. "'Twill be but a matter of time before he learns of Giric's release. When he does, Lord Dunsten will be furious. More important, he will track him down. Neither do I want you involved further. He is a powerful lord who could attack Ravenmoor Castle, or claim false charges against you to your king."

Nicholas pressed a kiss on her fingers. "Do not worry about me. I have rebuilt Ravenmoor's defenses, and I have the king's ear. King Edward would nae accept an enemy's claim without proof. As for your brother, he will be back in a few days. When he arrives, I will inform him of the situation."

"I could ride to Wolfhaven Castle and—"

"Your brother planned to take several of his men from Wolfhaven Castle with him."

Far from appeased, she studied Nicholas. From what little he'd divulged, she doubted that he would share Giric's destination. At the moment, there was naught she could do except pray for her brother's safe return.

There still remained an issue to settle between her and Nicholas. And wedged intimately with him in a tub was far from the setting she needed to discuss such a volatile matter.

Elizabet stood. The cool drops against her skin made her shiver. She stepped onto the floor and retrieved a blanket. Heart aching, she walked to the hearth, already missing his touch.

The slosh of water sounded as he exited the bath.

She braced herself for his anger. "I canna remain here."

The rumple of clothes sounded. "We have already covered that," he said with quiet calm. "You are to remain with me."

Furious she would dismiss her without question, she pulled the blanket up to her chin, stood, and faced him. "I canna remain now that you know that I am a woman." Heat stole up her cheeks. "Even after last night, 'twould nae be right."

She was driving him mad! Nicholas strode across the room and hauled Elizabet against him, claiming her mouth in a burning kiss. He broke free. "You are the most stubborn woman I have ever met. And you are staying here!"

Emerald eyes blazed and she stepped back. "I will nae be a mistress to any man, nae even for you."

Hurt cut deep at her accusation. "Is that what you think, that I would keep you as my mistress and offer you naught but disgrace?"

She swallowed hard, the pain in her gaze mirroring his own. "I think 'tis best if I leave." Her voice wavered.

He advanced a step.

Elizabet moved back, halted by the hearth. "Please . . . Last night . . ." She shook her head. " 'Twas a mistake."

The last shred of calm shattered. "Bloody hell it was!" With a growl, Nicholas tore the blanket from her. His hands roamed her body with a fierce need, touching, teasing as his mouth claimed her driven by the emotions she inspired.

On a moan, she trembled against him, then she began kissing him back.

Nicholas jerked away, his breathing harsh, his body coiled tight. "And was that a mistake as well?"

Tears gathered in her eyes. "Do nae do this."

He refused to allow her to destroy what they had found. "I love you," he said, cursing the timing, and with her, not surprised that she'd somehow found a way to undermine his plans to propose in a romantic setting. "I would never shame you. Ever! I had meant to ask you tonight with candlelight in your eyes, and with the love that fills my heart. But I am asking you now." He knelt before her, took her hand, and pressed it against his heart. "Lady Elizabet Armstrong, will you be my wife?"

He'd expected warmth or at least a semblance of a smile. Instead she grew tense. Terror whipped through him. She was going to say no! He stood and held her, afraid if he let go she would run. "Elizabet. Last night you said you loved me."

"I do," she whispered.

"Then marry me."

Sadness filled her eyes. "I canna."

Angst tore through him. "Is it because I am a knight and you are a noble?"

"Nay."

Her breath fell out in a panicked rush as she stared at him, and her eyes filled with regret. He picked up the blanket, and shoved it toward her.

She tore it from his hands and wrapped it protectively around her body.

"We will talk later," he snapped, angry at his foolishness. How could he have asked her to marry him in the middle of an argument? Was it any wonder she looked at him as if she would bolt? Until things between them calmed, until she revealed why she refused to wed him, he would have comfort in knowing she was safe. "When you are not by my side, a guard will be assigned to you for your protection."

She glanced around the chamber, her gaze pausing at the rumpled sheets. "I am such a fool."

"As well as I," Nicholas said. "But we cannot erase last night, nor would I want to."

"You do nae understand."

He glanced out the window. The sun was edging over the horizon. Blast it. The luxury of time had run out. "We will discuss *us* later. 'Tis time to break our fast and take care of the day's duties."

The all-too-familiar stubbornness filled her gaze.

"You can make this hard or easy." From her defiant stance, she would choose the latter. Nicholas caught her hand and led her where he'd removed her garb the night before, remembering all too well her naked body pressed against his. Desire filled him, and he began to harden. "Get dressed."

She eyed him, leaving the clothes untouched. "I do nae like it."

He couldn't help but smile. By God but she was beautiful when she was upset. "I never thought you would." He started to leave, paused at the door, and glanced back, her rumpled anger endearing, her sleep-mussed body wrapped in the blanket stealing his heart. "I will speak with one of the other women. Until we can have some of your clothes sent from Wolfhaven Castle, you will have to make do. And I will be by your side when the residents of Ravenmoor Castle learn the truth."

With a muttered grumble, she picked up a boot and tossed it at the door.

On a chuckle he slipped out, pulled the door shut.

A thump echoed on the opposite side.

Nicholas laughed, sure he was insane, more sure he was in love. For the next few days, until her brother returned, their time together would prove interesting. The challenge of melting Elizabet's anger heated his blood, of gaining her agreement to his proposal a challenge unto itself.

He smiled as he strode down the corridor. As much as she may wish, she wasn't immune to him, and the warrior in him prepared for the upcoming sensual battle. A siege he would win.

The lingering scent of porridge and ale from the morning meal hung in the air as Elizabet peered around the corner into the great hall. On a normal day only a few women would have cleaned up from the morning meal as the hounds scavenged through the rushes for the last morsel of meat or bread. Instead, a small crowd of knights and peasants had gathered within, which could have been a thousand as far as she was concerned.

At her side, Nicholas gave her hand a gentle squeeze. "All will be well."

Thankful for his presence, Elizabet released a slow breath and glanced up. "I am nervous." An understatement. She was terrified.

Though dressed in a fine linen gown of eggshell blue, found in one of Sir Renaud's many chests, and with her raven hair brushed until it shone and looking every bit the noblewoman, she felt like an oddity. How did one announce that the lad they'd worked alongside over the past several weeks was in fact a woman, a woman who was nobility, and one who had stayed within their castellan's chamber? God forbid if they learned she'd shared his bed.

Fear tore through her. This wasna going to work. If they didna eye her as some three-headed ogre, they would look upon her as a traitor, or believe her his whore.

"'Tis time," Nicholas said, drawing her forward.

"I am nae ready," she whispered. "A moment more."

With tender smile he winked. "You are too stubborn to be nervous."

She drew her shoulders back. And what did he know, the Sassenach. "I am . . ." At the love in his eyes, she realized he'd goaded her on purpose to make her forget her nerves. How could she nae love him, or even think of shaming him by acting with any hint of cowardice? Elizabet drew herself up. For him she would brave it all.

With a pleased nod Nicholas took her arm, then stepped forward with her by his side.

Sir Jon was the first to spot them as they entered the great hall. He turned to the throng milling about. "Pray silence for Sir Nicholas Beringar, Castellan of Ravenmoor Castle." His deep voice echoed throughout the large chamber.

Nicholas nodded as they walked past Sir Jon, but Elizabet could only nod. For once in her life words escaped her. The clack of their leather boots upon the wooden dais was like the beat of a drum, as if she marched toward the gallows.

At the center of the wooden platform, he halted. As if in slow motion, he turned with her toward the curious eyes of his knights. Nicholas's gaze swept over the audience. "Since my arrival I have seen Ravenmoor change, become a castle I am proud of. Negotiations to bring peace along our borders are well underway. But I stand before you this day and am honored to introduce you to a woman whose spirit is the essence of the Scots."

"She looks like the lad, Thomas," came a yell from the back.

Murmurs rippled through the crowd like a storm-fed wave, but their unsure eyes never left her.

And Elizabet wished the ground would open and swallow her up.

"That is because 'tis the guise she used to fool us all," Nicholas answered, his voice strong and proud.

A hush fell over the crowd, but her heart swelled with love. For her he'd braved humiliation.

As if daring any challenge, Nicholas scanned the crowd. "Though her means to gain entry into Ravenmoor Castle was extreme, her daring was to rescue her people locked within the dungeon." He turned toward her, pride warm in his heart. "I am honored to introduce to you Lady Elizabet Armstrong from Wolfhaven Castle which borders us on Scottish soil. Until recently, her brother, Lord Terrick, was held prisoner within Ravenmoor."

Grumbles of the earl's release ran through the crowd like the hum of angry bees.

Nicholas again held his hand up to silence any protest, proud of how Elizabet held her own when most women would have fled or never dared to enter. Aye she was nervous, but if he hadn't known her so well, he would never have seen it. "I released Lord Terrick because I believed his imprisonment to be unfair. He and his people were provoked by foul means."

"Sir Renaud said Lord Terrick was a reiver and murderer," a large man near the front called out. "A man nae to be trusted."

He held the man's gaze. "Sir Renaud's views are not my own," Nicholas replied. The last thing he would wish is to put Elizabet through this hell, but he would end untoward speculation here and now. She deserved that and more.

Nicholas took a step closer to the crowd; Elizabet remained by his side. "At my initial arrival, one had only to look around to see the shambles Sir Renaud had allowed Ravenmoor Castle to fall into. Upon further investigation, I discovered gross errors in the ledgers accounts. In addition, the previous castellan's actions toward his people and the border Scots have been cruel and highly improper, conduct I have reported to the king." He curled his hand upon the hilt of his blade and scanned the crowd, meeting his men's gaze. "If anyone finds they cannot accept my decision, you are free to leave. But if you remain, I will tolerate naught but respect toward Lady Elizabet. Her actions, though extreme, were inspired by love and devotion to her brother. If given her situation, would your actions be as courageous?" His voice echoed through the room, cascading into silence.

Each of his knights remained.

Relief sifted through him. Though he could ill afford to lose a single man, he refused to have any remain who harbored ill feelings toward Elizabet or his decision this day. "Are there any other questions?"

Silence.

He nodded. "Then let us be about our tasks." As he led Elizabet away, worry sifted through him. What would Lord Dunsten's reaction be once he found out Elizabet was staying within his home?

As the torches in the great hall illuminated the evening meal, Elizabet forced herself to swallow another bite of venison, thankful the day was over. She'd expected stronger resistance from the castellan's men to her presence within Ravenmoor Castle. Except for a few covert stares, nay more had been said. Their silence did nae erase the shock written upon their faces, nor their speculation. A lackwit could have deducted their belief—she was his mistress.

He asked you to marry him.

Mayhap, but caught up in her desire, she'd given herself to Nicholas before the rites of marriage and disgraced her family's name.

Laying the dagger by the trencher, Elizabet took another bite and forced herself to chew the tender meat. However much she wanted to flee, she refused to give any within the great hall the satisfaction of seeing her squirm.

Nausea churned in her stomach and she gave a covert glance at Nicholas, who sat at her side. With leisure, he sipped his wine as if he'd nae stood before his men, then the residents of the castle this day, and stated she was a woman and would remain as his guest for the next few days. Or the fact that after the meeting, he'd given her the responsibility of running the keep, normally the wife's task.

Oh, he was a sly one, claiming he needed her help as duties outside the keep required his attention. Though she'd agreed, once he returned she'd leave.

A lad approached and held up a bottle of wine. "More, Lady Elizabet?"

"Nay."

The lad moved to Nicholas's side. "Wine, Sir Nicholas?"

The castellan nodded.

He refilled his cup then moved away.

Nicholas glanced over. "You are quiet this eve."

She slanted him a glance. Curiosity shimmered in his eyes as well as determination. The hunter and she the prey. "I have naught to say."

He arched a brow as a slow, challenging smile touched his lips. "'Tis a first."

"You are reprehensible," she charged in a fierce whisper.

"And you are beautiful."

His flattering words softened her heart. She lifted her goblet and pretended interest in the wine, praying it would numb her body's traitorous response. How dare he undermine her anger with such ease, seduce her with such endearing charm. "I am tired and wish to go abed."

His eyes darkened with desire.

Elizabet set down the goblet. "Alone."

Pride shone in his expression. "You were wonderful this day, Elizabet. A lesser woman would have crumbled."

She lifted her head with a stubborn tilt, nae wanting his praise or the satisfaction that came with his words. "I am a Scot."

"That you are," he said with reverence. "And a beautiful one at that." He set his goblet aside and stood, then offered her his hand. "Let me escort you to your chamber. The day has been long and I am weary."

Her hand trembled as she laid it within his palm, aware of those around them who watched, his words of escort offered for propriety. Once the castle had settled for the night, she would slip into his chamber.

His fingers closed around hers, and his eyes held hers as he drew her to her feet. "I would give my life to protect you. Never doubt that."

And she didn't.

The hot August night embraced her as she entered his chamber hours later, the breeze sweet with the fragrance of heather, warm with a sultry promise. The soft orange glow melded with purple on the horizon.

Nicholas closed the chamber door behind her. It shut with a muffled thud.

His bed loomed between them. Uncomfortable she walked to the window. The hushed song of the crickets filled the oncoming night. She tried to rid herself of thoughts of the rightness of this moment, the intimate solitude that bound them, the endless comfort she found in his arms, or of her desire to never leave. "I was wrong to come."

Nicholas placed his hands on her shoulders, and she jumped. He turned her to face him. "What are you thinking?"

"Of leaving."

"Liar."

The layer of passion in his quiet accusation slid through her like a warm, honeyed mead. "We are nae wed. I should sleep in my room. By remaining here with you, I dishonor my family." The last stumbled out, filled with the nervousness she'd withheld throughout the day. Now, with the night upon them, her fragile wall tumbled, exposing her soul.

He brushed a strand of hair behind her ear, his dove-gray eyes never leaving hers. "Then marry me, Elizabet, for naught has ever felt so right."

"Please . . ."

He slid the pad of his thumb over her lower lips, then lowered his mouth until he claimed hers in a tender kiss. "Tell me you do not want me," he whispered, then skimmed his hands down the curve of her back, drawing her against him until their bodies fit tight.

She shuddered as he nuzzled her neck.

"Tell me now if you want to leave."

Waves of need swept her, smothering the reasons she shouldna remain. "I—I canna."

He nipped at the hollow of her neck then teased her with his tongue. "Come to bed. The hours will pass too quickly before you must slip to your chamber." He captured her nipple through the fabric.

She moaned.

"Let me make love to you, Elizabet. You fulfill my every fantasy, drive me wild with desire."

And she was lost. She was a fool. And she was in love.

Tiredness rolled through Nicholas as he again thumbed through page after page of the ledger, searching for an entry to prove Sir Renaud's deception. After a long and demanding day rebuilding walls and settling minor disputes, 'twould seem that he would discover only frustration, not answers within the previous castellan's records.

"Blast it!" He closed the leather-bound journal, sat back, and rubbed his brow. "I thought I would find some clue, but there is naught more than transactions one would find in any castle's ledger."

Elizabet studied the jumbled entries on the yellowed pages. "What exactly did you hope to discover?"

Beyond the closed door of the chamber, a woman's muted laughter broke into his musings. The tempting smell of roasting meat for the evening meal and the scrape and shuffle of trencher tables being set up in the great hall echoed in the adjoining chamber.

He shoved the worn book away and stood. "There is evidence that I am missing about Sir Renaud's underhanded dealings." With a frustrated sigh he paced the small room. Almost another full day had passed and yet they'd found naught more. When he walked to the desk again, he halted, staring at the thick-bound book he'd scoured for the last several hours. "I cannot explain why, but I believe proof is here, and for whatever reason, I am missing it."

"You have gone through every page," Elizabet said with understanding, "some twice."

"And naught. Where is it? What is the fact that I am too blind to see? I thought mayhap there was another ledger, yet I have found none." Another wave of tiredness swept over him and a dull throb began to pound at his temple.

" 'Twill be time to eat soon," Elizabet said. "There is little more that can be done this night."

He stared at the ledger, the pages jumbling in his mind to a haze. The tallow candle sitting upon the desk sputtered. He glanced over. It had burned to a nub.

"Nicholas," Elizabet softly urged. "As much as I, too, wish to find the answer, you are tired. 'Twill do nay good to continue this day. Please, put the ledger away."

She was right. Any answers it held eluded him. Tomorrow, rested and fresh, he would review the pages again. Mayhap then he would unveil its secrets. He lifted the bound pages. The smell of old leather and frustration combined in an unsettling mix.

Ready for this day to end, he jerked open the bottom drawer, tossed the book inside, shoved it shut. Wood scraped then jammed. As before, the drawer became stuck about an inch from closing. "God's teeth!" He wrenched the drawer back open.

Elizabet gasped. "Pull the drawer farther out."

Tiredness glazing his vision, he glanced up. "I was going to do that," he muttered. "I am not blind." The throbbing at his temple grew. " 'Tis old and needs to be fixed." Another problem he would take care of when time allowed.

She shook her head. "It may be old," she said with excitement, "but whoever crafted it knew their trade."

"Their trade?"

"We have a similar desk in my father's solar," Elizabet explained, "and it has a secret compartment in the bottom to stow letters of importance."

Stunned, he stared at the jammed ledger. "You mean the entire time, the other ledger was but inches away?"

"Aye."

He jerked open the drawer, tossed the exposed ledger onto the desk. In a trice he'd emptied the layer of yellowed papers stacked beneath. Hope built as he skimmed his fingers along the bottom of the wooden panel. At the third corner, his thumb slid over an irregular indent.

"I found it!" He placed his finger into the slight gouge and pulled. Smooth as silk the drawer lifted away. A musty stench of time and an airless mix of old paper greeted him as he exposed the book within.

The second ledger.

Thank God!

He withdrew the brown, leather-covered pages. Parchment crinkled as he shoved the other book aside, then laid the aged binding on the desk. Praying it held the proof he sought, he opened the cover.

Sir Renaud's name lay sprawled boldly across the top, arrogance emblazoned in every stroke.

Nicholas thumbed through a couple of pages. The entries were neater than those logged in the daily ledger, with each describing a detailed account of Sir Renaud's deceit against the crown, and the depth of perfidy involved.

On the third page he paused. With meticulous clarity the entries listed an assault on a Scottish village, the atrocities committed, and the names of those involved.

Page after page, crimes, often vicious in nature against England and Scotland, were listed in macabre detail with perverse indifference. As with every other raid, Lord Dunsten's name accompanied those who'd ridden at his side.

Anger crawled in his gut at the previous castellan's audacity; so sure he would never be caught, but these pages exposed the full extent of his treachery.

As Nicholas continued to sift through the yellowed pages, he noted a pattern. Twice a month a schedule was mapped out detailing locations of shipments and deliveries, along with contacts for future runs.

Paper scraped against his fingers as he scoured the notations. Several ports were listed over and again, obviously favored for the receipt of illegal goods, but that wasn't his biggest concern. The fishing village listed several times over on the river Annan at the mouth of the Solway Firth was Terrick's final destination. He riffled through the pages, anxious to find the most recent annotation, cursing what he might find.

Foreboding filled him as he turned to the final annotation. He flipped back a page and skimmed up the parchment until he found the start of the last listed entry. The date, two days before the castellan's recorded death. The entry compiled a complete list of the next two months' deliveries with the date of the next arrival.

Tomorrow.

The destination—the fishing village on the river Annan at the mouth of the Solway Firth.

He slammed the book shut, praying Terrick had become delayed in his travels. But he knew, from his brief time spent with the Scot, that Terrick was a man who finished what he started. Odds were at this very moment he rode toward the fishing village along the river Annan. In all probability, he had sent Elizabet's brother to his death.

His body shook with rage. Proof—he held it in his hands, but at this moment he would trade it without hesitation for a guarantee for Terrick's life.

"Nicholas, what is wrong?"

"'Tis here, all of it," he stated, the words thick and bitter in his throat.

She gave a slow nod as her eyes searched his. "But there is something else."

A hint of desperation edged her voice, and he longed to deny the fact. He released the leather journal, stood, and drew her into his arms. The kiss spoke of his love, his need, and of never wanting to hurt her.

Trembling, she pulled away. "Tell me."

"A shipment of goods is due to arrive tomorrow at a fishing village along the river Annan at the mouth of the Solway Firth."

"What has that got to do with . . ." Her face paled. "'Tis Giric's destination?"

He nodded, hating that in a sense he had failed her. "'Tis the last location on the list that I gave him to seek information." Nicholas rubbed his temple. "He was only supposed to ask questions, not be placed in danger," he continued, his voice harsh with his battered thoughts, "but if Dunsten sees him—"

"He will kill him!"

Angst churned in his gut. "I must leave immediately to warn him."

Fear sliced through Elizabet's heart for her brother, but the rawness of Nicholas's despair made her pause. "'Tis nae your fault."

"I sent—"

"Nay. Your decision was made in good faith. You freed my brother, gave him a chance to prove his innocence."

He stroked his thumb against her cheek, his gesture tender, his expression savage.

"If the conditions had been reversed," she whispered, "Giric would have done the same."

"That is not the point." His face twisted in pain. "I do not want to hurt you. Ever."

What if Nicholas reached Giric too late? What if he arrived in the midst of battle and was killed fighting to save her brother? And she realized that she was a fool to throw away a chance at love.

In the past she'd made decisions on impulse, her reasons to prove her worth. But she had grown. And she was wrong to compare Nicholas to her father or any other person in her life. He loved her for who she was. To doubt his love, to nae trust her own love to be strong enough, and to even walk away without a fight for what they had, was wrong. If Nicholas would still have her, she would give him what before she had only dared to dream. "Nicholas."

He lifted his head, his eyes stark and glazed with pain.

Elizabet pressed her lips to his, savoring this moment. "I love you."

His gaze softened, and he tipped his head forward to lay his brow against her own. "I know."

A half-laugh, half-cry fell from her lips. She shoved against his chest and pushed him back. "Nay, you dolt."

His brow lifted in a wry grimace. "You flatter me."

"Shut up so I can tell you that I will marry you!"

Surprise then joy flickered over his face. "You will?"

"Aye." She lifted her eyes to his. "I promise to weigh my decisions before I act, but my fear is that like I did with my father for so many years, and often with Giric, I will let you down."

He lifted her chin. A warm smile touched his face, and love glittered in his eyes. "You are intriguing, challenging, and at times frustrating, but you will never disappoint me. Is this why you would not agree before?"

Heat stroked her cheeks. "I know it sounds foolish."

"No, it sounds like a woman who loves deeply." He pressed a soft kiss on her lips. "I love you with all of my heart. Your father was wrong if he made you feel less of a person. I am not sure of his reasons, but he overlooked a wonderful and sensitive woman. Never doubt that."

With his belief in her, how could she?

"As much as I wish to remain and make love with my betrothed," he said with regret, "I must leave."

She laid her hand upon his cheek. "And I will be here when you return."

He lay her hand over his heart. "And I love you, Elizabet. Never doubt that." Somberness crept into his eyes. "Walk with me." As they entered the great hall, Nicholas called out orders to prepare to leave.

Knights jumped at his command and servants scurried to aid in their preparation.

A short while later Elizabet stood beside Nicholas's steed as his knights mounted and joined the formation behind him readied by the gate.

"Take care while I am gone. I have sent a missive to Lachllan to stay here and guard you until my return."

Her throat tightened as her fear for him grew. "I love you, Nicholas."

"I love you, too." After one last hard kiss, he mounted, kicked his horse forward. His men followed. Hooves rumbled like thunder as they cantered across the drawbridge.

A gust tugged at her blue linen dress, teasing it as she stood alone and watched them fade in the distance, dust churning in their wake. Nicholas was her world, the man she'd given her heart to without reserve. She prayed that he found Giric alive, for their safety, and upon Nicholas's return, for a future warm and bright.

Turning, she walked with dignity to the keep. Her future home, she corrected. She could envision a sturdy lad, their son running down to greet her. Fear that Dunsten would avenge her brother and slay Nicholas eroded the vision. Nay, she believed in Nicholas.

Good always won over evil.

But a sliver of doubt remained.

CHAPTER 17

Elizabet twisted and turned on the feather mattress. With a frustrated sigh, she opened her eyes. Darkness consumed the chamber, broken by the flickers of golden flames from the hearth. She reached over for Nicholas, and her hand slid along the rich brocade where he should have lain.

Where was he now? She doubted he'd reached Giric, but please let him be close. She shoved herself from the bed, walked to the window, and scanned the horizon. The chill of the late summer morning skimmed over her flesh, potent with the fragrance of the night, thick with the scent of the moors.

She glanced toward the bed. 'Twould be foolish to try to go back to sleep. She would only think of Nicholas. Gathering her borrowed kirtle, she dressed and smoothed the wrinkles from the sturdy but worn linen. 'Twas a bit overlarge, but until she had her own gown, 'twould have to do. Though it was nae yet dawn, she left the chamber. By immersing herself in the running of the keep, she could retain a degree of sanity until Nicholas and Giric returned.

The morning crawled past. Though she'd taken account of the larder, walked through the keep to survey the state of cleanliness and made a list of what needed attention, and then had spoken with the cook to plan the evening meal, she hadna been able to shake a sense of foreboding.

Elizabet turned her attention to the herb garden beside the new stable, determined to erase the chaos of weeds and turn it back to its thriving state.

A short while later, she tugged at another stubborn weed.

It didna budge.

Using both hands, she tore it from the ground and tossed the troublesome plant to the side in the growing pile. The essence of freshly turned earth and the pungent odor of volunteer rosemary, woven with the fresh fragrance of mint, scented the air around her as she worked.

Pride filled her. The small, weed-ensnarled thatch of ground was beginning to represent the makings of a fine garden. With care, the herbs she would plant would thrive, and would be a welcome addition to the otherwise plain fare.

Sweat slicked her brow as she worked her way over the unkempt ground. She wiped her brow and glanced up. The sun hung in a golden ball overhead, and white puffy clouds dotted the sky.

"Riders approach," a guard at the gatehouse called out.

Hope filled her. Had Nicholas met Giric returning?

"'Tis the banner from the Wolfhaven Castle," the guard yelled down.

Her spirits sank. Lachllan would give her a setdown, one hewn from worry. She tossed the weeds in her hand, dusted off her hands on her dress, and walked toward the entry.

The clatter of hooves echoed as the group cantered into the courtyard. At the front rode her steward.

The dam of emotions she'd kept at bay stormed her, and Elizabet ran to meet him.

The aged Scot pulled up and dismounted. Faded blue eyes swept her with concern. "Lass—"

"Thank God you are here." She threw herself into his arms.

Without hesitation he engulfed her in a fierce hug. "There now," he said, his gruff Scottish burr rough with emotion. "What have you done with yourself? When I left Ravenmoor you were dressed as a lad, I return you are now garbed as a lass?"

His gentle censure warmed her. She nodded. "'Tis a long story."

Lachllan gave a soft chuckle. "As if with you I would expect different? Now then, let me take a look at you." He held her at arm's length. A frown wrinkled his aged brow. He scoured the keep. "Sir Nicholas has left?"

"Aye. We must talk," she said, fighting to regain composure, "but nae here."

Understanding darkened his eyes.

A short while later, with the horses tended to and the men taken care of, she led him inside to the castellan's chamber adjacent to the great hall and began to explain.

Lachllan scrubbed his chin as she closed the door behind him. "A second ledger you say?"

"Aye. It holds names, dates, places of rendezvous points for the previous castellan's illegal activities. Which is why Nicholas left. A shipment is due to arrive today in a small fishing village along the river Annan at the mouth of the Solway Firth. 'Tis one of the destinations Giric was sent to in search of more information."

Lachllan's eyes narrowed. "Who is behind this, lass?"

"Lord Dunsten."

His weathered hands fisted tight. "A thieving scoundrel. I told your father we should have held him accountable for his crimes before, now look—" He mumbled a curse.

Her interest peaked. "What crimes?"

"'Tis long done."

Elizabet's thoughts spun to her youth, to the day when Giric and Dunsten had deteriorated from friend to foe. A day Giric refused to speak of. "I am nae a child. 'Tis Giric's life and perhaps Nicholas's that are at stake." She stepped up to him. "I will know."

His eyes filled with regret.

"Please," she said, her voice softening. "It has something to do with Giric and Dunsten's rivalry, has it nae?"

"Aye." He released his breath in a sharp hiss. "When Giric was ten and six summers, he and Dunsten came upon a lass in the woods gathering herbs when they were out on a hunt. After bidding her good day, they rode past. A short distance later, Dunsten said he didna feel well and was heading home. A sennight later they found the woman's body. She'd been raped and brutally murdered."

Horror swept through her. "Lord Dunsten killed her?"

"There is nay proof," he said with soft fury, "but Giric watched Dunsten ride off in the woman's direction. When your brother confronted him, Dunsten only laughed."

"I have never heard of a charge against him for her murder?"

"Nay," Lachllan spat. "Dunsten's guilt was never proved."

Nausea swept her. It explained Giric's loathing toward Dunsten and her brother's insistence that Elizabet nae wed him. "He is evil," she whispered, shaken by the man's depravity.

"Aye." Lachllan set his hand on her shoulder. "A bad one he is. We must hope Sir Nicholas reaches Giric in time."

Indeed.

He gave her shoulder a soft squeeze. "Now, tell me why I am looking at a lass now and nae Thomas?"

Heat stole up her cheeks. "Oh . . . I . . ."

A tired smile tugged at the corner of his mouth. He shook his head. "I can only imagine."

"'Tis nae what you think."

"Did I say anything?" But his eyes twinkled with humorous anticipation.

As she recounted the sordid tale, the expression on Lachllan's face shifted from shock to worry. Finding it prudent, she omitted the intimate details. If her mentor knew she and Nicholas had made love, he would be furious.

Her steward shook his head as she finished the tale. "And now?"

She held her breath as she lifted her gaze to his.

His eyes widened. "You love him?"

"Aye," she replied, her voice trembling. "He asked me to marry him, and I have agreed."

"Then why are you trembling?"

"I am afraid that I will let him down." She crossed her arms, the small chamber as stifling as her fears. "Nicholas thinks I worry overmuch, that my doubts are groundless, but he knows so little of me, hasna seen the countless times I let my father down."

He eyed her hard. "Is that what you think, you let him, us down?"

Elizabet dropped her gaze. "Though I tried to prove myself to Father, throughout the years, in the end I only earned his disappointment. Now 'tis too late. He is dead. I failed him."

"Oh, lass." Lachllan lifted her chin until he stared straight into her eyes. "Understand, 'twas nae you. Your father loved your mother dearly. When she died, he withdrew. He couldna deal with her loss."

"But I thought 'twas because Giric—"

"His withdrawal toward you had naught to do with Giric. You look too much like your mother," Lachllan explained. "Every day when he saw you, your father saw her. And it hurt."

Stunned, she shook her head. "But he never told me, he never . . . I only wanted to know that he loved me."

"I wish 'twas otherwise, but he couldna. He never recovered from your mother's death, and for him, seeing you each day was a haunting reminder."

She nodded, the woman understanding, the little girl still aching for her father's love, an acceptance and caring that now would never come.

"You must learn to forgive him. Your father was a man. Naught more. Naught less," he said quietly. "Though he never spoke the words, he loved you with a fierceness that none could compare."

Tears streamed down her cheeks. Loving Nicholas, she understood how her mother's dying could devastate a warrior even as strong as her father. And all these years, her silent tears, her endless attempts to gain her father's attention and affection were misguided. She'd believed herself a failure, unworthy of love based on her father's rejection, when he'd rejected naught but the reminder of the woman he'd loved. She wiped her cheek. "I am such a fool."

"Nay." Lachllan gave her a warm smile. "You are a lass who loves deeply, and I would have you nay different." Pride shone on his face. "Sir Nicholas obviously sees that. He is nae a fool, but a wise man who will bring peace between our lands."

Pride filled her. "I believe he will."

"And he is a man who willna lose what he claims. Be happy, lass. You deserve it."

"Thank you." She hugged him, then stepped back with a smile. "I would feel better had I my own clothes."

He grimaced. "Sir Nicholas's orders were to keep you out of danger."

Elizabet's smile fell. "He is concerned about Dunsten, who is miles away in Scotland." Hopefully leagues away from either Giric or Nicholas.

"I will have none of it. 'Tis nae safe for you to be outside the walls of Ravenmoor."

Anger kindled. "It has been over a month since I have seen my people. I will visit but a short while, gather some of my clothes, then return posthaste."

Weathered blue eyes narrowed.

She laid her hand upon his shoulder. "Do you think I would leave Ravenmoor Castle without appropriate guard? Nor will I tarry."

"A man could ride back for what you need," he said, nae budging an inch.

"If we depart now we will be back before dark. And I promise, upon our return I willna leave the confines of Ravenmoor until Nicholas and Giric return."

Lachllan's mouth thinned.

At least he hadna said nay. She gave him her sweetest smile. "And once we are back, I will talk the cook into baking you honeyed scones."

His eyes twinkled at the last. "Ouch, lass. You drive a hard bargain."

"We will take extra guard."

"I will likely regret it," he said with a grumble, "but aye, I will take you."

Overjoyed, she hugged him. "Thank you." A shiver of anxiousness slid through her, but she dismissed it, confident her worries over her brother and Nicholas spawned the unease.

Sweat melded with exhaustion as Nicholas urged his steed faster. He and his men galloped across the dense turf of the glen, adorned with foxglove, blooming ivy, gowan, and miles of sweet green clover. They'd rested a few hours during the night, departing at the first streaks of dawn to continue their journey.

The rolling valley curved up into a wooded hillock thick with oak and elm. Shadows of the forest engulfed him and his band as they entered, then wove their way through the stand of trees. When they crested the ridge, the small town along the river Annan came into view. Simple huts of turf and earth were scattered on the outskirts of the village, with a larger home standing alone overlooking the bank of the waterway opening to the Solway Firth.

Shielded within the trees, Nicholas signaled to his men.

They drew to a halt.

The scent of the water mixed with that of fish and the richness of the forest. He scanned the sleepy village for signs of suspicious activity as the ledger had indicated he should find, or the clash of blades, signaling Giric's discovery and confrontation.

Naught but the chatter of birds in the trees entwined with the faint echoes of daily life in a fishing village interrupted the tranquil calm.

He scoured the docks edging the shore. Except for several fishing boats pulled up on the banks, and another docked alongside a wooden extension, the piers stood empty. Unease shifted through him.

Had the shipment arrived early? Had he missed Terrick? Lord Dunsten? Their confrontation and resultant battle? Gut instinct denied the latter. There was only one way to find out. "Sir Jon."

The knight rode up to his side. "Yes, Sir Nicholas?"

"I am going to ride in and scout out the village."

The knight frowned. "'Tis too dangerous."

"And too dangerous to bring a contingent of English knights into the village and risk exposure," Nicholas said. "'Twill be—"

Sticks snapped, and the thud of hooves on turf echoed in the distance.

Someone was coming! Nicholas signaled his men to draw their weapons. The scrape of his blade on leather filled the moment as he withdrew his sword.

The steady thrum of hooves increased.

From the sound, a small band, ten, fifteen men at most. Mayhap a scouting party to ensure that all was safe before Lord Dunsten entered the village?

Nicholas held his position, prepared to intercept whoever approached.

The crunch of sticks and slap of hooves increased. The outline of men flickered through the breaks in the trees, then the group halted at the edge of the tree line, much as he'd done.

Curious at their hesitation, Nicholas watched. The sound of muffled voices reached him, then the men, seven to be exact, departed the woods.

Terrick.

Relief filled him. "Wait here." Nicholas kicked his mount into the clearing, and Giric turned, his sword drawn.

As he closed, Terrick sheathed his blade.

Nicholas's mount danced to the side as he drew up before the earl.

"My sister?" he asked, anxiety raw in his voice.

"Is fine." Nicholas glanced toward the woods. "My knights are hidden beyond the trees. Bring your men and join us."

The noble signaled to his men. Several minutes later they merged with Nicholas's band. "What brings you?"

"'Tis Lord Dunsten," Nicholas replied. "I came to warn you that he is scheduled to be here."

Terrick's eyes narrowed. "What?"

For the next several moments Nicholas explained about finding the second ledger and the contents.

"Saint's breath." Giric scanned the town through the trees. "It looks quiet. Are you sure Dunsten's down there?"

"The second ledger indicates a shipment is due to arrive today." Nicholas shrugged. "I have seen no sign of men preparing for its arrival. I was about to try to search out some information when I heard your approach."

The earl shot him a skeptical glance. "As I am Scottish, 'tis best if I go."

"'Tis my duty and I am going," Nicholas stated. "'Tis you who needs to remain here. If anything happens, Elizabet will need you."

"Bloody hell if I will." Terrick's mount snorted as he guided him to Nicholas's side. "You are nae going down there alone."

"Terrick."

He stopped short. "What?"

"I am in love with your sister, and I have asked for her hand in marriage. She said yes."

The earl's eyes darkened as he studied him. "I am still going."

"God's teeth, you are as stubborn as Elizabet," Nicholas said with disgust.

A wry smile touched his lips. "Consider it a family trait." He kicked his mount forward.

On a curse Nicholas followed, sure he was insane to marry into such a pigheaded family.

A short while later, with Terrick riding at his side, Nicholas slowed his mount to a walk as they turned toward the piers.

A band of fishermen worked in unison to repair a net at their approach.

Giric glanced at Nicholas. "Let me talk with them, 'twill raise less suspicion with me being a Scot."

He nodded.

Terrick rode up, halted paces from the men. "We are looking for a vessel that was to arrive today to help unload it."

The fisherman paused, the sturdy twine in his hands, and eyed him warily. "There be nay vessel in port."

"I have got eyes in me head," Terrick snapped.

Unperturbed by his ire, the man stitched another knot in his net then glanced up. "Who would be a-sending you?" he asked, shifting the bulky netting in his hands.

"Lord Dunsten," Terrick replied.

Shrewd eyes sized up the rider, and then glanced toward Nicholas. He shrugged. "The ships been delayed by a storm, but it willna dock here. Someone is sniffing around and making the Lord Dunsten edgy. He gave orders to clear out until he gives the word as to where the ship will pull in. Check with Blar at the stable. He will tell you where we will meet in a week's time."

Terrick nodded and rode away.

Nicholas followed, waiting until they were out of hearing distance. "Bedamned, he knows we're after him."

"Aye."

His body tensed as a terrifying thought slammed into his mind. "You do not think he is headed back to Ravenmoor Castle? What would be his purpose?"

"For me," Terrick said, his voice cold, hard.

"But you . . ." God in heaven! "Elizabet!"

The earl stared at him, confused.

"I told her to remain in the castle until our return," Nicholas explained. "She told me that he cornered her while she was playing the role of my squire, and he tried to kiss her. The bastard.

"Dunsten wants her to avenge me. If he learns of your engagement, he will want to hurt her to punish you as well." Terrick's eyes narrowed to dangerous slits. "He is nae a stranger to Ravenmoor Castle and may have connections within."

Nicholas dug his heels in his mount and raced from the village with the earl riding hard on his heels. Giric was right. Even with Elizabet locked within Ravenmoor, if Lord Dunsten wanted her, he would use his knowledge and connections to abduct her without a trace.

CHAPTER 18

Elizabet lifted her face to the sun, basking in the warmth, the race of the wind across her skin, and the freedom of riding across her land. Over a month ago she'd ridden the same path to Ravenmoor Castle dressed as a lad and terrified to learn the fate of her family. Now she returned a woman in love.

Sunlight shimmered like pixie dust across the loch's surface as she and her men approached. She slowed her mount, walked him to the water's edge, and loosened the reins. Her horse lowered his head and fluttered his nostrils over the water. With a snort, he began to drink.

Lachllan and the extra men they'd taken from Ravenmoor as an escort moved around her, each allowing his mount to the edge of the water to follow suit.

"'Tis a bonny day," the steward said, shielding his eyes as he looked toward the sky.

"Aye." Hints of gold flashed then shimmered across the water with a twinkling mischief. With ease she could envision fairies at play, skimming across the pristine surface with unbound delight. *A day for hopes, a time for dreams.* Warmth bubbled inside her that her mother's words should visit her now. Aye, everything was going to work out.

"We had best nae tarry." Lachllan turned his horse and started up the bank.

With a sigh, she followed.

As they cantered toward Ravenmoor Castle, a cool gust whipped across her face. Icy pricks danced over her skin, and the lightness of moments ago faded. Where was Nicholas? Had he reached her brother in time? Unease filled her as she remembered Dunsten's vow to avenge Giric.

The ground raced past her in a steady cadence. She drew in a deep, steadying breath. *Please let them both be safe.*

Brambles cluttered the edge of the forest as they closed like macabre sentinels to the silver birch and elm. Moments later, they rode into the deformed shadows of the trees.

A bird screeched in the distance.

On edge, she scoured the surrounding woods. Naught except for the snap and pounding of their mount's hooves. "Lachllan?"

He rode up by her side. "Aye?"

"I do nae—"

Sticks cracked and hooves pounded in their wake.

Elizabet turned, gasped.

A large band of men galloped at their heels, their banner well known.

Lord Dunsten.

From the riders pouring through the trees, they were outnumbered three to one.

"Ride, lass!" Lachllan shouted.

Heart pounding, she dug her heels into her mount.

Behind her, the clash of steel melded with cries of death.

Elizabet turned.

Dunsten's men fought with the knights in back of her ranks. Horses screamed as they collided. Riders tumbled from their mounts and their blood stained the earth. Those riding ahead of her turned to join the fight.

"Go!" Lachllan yelled, waving her away.

Elizabet hesitated. Then she withdrew her blade. "I will nae leave my men to die!"

An attacker charged her, then another. Panic grew as Dunsten's men swarmed around her like hornets.

She slashed toward the closest intruder.

The attacker pulled back.

"Lachllan!" She swung her sword at her aggressors in a wide arc.

Lord Dunsten's knights kept their distance, but managed to separate her from the protection of her guard.

Enclosed by the warriors, Elizabet caught but glimpses of the skirmish beyond, sickened as the earl's knights slaughtered her men with savage indifference. Bedamned!

A break opened within the wall of men.

She kneed her horse forward.

A curt order rang from one of the knights; the warriors sealed off any chance of escape.

Panicking, Elizabet whirled her mount.

Their blades readied, the knights held.

The cry of steel gradually stilled, and the forest fell into a macabre silence.

"Pull back," the earl ordered.

A shudder raced through her, then another as the knights surrounding her reined back.

Bodies littered the earth.

Fear tore through her. Lachllan! She searched the slain men. Tears burned her eyes as she couldna identify him amongst the butchered.

Astride his warhorse, Dunsten rode forward. His expression triumphant, the earl halted before her, sparing a perfunctory glance toward the massacre in his wake.

The broadsword trembling in her hand, she pointed it straight toward his heart. "You are naught but a butcher!"

With a caustic calm, he laid his claymore across his saddle as if ignorant of the blood smearing its steel. "A necessary though irritating detail."

"A detail?" she rasped, the rawness of her voice bordering hysterics.

Hard eyes narrowed. "If you had cooperated earlier, this bit of unpleasantness could have been avoided."

"Is that what you call murder?" Realization dawned with a sickening in her gut. "This isna about abducting me is it? 'Tis about your revenge on Giric."

Malice flickered in his eyes. "I have always admired your quick insight. 'Twill prove an interesting trait in our bed."

Nausea swept her as she recalled Lachllan's explanation of how Dunsten, with no conscience, had raped and murdered a young woman; neither could she forget his brutal kiss. She swallowed hard. What were a few more men or his abuse toward her for that matter? How many others had he slain who dared block his way? "I will nae marry you!"

Red slashed Lord Dunsten's cheeks. He nodded toward a man.

The knight rode toward her, and she lifted her blade. "I will die before I let a bastard like you take me."

"If you wish to see your brother alive," Lord Dunsten drawled, "sheathe your sword."

Fear tore through her. "You are going to kill him anyway."

"When I deem it appropriate. Your cooperation could gain him a day, a sennight. Or, mayhap we can come to terms and I shall allow him to live."

"A lie."

"Are you willing to risk a chance at saving his life?" He gave a nod.

From behind his man lunged, jerked the sword from her hand.

Nay! Elizabet kicked her horse forward.

Another warrior caught her mount's halter.

Frantic, she jumped to the ground, bolted.

Two of Dunsten's men cut off her escape.

Fighting to catch her breath, she halted. A low moan at her side caught her attention.

Lachllan lay to her right.

Mary, Mother of God! Tears rolled down her cheeks as she dropped to her knees and cradled his head. "Lachllan."

The steward's eyes flickered open. Pain wove in the aged blue depths. "Lass," he whispered.

A sob escaped, then another. She should have used caution as Nicholas had advised, but like a fool she'd believed Dunsten miles away. "I am so sorry."

He tried to shake his head, but moaned instead. "You couldna have known."

"It doesna change anything. If I had—"

A stick cracked as a knight dismounted. He seized her arm, jerked her to her feet.

She whirled and sunk her nails into his face, clawed with unleashed fury.

With a scream, the man shoved her back.

Elizabet stumbled and another knight caught her from behind, held tight.

"No one is to harm her!" Lord Dunsten snapped.

Pain shot through her arms as the knight jerked her roughly back.

"Release me!" She kicked and twisted to break free.

The earl rode up, halted. His gaze swept over her with malicious delight. "You intrigue me, Elizabet. A woman of persistence and passion. I have anticipated this moment for a long time." His eyes shone with twisted delight as his fingers traced over the leather whip secured to his mount. "I willna break you. 'Twould be a crime to ruin such spirit when it will undoubtedly bring pleasure to the bedding." He nodded to one of his men.

A blindfold was wrapped over her eyes. Before she had a chance to scream, a guard shoved a gag in her mouth, secured it, then bound a strip of cloth around her wrists.

Strong hands lifted her up and set her before a man in his saddle.

Steely arms wrapped tight around her waist. "Do nae fight me."

At Lord Dunsten's voice, her stomach lurched. With a muffled scream, she fought to dismount.

A hand clasped her throat, squeezed.

Blackness threatened as she fought to breathe.

"You are only making this more difficult on yourself," Lord Dunsten whispered in a soft threat as his other hand slid up to capture her breast. "But hear me well, Elizabet. I will have you. Continue to fight me and 'twill be here, before my men. 'Tis your decision."

She stilled.

He squeezed her nipple.

Humiliated, Elizabet refused to cry out, give him the satisfaction.

"The bedding will indeed be a divine pleasure."

His low laugh haunted her as he kicked his mount forward, and she knew she'd just entered her own private hell.

Hours later, a scrape alerted Elizabet someone opened a door, then she was jerked forward. Exhausted and terrified, she wove as she fought to steady herself. A sharp tug, and the blindfold was removed.

Cool wind rushed over her face as she squinted, taking in the candlelit interior. Vaguely she remembered this room from their childhood play so long ago. Except naught existed of the friendship they'd held in the past.

The earl dismissed his men. The last guard shut the door leaving her alone—with him.

Her heart pounded. Numbness throbbed in her hands still bound tight. She tried to wriggle her fingers, but the rope bit into her flesh and pain rewarded her action.

Dunsten turned toward her and advanced. Candlelight flickered over his face illuminating the harsh angles that carved an angry path to his eyes.

The echo of waves crashed on the jagged cliffs below in a sinister backdrop.

A pace away he stopped. His hand shot out and caught her jaw.

Almost losing her balance, she cried out, her gasp muffled by the gag.

He ripped away the offensive material.

Her skin tingled as blood rushed through the numbness. She dragged in a long breath; the briny ocean air rushed down her throat in a raw slide.

"You believed that you could escape me," he spat, his eyes bright, his tone ragged, deranged. "You will learn that I always get what I want."

Her stomach lurched at the thought of his touch. She shook her head. "Please—"

Dragging her body against his, he caught her mouth in a rough kiss.

She balked. His fingers squeezed her face tighter, and she tasted her own blood.

Dark, cold eyes filled with satisfaction lifted to hers. "'Twould be extremely satisfying to remain and take you until you scream, but my tasks this day are far from through."

Repulsed, she wiped her hand across the back of her mouth. "Giric will never come!"

He gave a cold laugh. "Your brother would do anything to save you."

And Giric would. She had to stop Dunsten. Mayhap she could bluff. "Nicholas will kill you—"

His eyes narrowed to slits.

She stilled. She'd nae meant to bring Nicholas into this convoluted mess.

"Nicholas?" Shrewd eyes studied her, growing more ominous, if possible. "You care for the English bastard!" With a curse he shook her until her teeth rattled, then without warning, stopped. The rage in his eyes tilted to madness, and his expression slipped into a surreal calm.

Elizabet's panic of moments ago avalanched into a morbid fear. He was insane.

The earl stroked his fingers through her short hair, catching the end to twirl around his index finger. "When I am through with you," he said in a soft caress, "Sir Nicholas will be but a fleeting image in your mind." He ran his thumb tenderly over her lips bruised by his roughness.

She jerked from his touch.

A cold smile touched his mouth. "You will delight me until the end, Elizabet. Your spirit is mine, now and forever." He released her.

Trembling with fear, she stumbled back, needing the distance, trying to quell her panic from learning that his stability matched that of a crazed boar.

Dunsten, his smile askew, strode forward, and released the ties.

Pain burned through her arms as blood sped to her fingers. She rubbed her hands and glanced out the window where night was descending, and where, somewhere, miles away, Giric and Nicholas rode ignorant of Dunsten's lethal intent.

"They will come." The earl gave a cold laugh. "The beginning of their end."

Elizabet remained silent. Any challenge, verbal or otherwise, would incite him further. She must find a way to escape.

Dunsten nodded. "You are a quick learner, a trait that will keep you alive." Turning, he strode from the chamber.

The guard followed, pulled the door shut. Numb, she walked to the window and stared into the twilight.

With a distant rumble, breakers slammed the weathered rock below with a crushing force, and water spewed high into the air. In the shimmering blue haze of the sky, the first star appeared.

A sign? She closed her eyes and prayed that somehow if she didna escape in time that Giric and Nicholas would find a way to storm Hardwell Castle. As if either had forces to conquer Dunsten's significant stronghold.

Through the tears, another star shimmered in the blackening sky. A wolf howled in the distance, a sad mournful sound. Her body trembled as she turned and slid to the floor. Fighting for hope, Elizabet laid her forehead upon her knees. Mayhap destiny carved her another path.

Fading sunlight trickled through the leaf-filled branches, casting fractured shadows along the forest floor. Nicholas's horse snorted as he guided his mount through the stand of trees, exploiting the last fragment of dusk in an effort to find Elizabet and her escort. "Elizabet." His voice ripped through the stillness with harsh desperation, the hours they'd searched taking their toll.

A light wind answered his call, fresh with the taste of dew, devoid of any sign of her.

"If she is out here," Terrick said, his tone somber, "we will find her."

The muted thump of hooves sounded against earth. "Why did she not remain at the castle until my return?" Nicholas snapped, clinging to the anger. Anger he could deal with, forge into purpose.

"She believed Lord Dunsten was miles away," the Scot returned. "As did you." He guided his mount around a decaying stump overrun with ivy and brambles. "How could she have known he hadna traveled to the village along the river Annan as planned?"

Terrick was right. When he'd departed, he along with Elizabet had believed Lord Dunsten was at least a day's ride away. A low ache began to throb in his temples, and he rubbed his brow, remembering her apprehension at his leaving, her concern for her brother and his journey, but through it all, her unfailing love and support.

"We are not sure that the Earl of Dunsten has her," Nicholas said, holding a vague hope that she was delayed in her return to Ravenmoor Castle for an innocent reason.

Giric grunted. "I pray you are right, but I have my doubts."

As did he. Nicholas guided his mount through the stand of trees, and they rode into a break in the forest. Orange-gold shards of light rippled across the sun-ripened leaves, a stark reminder of the fleeting day. He drew to a halt, listened for a sound of voices, the snap of a twig. Naught. Where was she? Where was her guard?

On their initial ride back to Ravenmoor Castle, a sense of urgency had haunted him. He'd owed it to finding Dunsten absent at the village along the river Annan. But upon their arrival, Sir Jon's report of Elizabet's departure with Lachllan and an escort to ride to Wolfhaven Castle to retrieve a few of her items had ignited a deep-seated fear.

After changing to a fresh mount and adding twenty men to his ranks, he and Giric had departed to find them. They'd arrived at Wolfhaven Castle and learned that Elizabet and her men had left hours ago.

Now, with the sun easing from the sky, they were no closer to finding her.

Had they missed seeing her during travel, and had she and the men arrived at Ravenmoor Castle? Were his efforts, concerns for naught? He prayed 'twas so, but a foreboding gnawed at him like a festering wound.

They rode into a denser stand of woods.

"Over here," a guard yelled.

Nicholas kicked his horse toward the guard, Terrick riding at his side.

The scent of death rose around them in a nauseating swirl. The blurred shapes grew into bodies smeared in blood, the bodies of his men. Panicking, he scoured the dense forest, each darkening shadow mocking his effort. "Elizabet!" His desperate call faded into the morbid silence. Blast it, where was she?

Hooves scraped against the earth as Giric rode in a wide circle, then pulled to a halt. "Lachllan!" He jumped to the ground beside a twisted body.

Nicholas made out the elder, the red of his hair barely discernible in the fading light. God's teeth! He dismounted and rushed to Terrick's side.

A harsh breath rattled from the Scot, then another. His eyes flickered open and regret dwelled within. "I didna know if you would arrive in time."

Giric knelt beside his steward. "We are here."

Sadness wrenched Lachllan's face. "She should have run. I told the lass to go."

"Where is she?" Giric rasped.

"Dunsten has her," Lachllan spat.

Terror ripped through Nicholas's heart. "How long ago?"

The steward glanced toward him. "Several hours now." He tried to swallow, but ended in a fit of coughing. "She fought him. A brave lass, but he—"

"Rest easy now," Terrick said as he scanned his injuries. "We are going to take you to Wolfhaven Castle and tend to your wounds."

"We are closer to Ravenmoor," Nicholas said. "We will bring him there."

The earl met his gaze. "My thanks."

"Lady Elizabet," Lachllan whispered.

"We will bring her back," Nicholas said, his eyes locked on Terrick's. The slow fury burning in the Scot's gaze matched his own. "Over Dunsten's dead body if necessary." He strode to his mount.

Giric caught his shoulder as he reached for the saddle. "Where do you think you are bloody going?"

Blinded by rage, Nicholas turned. "You know bloody where!"

"Aye," Giric spat. "Dunsten would like you riding in mad as a wounded badger and ready to skewer everyone in your sight. Like a lamb to slaughter you would be."

Nicholas shoved him away, staggered by the pain, needing to take charge of the situation. "Go to Hades."

Terrick's eyes narrowed. "If you leave now, you will be on your way right quick enough."

"Do you think I am going to lose precious hours by returning to Ravenmoor Castle with Lachllan and any others who survived when the task can be taken care of by my men?"

"What I know," Terrick said with a hard bite, "is that you are going to wait until the crack of dawn guides you, and you have had a bit of rest beneath you, and Dunsten doesna have all of the advantages."

Emotions pounded him with each breath as Nicholas slowly regained control. The cost heartbreaking. That bastard had her. If he touched her . . . If he harmed one inch of her . . . Blast it! Never had he felt so helpless.

"Look at this, will you," Terrick said with disgust. "I am telling a bloody Sassenach nae to get killed."

Nicholas met his gaze, the bond between them solid. "You are a sorry lot to be sure," he said, finally able to find logic through the fury. "For a moment I went crazy."

A grim smile carved the Scot's lips. "My sister can make a man act that way."

"And when I get hold of her—"

"You are going to love her." The earl shook his head. "You will nae be telling me any different. I have threatened her too many times, and forgiven her the same."

A degree of levity wove into the moment, enabling Nicholas to put the situation into its proper perspective, and finding a friend and more in the Scot. "My thanks."

Terrick extended his hand. "A Sasanach you may be, but you are a good man all the same. And if I thought there was the slightest chance, I would ride alongside you this night to Hardwell Castle."

Of that Nicholas had no doubt. He took Terrick's hand, accepting the friendship and the loyalty offered. "'Tis time to be getting the men back." He nodded toward where the guards lifted the wounded. "Once they are settled at the castle, we will make a plan to free Elizabet."

"Aye," Giric agreed.

As the night consumed the last remnants of the day, Nicholas worked beside the Scot, tending to the men who'd survived and helping to bury those less fortunate. Once makeshift gurneys were made, they rode toward Ravenmoor Castle, their pace hindered by darkness.

This night his purpose was his men, but on the morrow, Lord Dunsten would regret his attack.

No one touched what was his.

CHAPTER 19

With the first rays of sunlight filling the chamber, Elizabet glanced toward the door. The night had passed with a foreboding silence. Whatever his twisted reasons, Dunsten hadna returned, but his ominous presence tainted every breath. She shivered.

She must escape before Giric and Nicholas came for her. And they would, damn their hides. Her brother was a stubborn, pigheaded, loving fool, and Nicholas was nay better.

Childhood memories tumbled back in a vicious slide as Elizabet searched her prison. The times she, Giric, and Dunsten had played in this very room and had hidden throughout the many corridors of Dunsten's ancestral home.

And the day she'd almost died within these same walls.

She shut out the horrific memory, struggling to recall the castle's layout. Vague images flickered through her mind, naught more. Blast it, there was something she was forgetting! Closing her eyes, Elizabet fought to remember.

The door scuffed open.

She glanced up.

Dunsten entered.

Elizabet froze.

Clad in mail, his claymore secure in its sheath over his back, and a dagger fastened to his belt, he strode in with a confident swagger. "Good morning, Elizabet." His eyes raked over her. "I trust you slept well."

An involuntary shudder swept through her, but she stayed the urge to wrap her hands around herself. "As well as anyone held against their will."

A smile crept to the edge of his mouth. "Your defiance endears me. An admirable trait." He took a gauntlet in his hand and pulled it on. "Sadly, I do nae have the time to tarry. As we speak, your brother and Sir Nicholas approach."

However much she longed to run to the window and see if she could make them out in the distance, she refused to give Dunsten that small twisted pleasure.

Seconds passed.

He quirked a brow. "Are you nae curious as to their fate?"

"Will it matter in the end?" A sense of victory stole over her as a red slashed across his cheeks. So caught up in the attack and her resultant imprisonment, she'd nae considered the possibility of him having a weakness—until now.

All through their childhood he had lived for praise, to always be the best. Stroke his ego. Exploit his weakness. This was her only hope.

"You are planning to murder them?" she asked, keeping her voice calm.

"They have interfered with my operation." He pulled on the second gauntlet. "I canna risk exposure." He shrugged. "You, I meant to have anyway. Your brother as well as the castellan are an unexpected boon."

"But you have me."

He tugged his coif on his head, eyeing her all the while. "Aye, I do."

A ribbon of nerves wove through her at his hard stare. "Why do you need to kill them? You could offer them—"

"Elizabet, you as well as I know that neither your brother nor Sir Nicholas would consider joining me. Though," he said with a weighty pause, " 'tis an intriguing thought."

Time, she needed more time.

"I will be away for a few hours. Upon my return, your brother and the castellan will be in my custody." His eyes narrowed. "Until I decide on the best way to dispose of them, I will lock them in the dungeon. Pray they do nae decide to be difficult. If I havena returned by Terce, the guard has orders to slit your throat." With a curt nod he turned and strode toward the door.

Panic rolled through her, and she ran to him. "Dunsten."

His boots scraped as he halted by the door, his look hard. "'Tis too late. You had your chance to save them." Without warning he approached, ripped a strip of the pale fabric from the shoulder of her dress.

Stumbling back, she pulled the torn garment to hid her exposed skin.

With a cold laugh, he exited, tugged the door shut.

Her mind churning with desperation, Elizabet tied the ragged ends of the remaining cloth into a makeshift knot over her shoulder.

Several moments later, the clatter of hooves echoed from outside.

She ran to the far window.

Below, Dunsten led a large contingent of men through the gates. Dust swirled in their wake, then was cast away by the ocean breeze.

Heart pounding, she searched beyond the castle walls to the rolling hills green with life. And she was locked within the chamber unable to warn Giric and Nicholas or to halt Dunsten's madness.

Trembling with anger, she curled her hand on the stone sill. Again she'd failed those she loved.

Are you going to give in, girl?

At her father's voice she whirled. Except for the fire crackling in the hearth and a small hay-filled pallet for her bed, the chamber stood empty.

She gulped a breath, then another, his gruff words echoing in her head. Shame filled her that she'd allowed herself to doubt. Lachllan's words of reassurance as to her father's love came to mind. 'Twas a time to forgive, to accept a man who dared to love with abandon. Caught in her own pain, she'd overlooked his own.

"Nay, Father," she answered into the silence. "I will fight for those I love." She swallowed, the emotions of the moment taking their toll.

"I am sorry for all of the years we lost. I was angry, and if the truth be told, bitter." The flames jumped, twisted before her. "I rebelled, but I guess you knew that as well, and caught in your own pain of loss, you didna know how to reach out." She swallowed hard. "I am sorry."

A gust of wind swept into the room, tugged at the hem of her skirt, then swirled to capture the plume of smoke rising up the flue. The flames of the fire jumped and sparks snapped in a magical swirl.

Elizabet knelt before the fire, sensing his presence, and an inexplicable warmth. "You loved me in the only way you knew how."

Embers spit up into the flames as if he'd answered the same.

"Now I understand. Father, I love you." Warmth invaded her soul, and a peace she'd longed for over the many empty years filled her heart. "I willna give up, and neither will I let you, Giric, or Nicholas down."

Determination filled her as she rose. Though the years hazed her memories, there was a time when she knew every inch of this castle, including the dreaded secret passageways. Her pulse sped at the reminder of being lost within the darkened tunnels.

Elizabet focused on the need to escape, on the lives that depended on her. The matrix of passageways ran to all of the master chambers, but she couldna remember if they extend to this room. Fighting for calm, she scanned the wall looking for a camouflaged panel.

Naught.

Sunlight poured into the room, warming, illuminating the walls as she ran her hands carefully over the rough, abrasive stone. Time slipped by like a thief as she continued her painstaking search. As she smoothed her fingers over the next stone, they dipped into a small indent.

Excitement shooting through her, Elizabet tugged at several crevices around the tiny fracture, but only broke a nail and discovered naught. She sagged against the crafted stone. Mayhap as she'd feared, a secret passage leading to this chamber didna exist.

Boots clacked outside her chamber door.

Her heart slammed against her chest. Had Lord Dunsten returned?

A guard murmured to the other.

The other man gave a quick, low laugh, and then the guard left.

The slight shuffle of the new guard's movements echoed outside.

Was he deciding to check on his prisoner? Had Giric and Nicholas rebelled and now he was to carry out his orders to end her life?

Every gust of the wind through the window, the muted outside voices in the courtyard, and daily sounds that made up castle life echoed around her with haunting clarity.

After the guard remained outside a length of time, she gave a relieved exhale. 'Twas only a changing of her guard.

With steely determination she resumed her search. Another wash of cool air drifted over her, thick with the scent of the ocean. She glanced out the window expecting to see clouds covering the sun.

The sky was clear.

Elizabet frowned. Where had the chill breeze come from? She glanced back. It must be coming from the tunnel! Pulse racing, she felt along the stone. Her finger slid between a needle-thin slit that ran up the wall between the carved stone, the breeze strong.

She'd found it!

The chilly air sifted through her fingers as she inched over the opening, searching for the indent that would gain her access to the passage. Midway up, her thumb edged into a slight irregularity. Thank Mary! She pulled against the cleverly hidden door.

The panel moved a degree.

"Come on!" she breathed.

She tugged again.

Stone scraped.

Elizabet glanced at the door.

Silence.

Adrenaline spiked as she moved to a better angle. She pulled.

The panel slid open a hand's width.

Again she checked the door to ensure the guard didna investigate. A moment passed, then another. She tugged again.

The door moved another inch.

At this rate she would be here all day. Bracing her body against the door and her foot on the wall, she pulled hard. The entry opened wide enough for her to slip through. She peered into the tunnel.

A shaft of darkness beckoned her with morbid invitation, and her skin crawled at the thought of entering the narrow passage, trapped by sheer rock as impenetrable as unforgiving.

She fought to shake off the bout of nerves. This wasna the time to remember or to fear. After a deep breath, she slipped inside the shaft. Blackness consumed her. Moisture tinged the air, and the quiet rush of emptiness filled the dank void.

She gulped a deep breath, then another, allowing her eyes to adjust to the swath of light spilling into the murky gray before it, too faded in the dark.

Now to find the candle that was hidden on a shelf inside each entrance.

As she stepped forward, she skimmed her fingers along the uneven shelves of stone to follow the tunnel. Another step, and her fingers tangled in a silky mass. Visions of a spider crawling within the web skewered her mind. She jerked back.

Trembling, she fought for calm.

She couldna do this!

Stop! Focus!

Hand shaking, she moved her fingers over the surface, rough, slick, and damp. Her fingers slid into the indent and bumped against the tallow candle. Thank Mary! Snatching it from its hidden pocket, she hurried from the dark confines.

For a moment she stood in the chamber, absorbing the light, warmth, and the freedom around her. She peered toward the narrow opening, swallowed hard. She had to go back.

Elizabet focused on her mission, nae the blackened and restricted route she must take. Kneeling before the hearth, she lit the wick. Shielding the flame, she slipped into the tunnel.

At the distant clack of hoofbeats she turned toward where the shaft of light stroked the rough edges of darkness.

The candlelight wavered then flickered out.

Terror seized her. She bolted for the light, then ran to the window.

A large group of men cantered toward the castle. Surrounded by Dunsten's men rode Giric and Nicholas.

The room spun around her, the sense of panic and loss staggering. The candle trembled in her hands. Numb, she stared at the blackened wick.

Sparks crackled in the hearth in a scolding snap.

With one last look at the approaching party, she hurried over and knelt before the hearth.

Dunsten was right. This was nae over. But she was determined that the ending would be far from what he had planned.

Elizabet moved to the entry, paused to let the sun warm her face one last time, then stepped inside the blackened tunnel, and closed the entry.

The figure in the upper window disappeared, but Nicholas knew Elizabet's every detail. Blast it! Like a fool he'd believed when they confronted Lord Dunsten and his guard they would have time to react, to find some way to overpower the earl and gain entrance into his castle.

In the end, they'd met at the first break of dawn. With the wind rolling over the moors, Lord Dunsten had ridden forward without pause with a large force; a man in control, a warrior who held the upper hand.

Nicholas glanced at Terrick, riding at his side. Their eyes met, reflected the fury for one man, Dunsten. He looked toward the castle window where Elizabet's face had appeared moments ago.

Empty.

His gut wrenched. Thank God Terrick was right that she was alive. What had she endured since her capture? With disgust, he glanced at his hands, bound, raw, and burning from his struggles to escape. However much he wished to flay Lord Dunsten inch by bloody inch, at the moment he could do naught.

As they continued to ride, the pounding of the surf grew. He glanced toward the shore. Foam-tipped waves stormed the beach, tumbling up the sand to slam against the arched wall of stone that pillared the fortress of Hardwell Castle.

They started up the steep incline. The narrow path wove erratically making it difficult to ascend, and all but impossible for an attacking force to penetrate. An excellent defense. 'Twould seem in all matters Dunsten left little to chance.

Shadows engulfed them as they rode beneath the gatehouse. Echoes of hooves, the smell of dust, sweat, and the ocean permeated each breath. When they drew to a halt inside the courtyard, Nicholas glanced up, praying to find Elizabet's face.

The window stood empty.

A sated smile touched Dunsten's mouth as he followed Nicholas's gaze. "Take them to the dungeon."

Guards caught their mounts while others hauled Nicholas and Giric to the ground.

"Wait." As the guards held Nicholas and Giric tight, Dunsten walked over. Malicious delight glittered in his eyes as he withdrew a ribbon of pale linen tucked beneath his belt.

Nicholas stilled. A portion of the dress Elizabet had worn the day he'd left.

Lord Dunsten's thumb slid over the fabric in a slow caress. "She screamed when I took her," he drawled as if savoring the memory, the touch, and the taste of her flesh. He lifted the cloth to his nose and inhaled, his eyes never leaving Nicholas. "'Twas a pity I had to leave her tied naked in my bed, but with you and her brother taken care of, I will be free to return and sample her pleasures."

He'd known anger in his life, but never this sharp, this biting. Nicholas lunged toward Lord Dunsten. "I will kill you!"

The guards held him back.

"You will kill him only after I have wrung his bloody neck," Terrick yelled as he fought his captors.

Nicholas kneed the guard closest to him.

The man doubled over.

Another knight moved in, drove his fist into Nicholas's jaw. The metallic taste of his blood filled his senses. A sharp punch landed, this time on his gut, then another to the side of his head. Pain slid through him, and he sucked in a harsh gulp of air, then another.

With a cold laugh, Dunsten quirked his brow in delight. He dropped the pale linen, ground it into the dirt with the heel of his boot. He glanced at the guard. "Take them to the dungeon and beat them. When you are done, shackle them in a cell. I wouldna want anything to happen to them while I take care of an unfinished matter. After, I will be down to deal with them, personally."

His laughter echoed in his wake as the men hauled Nicholas and Terrick away.

The ringing in his ears matched the pounding in his head, but Nicholas kept his feet, barely.

A guard's fist plowed into his gut as they entered the dungeon.

Nicholas stumbled backward as another guard's boot slammed in his face. Pain, raw, burning, raced through his body. Even breathing hurt.

A guard shouted to the other man near his side who pummeled Terrick. With a nod, the man hauled Giric past Nicholas into a cell.

A burly man shoved Nicholas inside the cramped confines, then pinned him against the wall. In quick, efficient movements, he shackled his arms and legs, tested them with a jerk. With a satisfied grunt, he posted himself outside the door.

His head pounding and pain wracking his body, Nicholas pulled against the metal bands. They rattled and cut into his flesh. "God's teeth."

"The bastard," Terrick growled, testing his chains.

Footsteps echoed up the turret with a steady clip.

Nicholas looked over. Between the bars, Dunsten's stocky frame came into view. As he walked toward them, his shadow raced ahead like black fingers raking across the bars of the empty cells.

Dressed in finery befitting his station, a crisp linen shirt below the deep green tunic adorned with his family crest, the earl could have mingled amongst royalty, fit in with the elegant, the elite. But the stark setting, designed for death, stripped away the elegance. His ornate finery became somehow tarnished.

A length from their cell, Dunsten stopped. In silent toast he lifted a goblet of wine, drank deeply as if savoring this moment, his victory at their upcoming deaths.

An odd sensation swept through Nicholas as he studied the brutal man. For all of his arrogance something was amiss. Beneath the gleam of success lurked the hard glint of anger, and his fingers clenched the cup until his knuckles turned white. Why?

Elizabet?

That she'd resisted this madman went without question. But to what degree? In her fervor to resist, had he crossed beyond the realm of rape and stumbled into murder? Panic swept him. *Please let her be alive.*

Dunsten took another step closer, took a large gulp of wine, then tossed the cup. The goblet clattered across the stone and wine splattered onto the floor like blood.

Nicholas clenched his hands, needing to know her fate, wanting to serve Lord Dunsten his own brand of justice.

"My sword," Dunsten snapped.

A guard rushed forward and handed him a claymore.

The polished steel glinted in the torchlight as Lord Dunsten wrapped both hands around the hilt. With a growl he moved through several maneuvers, hacking with a wild fury. He stopped, his breaths rough, and his eyes wild. "Release Sir Nicholas first."

The jingle of keys raked the silence as the guard shoved the door open, then entered. The knight unlocked the chains securing him to the wall. "Move."

Nicholas glared at Dunsten. "Is that how you serve justice—murder the innocent? Not give them a chance to defend themselves?"

Crazed eyes darkened. "Bring him to me!"

The guard cursed, shoved hard. "Move."

Weak from the beating, Nicholas stumbled forward.

The guard kicked him.

Chains clanked as Nicholas fell to his knees. His entire body screaming with pain, he pushed to his feet. Blast them all. If he was to die, however cowardly served, 'twould be looking at his enemy straight in the eye.

"So brave," Lord Dunsten said with disgust. "And for what? A king who serves only himself?" A sadistic smile touched his mouth. "Or is it for a woman who now serves me . . . on her knees?"

With a roar, Nicholas lunged.

The guard tripped him.

Nicholas slammed to the floor. Body raw with pain, he shoved to his knees. "I will kill you!"

"Will you?" Angling his sword, Dunsten swung it inches from his neck. With a twist, he streaked it across his shoulder, curled the blade, then pressed it under his jaw.

The bite of steel pressed against his pulse. Nicholas held, aware death was but the flick of the wrist away.

"You are nae afraid are you?" Lord Dunsten said.

Nicholas remained silent, refusing to give him any final satisfaction, pleased when Lord Dunsten's eyes narrowed.

With a curse the Scot withdrew the blade. "Unchain him and give him his sword. "'Twill be most enjoyable to diffuse your anger with my sword, and end your miserable life in the light of battle."

A chance. Nicholas fought to ignore the pain racking his body.

The guard approached with keys to unlock his shackles.

"My lord!" another guard called as he rushed through the entry. "No one has found Lady Elizabet. She must have somehow escaped."

Molten rage infused Lord Dunsten's face as he stalked toward the man. "Your orders were to report to me—in private!"

The guard's face blanched. "My Lord I—"

With a curse, Dunsten sank the claymore into the knight's heart.

Eyes widened with pain as the guard staggered back. On a groan he crumbled to the floor.

"Incompetence!" Dunsten waved toward the guard on his right. "Lock Sir Nicholas in the cell! I will deal with him upon my return." He stormed from the dungeon. The slap of steps and his faint curses echoed through the turret, then fell to silence.

She'd escaped. Thank God.

"Move," the guard demanded.

His body revolting with each step, Nicholas half-walked, half-stumbled back to the cell.

Chains rattled as the guard secured him to the wall. "Nae think you have escaped death. Once he finds her, then you will die." The guard exited, shoving the door shut with a clang.

As if the guard's word mattered? Trembling with relief, Nicholas laid his head against the cool stone, turned toward Giric. "She's escaped," he said, the words thick with emotion.

"Aye," Terrick replied. Worry flickered into his eyes, tainting the thrill of hope. "As long as she doesna do something foolish like try to come and rescue us."

Nicholas's heart stopped. The elation of moments ago swirled into fear. Bedamned, she would!

CHAPTER 20

Fear whipped through Elizabet as she stood in the dark confines of the tunnel. *Go, Nicholas and Giric are counting on you!* She dragged in a cool breath, tainted with the salt and the sea and the scent of time. Her hand shaking, she lifted the candle. The golden glow trickled through her cupped hands, slanting eerie shadows down the narrow passage, then faded into the smothering blackness.

Sand and rock crunched into the foreboding silence as she forced herself to take a step, then another. She must stay calm.

Yellowed candlelight scraped the smothering black, and the years rolled back. Again she was a child playing within these tunnels.

It had been a game.

She'd always loved the chase, the excitement of hiding from Dunsten, and the ultimate win. Except on her last journey so many years ago, somewhere she'd taken a wrong turn. The tunnel had narrowed, slivered into a ragged crevice, and ended.

She'd laughed with the innocence of youth and made her way back. Except, as she had retraced her steps naught had looked familiar. With a shrug she'd returned to the point where she'd realized her error, or tried.

Hours passed as she worked along each new inky path, her hopes and her spirit burning as low as her flame. Until, with a shaky flicker, that too had extinguished.

Then came the fear.

Cold.

Brutal.

Consuming her in a panic all its own. Lost and terrified, she'd huddled into a ball and caved into her terror.

Yellowed light sputtered before her. Elizabet shook herself from her memories, angry she'd given in to the moment of panic, allowed her fears to paralyze her.

A child hadna known any better and had awaited her rescue—a delivery that'd arrived many terrifying hours later. But she was an adult, with her past far behind. Nicholas and Giric didna need a woman trapped by the fears of a frightened child. Any hopes for their survival was up to her.

With her courage patched up, she advanced.

A low moan howled in the distance, then a soft, cool breeze sifted over her. The flame wavered and rolled wildly then went out.

Blackness engulfed her.

Her confidence crumbled, and a scream built in her throat as her fears unleashed.

Focus or die!

She closed her eyes, fought to subdue her terror. The sharp tang of panic, the burning horror, threatened to infuse every inch of her mind.

A second passed. She held on to sanity by a thread. Another moment slipped by, then another. Slowly she regained control.

The coolness of the breeze washed over her face, rich with the scent of the sea. So caught up in her fear, she'd missed the obvious, she was near the exit! Elizabet skimmed her fingers along the walls of timeworn rock, felt the cool trickle of seeping water and the rough scratch of moss as she forged ahead.

A sliver of grayed light wavered in the distance.

She stumbled toward it. As she turned the next corner, sunlight streamed down the tunnel, which opened to a large cavern facing the ocean. Waves rolled in, crashed onto the sand and tumbled up the foam-slicked expanse in a wild rush.

Relief swept her as she hurried forward. Water licked at her feet, biting into the scrapes at her knees. Sand tumbled down the slope as water tugged at her feet in its retreat. She followed the outgoing wave, and exited the cave. Sunlight streamed over her, erasing the cold fear.

With a steadying breath, she scanned the angle of the sheer stone. Atop the massive gray wall loomed Hardwell Castle. And locked within were the two men she loved.

"Nicholas, Giric," she whispered. "Please, do nae let me be too late."

Lifting her dress, she turned and ran.

Hours later Nicholas stared out the distant window, where streaks of orange melded to a blood red. Where was Elizabet now?

"Do you think she has escaped?" Terrick asked, his voice rough, edged with the taste of desperation.

Nicholas met his gaze, needing to believe she had. "Yes."

His Adam's apple worked as Giric swallowed. "She used to play here as a child." He shook his head. "My sister ran through the castle like it was her own."

Hope ignited. He shifted, his body aching from the long hours of being held against the wall and the beatings. "Here?"

"Aye," Giric replied.

Nicholas listened with curiosity, then disbelief as Terrick related the closeness of their families, and then the horrific event that'd severed close ties.

"After they discovered the woman's mangled body, the Scots were in an uproar and rightfully so. The rape, the murder"—Terrick swore—"both were brutal. But I knew who had taken her innocence and then her life. When I confronted Dunsten, the bastard laughed. Only because he was a noble's son did he escape justice. If I could have found a speck of proof, I would have slain him myself."

Nicholas laid his head back against the hard, cool stone, amazed how some men had no respect for life.

Distant footsteps slapped against stone, grew louder.

Nicholas turned toward the door.

The heavy crafted entry scraped open. Illuminated by torchlight, Lord Dunsten stepped inside. Slashes of red cut his cheeks, his anger easy to read. "Release Sir Nicholas and give him his sword!"

His body tensed as Nicholas met Terrick's glance. He arched his brow in question.

"'Twould seem," Terrick whispered, "he would like us to believe he has caught my sister."

"Aye," Nicholas answered. Thank God she had escaped.

Metal scraped as the guard unlocked, then opened his cell. He jerked Nicholas's cuffs and glared at him. "Try something like before and you will feel my boot in your arse."

Nicholas held his glare, but he remained silent. After his earlier beating, then being chained to the wall, he was exhausted. He would save his remaining strength for the upcoming fight with Dunsten.

The guard unlocked his legs. "Move."

His legs wavered as the guard shoved Nicholas forward, his hands still locked within the forged steel.

The earl gestured to the chains as they exited the cell. "Take them off. Be quick about it!"

The guard hurried to comply.

Moments later, he was freed, and the forged metal trembled in his hands. Nicholas balanced the broadsword, felt the play of power within the blade.

With a grimace of impatience, Dunsten waved him forward.

Nicholas readied his blade. The moment was his. If it served his death, 'twould not be without a fight.

Crouched in the shadows, Elizabet caught her breath. Her heart squeezed as Nicholas lifted the broadsword to match Dunsten's, then swayed.

Their blades clashed, separated.

A hand laid on her shoulder, and she glanced back.

"'Twill be a bit longer before everyone is in place," Colyne MacKerran, Earl of Strathcliff whispered.

She nodded, thankful to have met Colyne en route to Wolfhaven Castle. That he'd agreed to aid her was a relief, more so that he'd sent a runner to both Wolfhaven and Ravenmoor for more help. Still, guilt swept her as she'd caught his searching look, that of a man still in love with her. However much she loved him, 'twas only that of a friend. Never could it be more. Her heart belonged to Nicholas.

Lord Dunsten cursed, jolting her back to the fight.

Elizabet swallowed hard. She and Colyne's men had nae come this far to chance losing it all now. A moment more, then they could attack.

Nicholas ducked; his adversary's blade sliced inches over his head.

The guards moved back, their attention locked on the combat centered in the dungeon.

"My man just signaled me all is ready," Colyne whispered. "Go." Lifting her sword, she crept forward with the others. They moved past the body of the guard they'd subdued and kept to the shadows, pressed as close to the cells as possible.

Nicholas's face became clear as did the sweat and his exhaustion. Blood stained the shredded tunic at his shoulder and streamed from several other gashes on his chest.

With grisly enjoyment, Dunsten toyed with him, keeping him at a sword's length.

Heart aching, she long to rush them, but to keep the element of surprise, they must move closer.

Two more steps forward, then she, along with the men, pressed against the cold bars, hidden in the half-light of the waning sun.

Dunsten's guards' attention remained on the fight.

Thankful, she clenched the hilt of her sword. A moment more—

Chains rattled with a sharp jerk.

She glanced toward the left.

Her brother's eyes burned into her.

"Giric," she whispered.

"I see him, my lady," Colyne replied.

On edge, she mouthed to her brother to wait.

Giric nodded, then banged his cuffs against the wall over and again.

Lord Dunsten shot a cold glance toward Giric. "Silence him!"

* * *

At Dunsten's distraction, Nicholas charged. His blade sank into Dunsten's side, then jerked his blade free.

The earl's eyes widened, then narrowed to fury at the stream of blood running. "'Tis the last you will touch me, Sassenach!" He attacked.

Nicholas met him swing for swing, shoved him back. If he couldn't kill the bastard, mayhap he would weaken him for his duel with Terrick. He raised his sword to yield his next blow.

Yells burst through the chamber.

He deflected the earl's next swing, glanced back. Elizabet along with men he didn't recognize charged from the shadows.

The guards whirled, drawing their swords. The clash of blades filled the dungeon, then the screams.

Blood surged hot in his veins as Nicholas faced Dunsten.

A guard ran toward him.

Nicholas drove his blade into the man's chest, shoved him away.

Another guard charged.

Sweat melded with blood as Nicholas carved his way through the melee, fighting to keep Lord Dunsten in sight.

The guard before him swung then lifted his blade.

Nicholas slashed his sword across the man's neck.

Eyes wide, blood pouring down his chest, his adversary dropped.

A hand touched his shoulder; Nicholas whirled. "Blast it!" he snarled as his gaze fell upon Terrick. "I almost ended your bloody life."

"Where is Dunsten?" Giric asked as he scoured the melee.

"I saw him a moment ago," Nicholas replied.

"Watch out!" Terrick yelled.

Nicholas turned as another guard attacked. He finished off the aggressor then quickly scoured the chamber. Dunsten was missing. Elizabet? Panic swept him. She'd fought by his side moments ago. Bloody hell, where was she?

Torchlight flickered like ragged fingers over the dying, and the dead sprawled within a pool of blood. His heart pounded as he strode along the cells. "Elizabet!"

The clash of the last remaining resistance answered his call.

"Where is Elizabet?" Terrick yelled as he ran toward him.

Fear choked Nicholas's reply as only one deduction made sense. "Dunsten has her!"

The tang of blood and smoke tainted each breath as Elizabet struggled to free herself from Dunsten's brutal grip.

The earl tightened his hold as he dragged her farther from the fighting.

The blackness of the tunnel began to envelop them; the shards of orange-red flame fading in their wake. After everything she and Nicholas had overcome, the love they had found, it couldna end like this.

A shout.

The scrape of blades.

In the distance, Nicholas turned and engaged against a combatant.

"Nicholas!"

Absorbed in the fight, he never glanced her way.

Despair clawed at her hope. Their footsteps echoed into the growing quiet, and the last glimmer of light faded as they rounded the corner of the dank, musty shaft.

Once darkness encased them Dunsten halted, caught her shoulders in a painful grip. "Yell, lass," he shouted, his words twisted with insanity. "They will never hear you. And we will be long gone before they realize we have left."

He spoke the truth. With a last, futile glance back, she started to turn.

"Elizabet!"

At Nicholas's faint call, hope rose. He'd discovered her absence, but had he or Giric noticed which route they'd taken?

Dunsten yanked her hand. "Move!"

She struggled to break free.

"I was a fool to think you would nae try the tunnel to seek help." He gave her a hard pull.

Stumbling forward, she skimmed her hand over the rough walls to help guide her along the inky path.

They wove through the darkness, and for the third time that day she battled the fear that haunted her over the years. As they rounded the next corner, Elizabet listened for the sound of steps behind them.

Naught.

Somewhere ahead the drip of water echoed, grew.

A shiver rippled through her, then another. She smothered her panic, refusing to give in to her fears. As she took the next step, her foot rammed into a rock. With a gasp, she fell, slamming against the gravel and sand floor.

With a curse, Dunsten hauled her to her feet. "You are more trouble than you are worth, but that bastard Nicholas will never have you."

Furious, she tried to shove him off balance. Failed. "Nicholas is nae the bastard, you are!"

With an oath, Dunsten's fist connected with her cheek.

Pain streaked through her and she dropped to her knees. The salty taste of blood tainted her tongue.

With an angry curse, he hauled her up and slung her over his shoulder.

Elizabet worked to catch her breath as the void of unconsciousness lured her. If she succumbed to the darkness now, any chance to escape, however remote, would be lost.

The blackness hummed around her as Dunsten continued through the maze of tunnels at a slow but steady pace. The smell of the sea grew. The rush of water magnified, filling the inky darkness like thunder.

A shimmer of light appeared in the distance. With her each step, it grew brighter. Elizabet gained her bearings. Nay! By all the saints, he couldna be headed there!

She'd believed that he would make his way along the seawall and resurface near the orchards where she'd entered earlier with Colyne's men, and where he'd left a small contingent outside in case Dunsten somehow tried to escape. In the commotion, she'd forgotten this second escape route!

The last hints of dusk sifted through the wide opening as the earl moved into the cavern carved by the sea.

Trying to maintain a degree of calm, Elizabet weighed the situation. The tide was coming in. At high tide this exit became blocked. If they made it out of the tunnel, chances of anyone following them ended.

She glanced back.

Gloom fell away to blackness.

Where are you, Giric? Nicholas? Water sloshed and swirled around her legs as Dunsten dragged her into the foamy waves. Gulls echoed beyond the sea-borne entrance, their high, screeching calls piercing her senses.

If she didna stop him . . . Nay, she refused to doubt herself now. Twisting in his arms, Elizabet kicked him between the legs.

He howled in outrage. "You bloody wench!"

The oncoming wave slammed him, and he started to stumble.

This was it! She shifted all her weight toward him.

Dunsten slipped. Water sloshed around them as he landed onto the water-packed sand with her on top.

She dug her foot in the sand, pushed away.

"Nay!" He jerked her toward him as the next breaker swept in, catching them both.

The rush of water battered her, but she continued to fight to break free.

With a curse, the earl surfaced, dragged her to feet by a fistful of hair, slammed her into the incoming surf.

Water pummeled her.

His face twisted in outrage, he caught her neck and held her under.

Panicking, Elizabet struggled to reach the surface.

He hauled her up. Veins popped out on his face, carving intricate paths of rage. "Do nae fight me. I can give you everything you want and more."

"Rot in Hades. Nicholas is a better man then you will ever hope to be."

"Then that is what you shall have. For if I canna have you, no one will."

Water surged into the cavern sloshing up the time-worn walls. She barely caught her breath as he shoved her to the sandy floor. Salt and sand filled her mouth as the wave crashed over her. The water began to recede, and the current tugged at her mercilessly, trying to wrench her from his unyielding grip. Her eyes stung. Nausea and fear collided, threatening to extinguish her last hope. She pulled at his hand, fought to loosen his grip as her world spun, then faded to blackness.

CHAPTER 21

Dizziness threatened, and the taste of blood stung Nicholas's senses. He clutched the wall, tried to focus, to listen to the faint struggle ahead that he had followed this far.

He drew in a ragged breath, then another. His legs trembled. The pounding in his head slammed like a smith's hammer to his skull. He closed his eyes, fought against the pain. Doubts toppled onto one another as blackness threatened. Mayhap he should have bid Terrick to come instead.

Bedamned, the time for regrets was long past. He'd not made it this far to lose her. He shoved from the tunnel wall, staggered forward.

Elizabet's scream echoed in the distance.

Blackness tangled around his consciousness like demons. Nicholas clawed his way along the damp, cool walls, cursing each twist and turn that threatened to lay siege to his goal.

Murky gray light wove before him like a silken promise. Shapes jutted from the sand. Water, dark and angry, churned up the steep incline like an outraged lover.

The stain of dusk slashed through the tidal chamber as Nicholas stepped inside. In the sky beyond, reds clashed with orange and then wove into hard shadows of black.

A splash to his left.

Nicholas turned.

Hip-deep in the surf, Elizabet flailed as Dunsten pinned her beneath the surge of water.

Rage, hot and sharp, tore through Nicholas as he sloshed into the water. "Dunsten!"

Still holding Elizabet's head under, the earl turned. His eyes narrowed. "Bedamned!"

For a split second, his grasp loosened and Elizabet surfaced. Her strangled cough was lost in the crash of the next wave.

Nicholas lunged.

Dunsten released Elizabet, withdrew his dagger.

With a growl, Nicholas caught the hilt of Dunsten's knife. "You"—he tore the blade free; it slipped into the churn of water—"will"—he slammed his fist into the earl's face—"never touch Elizabet again!" He drew his hand back; the next breaker hit him.

The rush of the surf filled his ears, salt and sand stung his cuts and scraped over his body. Nicholas held on as the wave jerked them back, refusing to lose Dunsten even to the sea.

Water receded and Lord Dunsten pushed to his feet. "You bloody Sassenach!" Eyes wild, he turned toward Elizabet.

The next breaker raced around Nicholas in a mad swoosh, chased by the hiss of foam and rolling sand. He dove on top of Dunsten.

The roil of water swept them under as the earl twisted in his grasp, his hands searching and finding his neck. He squeezed tight.

Darkness threatened Nicholas as he tried to kick to the surface. Bedamned! He shoved Dunsten's chest, then moved to the earl's neck. He squeezed.

The noble's hands tightened.

Another wave of blackness threatened, and Nicholas twisted his fingers deeper.

The earl's hold loosened.

The bastard! In the rush of water, Nicholas tightened his grip.

Dunsten's hold fell away.

Nicholas kicked to the surface. Air, clean, cool, surged through his lungs. A gulp. Then another. His head began to clear.

Without warning, the earl's hand caught his leg, hauled him under.

Water raced down his throat. Sand lashed at his body. Nicholas barely caught a breath as another wave washed in, ripping at his feet.

Dunsten caught his arm.

Water rolled back, allowing Nicholas to breathe.

"Nicholas!" Elizabet's scream sliced through his pain-fogged mind.

Clenching his teeth, Nicholas jerked the nobleman's hand free. "Stay back, Elizabet!" He slammed his fist into the noble's jaw.

Rage and pain dredged the earl's face as he staggered back. With a curse, Dunsten wrapped his hands around the hilt of the claymore on his back, tugged. The sodden leather gushed. The weapon moved a hand's length. His face carved in outrage, he withdrew a second dagger from his belt, waved it like a madman.

Nicholas started to move forward, then his vision grew blurry.

As Nicholas's body began to weave, panic swept Elizabet. She had to help him! Water sloshed around her legs as she staggered to her feet, hurried forward.

Dunsten raised the blade.

The next wave rose up, crashed to shore. In a violent rush, the water ripped both men back.

"Nay!" Elizabet moved deeper into the ocean.

In the distance they surfaced.The next wave pulled them under.

Stunned, she scanned the churn of water. In the mix of waves, blood stained the frothy caps. A scream built in her throat as she searched the roiling water, wading deeper.

A shape rose from the depths.

Thank God! "Nich—"

Dunsten surfaced.

God nay!

He swam toward her.

Heart pounding, she scrambled for shore. As she reached the sturdier sand, Dunsten's hand caught her shoulder. "Release me!" She fought to free herself, but his fingers bit deeper into her flesh. Desperate, she searched for a rock, stick, anything to use as a weapon.

Dunsten turned her toward him, curled his hands around her neck, tightened. "He is dead!"

With all of her strength, she fought to break free.

Malice filled his eyes. "Now you will die—" On a gasp, Dunsten's eyes widened, then he fell back. Dazed and coughing, she rolled away in case the earl lunged for her.

Instead, Nicholas stood in the rush of water, his hand pulling Dunsten deeper.

Another breaker rolled in, hauled both men under.

Emotions stormed her as she shoved to her feet. "Nicholas!"

The next wave crashed, rolled in, then slid out.

One man stood.

Alone.

Nicholas walked toward her.

"Thank God!" On trembling legs she ran toward him, thankful as he wrapped her into his embrace.

His mouth took hers. The first taste claimed a fierce, hungry need. The second slid into a warm seduction.

He skimmed his hands down her back to press her full against him as his mouth grew demanding. In shuffled steps, Nicholas guided her to the shore, where the water nipped at the beach. He pulled her to the ground with him, rolling so she lay within his arms. "I—I thought I had lost you," he whispered, searching her eyes, his own laced with anguished desperation.

Emotions storming her, she shook her head. "'Tis over." The fears that had threatened burst. Her first sob rolled through her, then the next.

Ignoring the pain, Nicholas caught her mouth in a tender kiss, drinking her tears, tasting the fear, but above all her love.

The sizzle of foam brushed against his legs as he pushed her against the sand and touched her, because he could, because life had given him another chance. He lifted his head, drank in the sight of the woman he loved with all of his heart. "I love you, Elizabet Armstrong."

Her eyes shined bright. "Nicholas I—"

"Say you love me," he urged on a half-laugh.

With a smile, Elizabet laid her hand on his chest and pushed him back. "I love you, but do nae let it go to your—" Nicholas smothered further words with a tender kiss. "I am man enough to know that I hold the woman who is my heart and necessary to my life—one that I will cherish always."

Delight twinkled in her emerald-green eyes. "And now you think pretty words will make me love you forever?"

His heart pounded in his chest, but he wanted this tenderness, the lightness of the moment. "I am hoping so." Her warm laugh had him melting. "Is it working?"

"Nicholas I . . . Aye." She wrapped her hands around his neck and drew him close, her eyes darkening with sultry promise. "Kiss me."

And he did, savoring the rightness of this moment, and the gift of her he'd been given. When he pulled away, her finger traced his face, pausing at the sharp angle of his jaw.

Elizabet frowned at his shoulder, then her eyes lifted to meet his. "We need to return. Your cuts need to be treated and . . .Giric."

Nicholas smiled. For the moment he too had forgotten her brother. The rumble of water echoed around them as he brushed back a damp lock from her cheek, knowing with her he could never get enough. "He will be worried." That Terrick had entrusted him with saving Elizabet's life left him humbled. "One last kiss then we will go."

She laughed. "One kiss is it? Nay, one will never do. You will be begging me for more."

He grew serious and cupped her face. "Only for you."

"Nicholas—"

At the slap of footsteps over sand and rock, Nicholas glanced toward the tunnel. A faint golden glow flickered from deep within the shaft.

The jagged light steadily grew. Breaths, rough, harsh, blended with the jostle of leather and steel.

"Hurry, get up," Nicholas said. Sand shifted as they shoved to their feet.

Seconds later, Terrick, holding a torch, followed by a small contingent of men, burst into the chamber. He halted, and his expression of fear transformed to amazement. "Saint's breath!" He eyed them both as he sheathed his sword.

The men behind him secured their blades.

Giric strode to the edge of the incoming tide, stared out the near-filled tunnel at the incoming breakers.

Understanding, Nicholas drew Elizabet up against him.

"He is dead?" Giric asked as he stared at the sea.

"He is," Nicholas replied.

Terrick glared at Nicholas. "I almost broke my neck running through the tunnel with—" he made an angry gesture toward the torch, "—with that measly piece of stick dabbed with a flame! And why?" He threw out his hands in exasperation. "I was thinking your bloody carcass was in trouble."

Nicholas eyed him, understanding his fear, having lived with it through the past several hours as well. The tension that'd haunted him dissolved. He laughed, enjoying the warm sound in a chamber that moments ago had echoed death.

Terrick opened his mouth to speak, and then snapped it shut.

Elizabet's sweet laughter blended with his.

The Scot's eyes narrowed. "I bloody well almost got killed. The next time I will leave you both to—"

"Giric," Nicholas said.

"I thought you were in trouble," the earl repeated, but the anger in his words had faded.

Nicholas winked at Elizabet. "I am. Watching over your sister is likely to be the death of me."

His mouth curved in a smile. "Aye, that she will be." Giric offered his hand. "You look worse than a grime-covered pig."

Nicholas shook Giric's hand. "You are not much better to look at."

Mischief danced in Terrick's eyes. "Well, we will have to fix that, then."

Elizabet moved between them. "What are you—"

"A pint it will be," Terrick said as a smile broke onto his face.

She punched his shoulder but he only laughed. "'Tis nae funny, Giric Armstrong!"

In answer his smile widened.

"Come on, lass," Nicholas said in his best deep Scottish burr.

Her eyes sparkled, filled with love. "You are lucky I love you or I would be tossing you in the sea."

Nicholas drew her near until his lips hovered a breath away from hers. "I am at that."

CHAPTER 22

Candles lined the walls, casting flame-softened light over the room like magical fingers. Fragrances reached Elizabet, those of the heather, gowan, foxglove, and the myriad of other blooms placed in baskets throughout the great hall. Elation filled her as she absorbed it all.

A golden shimmer glistened among the thick swath of heather near the window. She smiled, imagining fairies dancing within. 'Twas as if they had indeed cast their spell over this moment.

"Let me look at you, lass," Lachllan said as he stepped forward. Weathered blue eyes scanned her face, eyes blurred by tears. "A picture of your mother you are. And you couldna mean more to me if you were me own daughter."

She sniffed as a tear rolled down her cheek, then another.

Lachllan drew her against him. "There now, lass." He stroked his hand over her hair. "There is no reason to cry."

"I almost lost you," she said on a sniff.

"Now do nae be fretting over the past. I am fine as you can see."

"When we left you in the woods . . ." Fear stole her words.

"'Tis your wedding," her steward gently chided. "I will have nay more tears."

"Elizabet," Giric said, striding up. "I will nae let Lachllan keep you all to himself." He paused, shot a questioning look at the steward. "Is something wrong?"

"Nay," Lachllan replied, "the lass is being sentimental."

"Again?" Giric grimaced. "Do nae be telling me this is the same woman who dressed as a lad to save me?"

Her heart warm, Elizabet batted his hand away with a laugh. "You do nae have a sentimental bone in your body, Giric Armstrong."

"I am a man who has vowed to set his own home to rights," Giric said with mock outrage.

She softened, remembering his pledge to give up his reiving ways and rebuild their ancestral home. "Mayhap I will overlook your shortcomings."

"Will you now," her brother said. "And mayhap I will forgive you for marrying a Sassenach."

She smiled, far from worried. For all of his fierce words, the bond between Giric and Nicholas was as strong as if they were brothers.

With a somber look, Giric held out his hand. "Colyne MacKerran wanted me to give you this after he left."

Tears filled her eyes. "If I had nae met up with Colyne and his men, you would have died."

"'Twas fate," Giric agreed.

"Indeed," Elizabet agreed, "but never did I wish to hurt him. I tried to love him, I swear it."

"Shhhhhh, lass," Lachllan said. "We know, as does Colyne. Neither does Colyne hold it against you."

"And now you have Nicholas." Giric smiled. "One day, Colyne will find a woman who loves him as well."

"I pray so." She paused. "You said he left. Where is he going?"

"With the unrest in Scotland," Giric replied, "he is returning to his home in the Highlands, Taigh Castle. Do nae worry about him, Elizabet. At times the love we wish canna be." With a resolute sigh her brother hugged her one last time, then let go. "Now, onto happier things. I am proud of you, and I will always be wishing you the best."

Tears welled in her eyes. "I will be crying again in a minute."

He gave an exasperated sigh. "And 'twill nae be my doing. I am going for another cup of wine." Giric strode off.

Lachllan cleared his throat. "I think he will be needing company."

She smiled as the steward caught up to Giric, slapped his hand on her brother's back, then whispered something in his ear. No doubt her brother would rebuild Wolfhaven Castle to its previous grandeur.

Hands stole up to cup her shoulders. She shuddered with anticipation, knowing his touch before she even looked behind her.

"I heard you were missing me," Nicholas murmured as his lips playfully nipped her neck.

She arched to allow him better access. "Mayhap." Every nerve tingled in anticipation for the upcoming night.

He turned her slowly as his mouth grazed up her throat, nipping along her jaw, then edging along her ear. "I am planning on seducing you."

At his rough whisper thick with promise she shivered.

"And, planning on touching you . . . everywhere."

She moaned with pleasure as he claimed her mouth, hot and hard.

Longing ripped through Nicholas as he drew away, staring at her mouth swollen with his kisses, tempting him back for more. "Come away with me, Elizabet. I am wanting to make love with my wife, and I find my patience is at an end." The warm flush creeping up her cheeks made his body ache for her.

Her eyes shifted to their guests filling the great room, most well into their cups. "'Twould be rude to leave. 'Twould be . . ." Her breath hitched. "Nicholas, I canna think when you are staring at me that way."

"I am not wanting you to think." He linked their fingers together. With a glance toward the merrymakers, he drew her with him. In seconds they'd reached the coolness of the turret. "We made it."

She laughed. "I feel like a child sneaking sweetmeats."

"Mmmmm," he said. "And you definitely taste more delicious."

"They are gone!" An indignant shout roared from the great hall.

"Run!" Nicholas pulled Elizabet with him as they raced up the stairs.

"I see 'em!" a sodden voice called out.

The stairwell buzzed with the echoes of the exuberant crowd, and Elizabet laughed as she kept pace. "They are gaining on us!"

Nicholas slammed the door shut seconds before the drunken

crowd topped the steps. The clamor and shouts increased as he slid the wooden bar into place.

"They will give up and go back," he said with much more bravado than he felt.

She chuckled. "They are Scots out there as well, nae just weak-willed Englishmen."

"Weak-willed is it?" he challenged, backing her against the wall, and trapping her with his body. The sheer delight that jumped in her eyes had him burning with need.

Elizabet squealed as the first of the rabble-rousers pounded on the other side of the oak door.

"Open up!" a deep voice demanded. "We have a right to see the bride."

Nicholas held her gaze, wanting to see the thrill, the excitement of every moment. "You have seen her all that you will see her this night!"

Her throaty laugh melded with the thick drunken outrage. "Oh, you are a brave one, you are."

He shot her a wink. "Aye."

"He is keeping her," a deep male voice yelled.

A rush of disgruntled shouts whipped through the crowd. For the next several minutes the mob laid siege to their door. It rattled, trembled, and groaned beneath the assault.

"We will replenish ourselves with drink and return!" a drunken voice boomed over the lot.

Yells of agreement fragmented into one another. Slowly the procession faded from outside the door.

The play of laughter and knowing in her gaze had Nicholas's body hardening. "About this weak-willed Englishman you were speaking of?"

Her eyes widened with feigned confusion. "And who would be spouting such drivel?"

The fresh scent of heather and woman seduced his senses as he leaned closer to nuzzle her neck. She shivered as he tasted her silky flesh. "Who indeed." Nicholas slid his hands up her arms, cupping her face, grazing his lips against hers. "I think they have left."

"For a time," she said in a breathy reply, her eyes a bit desperate as they searched his.

He loosened a tie on her gown, enjoying watching the humor fade to raw need. "I am going to make love to you, Elizabet." He undid another tie and pushed the fabric back to expose her shoulder. Candlelight caressed her skin with a golden flush, flickered across the seductive swell of her breasts. "Here. Now."

"I—Oh." She glanced back toward the bed.

Desire seared him. "There too." He slid his hand under the soft fabric to cup her breast, rubbing his thumb over the proud nub.

Emerald eyes darkened to liquid pools. She nodded as her tongue peeked out to sweep over her lips. "I would be liking that."

Maybe it was her throaty reply that all but drove him to his knees, or her tiny shivers at his touch. At the moment he couldn't say which or care. She moved him as no woman had—ever.

Since his arrival, Elizabet had managed to turn his life upside down, often in the most unexpected ways. Yet in the end, through her love, determination, and compassion, he'd learned more than he'd ever expected. Forgiveness for his father, acceptance of Dougal's death, then she'd shown him love.

He trembled at her taste, savoring every moment, every touch. This woman—magnificent in her beauty, fierce in her love—had guided him to his heart's desire.

Nicholas pushed the silken gown away, needing to feel her quake beneath him. The soft garb pooled on the floor with a delicate swirl.

A thin chemise as pale as a winter's snow willowed along her slender frame in a gentle caress. Hints of her taut, ruby nipples strained against the silken fabric, tempting and teasing him with innocent guile.

His body coiled tight, urged him to take without caution. Fighting to maintain control, he drew a steadying breath, then another. In this as all things, she would come first. He caught her nipple through her chemise, and she arched against him on a moan. Slowly he teased her, wanting to watch her as her eyes glazed, and she fell apart.

On an unsteady breath he peeled away the last remaining fabric covering her.

Naked she stood before him, proud, challenging with a glint of need in her eyes.

He skimmed his fingers down her warm flesh, through the mist of downy soft curls and cupped her. She was already damp.

He grew harder as he slid his finger between her soft folds and into her slick heat. With gentle strokes, he urged her up, guiding Elizabet to her sensual crest.

As her body convulsed into a frenzied state, he trailed his kisses across her skin to her most sensitive place and slowly began to taste.

"Nicholas!"

He stroked her with his tongue, and her body trembled.

She moaned. "I—I . . ."

Lazily he suckled on her swollen flesh, stealing her words, wanting her complete surrender.

On a gasp, her muscles tightened, and her pants grew desperate.

Watching her, he slid his tongue deep.

On a scream, she arched and fell over the edge.

As tremors swept through her, he kissed his way up her body, capturing her mouth to swallow her cries as he lay his body over hers, then drove deep. Nicholas thrust long and hard, taking her back over the top. As she convulsed around him in violent demand, his hard-won control shattered.

Breaths coming fast, he lay against her. "We have not even made the bed yet."A sated smile curved her lips. "You promised we would," she said with love in her eyes.

He nipped playfully at her neck as his mind shifted back. "And I am a man who always keeps his word."

"Mmmm." She skimmed her hands along his chest. "When I first saw you through the branches, I thought of a predator, sleek, mayhap a bit wild." Her eyes searched his with sensual delight. "Dangerous," she added on a teasing growl.

He laughed as he remembered the exact moment he'd spied her through the trees, and then the exact moment when he'd saw in the water that the ragged urchin had turned into a beautiful woman.

After a deep kiss, Nicholas lifted her into his arms and strode toward the bed, already needing her again. "What would you have done if I had come up the tree after you?"

Emerald eyes sparkled with delight, with the fire of passion that would always be an innate part of her. "I would have given you a merry chase," she said with a laugh.

As he laid her on the bed before him, her laughter faded. "And I would have caught you."

With a mischievous twinkle she cupped his face, her look stubborn, daring. Then her gaze softened, and the love there humbled him.

"Aye, my husband, I believe you would."

Keep reading for an excerpt from

An Oath Broken

The next book in The Oath Trilogy

Available in June 2015 from

Diana Cosby

and

eKensington

CHAPTER 1

England/Scotland border, 1292

Lady Sarra Bellecote crumpled the missive and flung it to the chapel floor. "He can go to the devil!" Blood pounding hot, she swept past the aged bench, halted before the stained glass window.

The angry slap of the January wind against the crafted panes matched the fury pounding in her heart. Her home, her decision to marry was being torn from her. She closed her eyes against the rush of betrayal.

How dare her guardian issue her such an ultimatum?

A hint of frankincense and wood filled her every breath. After a moment, Sarra regained a measure of calm, and on a long exhale opened her eyes.

The stained glass portrait of the Blessed Virgin, crafted within the blue, pearl, and gray panes, stared back at her. Calm and reassuring, at a time when she didn't know whom to trust.

Faith, her mother's voice of long ago whispered in her mind.

Bitterness curdled in her throat. As if after all of these years God would choose this moment to offer a token of hope?

Sarra turned from the stained glass portrait and clasped her hands tight before her. But she did not pray. Her belief in God, as in most things in her life, had long since fled.

Soft footsteps sounded behind her, accompanied by the swish of vestments.

"My child." Father Ormand's gentle entreaty spilled through the brittle silence.

For a moment, the child whose faith had once guided her responded to his entreaty. Then, like her hope over the years, she flickered and died.

Sarra lifted her head and stared at nothing, feeling everything. "Why should I yield to my guardian's request to marry his son or forsake my holdings and be exiled to a nunnery?"

Father Ormand cleared his throat. "Lady Sarra, your guardian knows not your feelings about—"

She whirled, aware her action bespoke poor manners toward a revered man of God, but at the moment hurt overrode decorum. "As if Lord Bretane would care?"

Thick lines sagged across his brow as his solemn brown eyes studied her. "Your father would have wished this, my lady."

"You are wrong. A marriage based on threats and conditions is not a union my father would have sanctioned."

"Lord Bretane was your father's best friend," the priest said quietly. "Your father was the godparent to Lord Sinclair, the man you are to wed." Father Ormand shook his head as his worried gaze searched hers. "Arranged marriages are expected. Feel blessed that your guardian, a man your father trusted enough to leave your keeping to, chooses your husband. With the wealth of your holdings, the king could have easily intervened and selected your betrothed."

A part of her acknowledged that she should be grateful. King Edward's matches often served his own gain. But her guardian's writ commanding her to wed his son by Midsummer's Eve was a directive she loathed to obey.

Since she'd witnessed the savage murder of her parents at the age of eight, her hopes and dreams had crumbled one by one. To think her last desire, to marry for love, would be seized from her in a forced marriage to a Scot was unacceptable!

She shuddered as youthful images of her betrothed, a dark-haired child smashing falcon eggs, scraped through her mind. "Drostan was a contemptible lad. I must speak with Lord Bretane and request that he reconsider."

"Lord Sinclair was but a child when you knew him," Father Ormand offered. "Boys make mischief, but boys turn into men. Ten and one years have passed since you have seen Lord Bretane's son. 'Tis unfair to judge what we cannot see."

Mayhap, but beneath Drostan's title of baron lay the blackened ugliness of his ancestry.

A reiver.

The name punctured her mind like a bolt of a crossbow—lawless raiders who pilfered, raped, and murdered. The border savages who had attacked and killed her parents. *And for what?* The paltry pieces of gold they carried.

Several wisps of her golden hair slipped from her braid. Sarra secured the wayward locks into the tight plait, her own life as confined by convention as the strands she fought daily to keep within their bounds.

"Come," Father Ormand urged. "Lord Bretane's escort is expecting your reply. We have kept them waiting overlong."

However much she wished to send the priest to deal with the entourage of Scottish knights in the courtyard, as mistress of Rancourt Castle, 'twas her duty.

With a nod, she walked toward the exit, refusing to succumb to her fears. Determination and pride had allowed her to persevere since her parents' tragic death. The same resolve would serve her well in her upcoming confrontation with her guardian.

She abhorred the thought of the arduous travel ahead at this miserable time of year. For her sanity, she must believe the man she remembered, the man who had bounced her on his knee and had offered warm smiles during her childhood, would never condemn her to a life with a man she didn't or couldn't love.

Angry clouds boiled overhead, spitting fat flakes of snow. Wind, sharp and brutal, tugged at the cloak of Giric Armstrong, Earl of Terrick. He remained motionless astride his destrier, positioned before his small contingent of men.

Waiting.

Through thick, black lashes, Giric scanned the courtyard of the English fortress, dusted with a fine sheen of snow. He took in the well-maintained grounds, the sturdy walls, and the skill of the knights training in the practice field as the clash of steel echoed throughout Rancourt Castle.

Envy shot through him at the quality of their armor and the swords they wielded. He smothered his discontent. The gold he would earn on this simple task would make great strides toward rebuilding his home, Wolfhaven Castle, feeding his people, and furnishing his knights with sturdy blades of steel and fine-crafted mail. And prove to his people that he was a noble they could respect.

The slam of the keep door at the far end of the castle caught his attention. A gust of wind swirled up, billowing into a white cloud thick with snow. Two cloaked figures emerged through the wintry haze. Another icy burst exposed a hint of vestments worn beneath the black cloak of the larger form.

A priest? Giric studied the smaller figure lost within the rich folds of a burgundy cloak. The hem of an ivory gown peeked from the border. Lady Sarra Bellecote? He frowned. Aye, he'd expected the lady of the castle, but accompanied by her guard. Why would she require the aid of a priest? Only one reason came to mind—she'd refused the match and had requested sanctuary from the church.

Giric dismissed the notion, confident his desperation for cash spawned such dismal thoughts. Many reasons could exist for the vicar's accompaniment. Mayhap a devout Christian, Lady Sarra sought the blessing of her priest.

He relaxed in his saddle. 'Twould make their journey easier if his ward was a softly spoken maiden of God.

The pair closed on his entourage.

Several paces away, the woman motioned toward the priest. The vicar halted, yet the slender figure continued forward. A length before Giric, she stopped.

Wind tugged at the hood of her cloak as the woman slowly raised her head. Framed within porcelain skin, eyes as gray as a winter storm locked on his clan brooch, darkened as they cut to him.

Giric's breath stumbled in his throat. Draped within the oversized cloak, most women would appear nondescript within the numerous yards of wool. This woman's regal bearing, as well as the mix of innocence struggling against the fear in her eyes drew him, conjured forbidden thoughts of her silky skin warmed by sunshine as he slowly peeled each garment away, touched her every secret place until she begged him to make love with her.

Stunned, he squashed thoughts he had nay right to entertain. He was hired to escort her to her betrothed. And she was an innocent. "I am Lady Sarra Bellecote, mistress of Rancourt Castle. You are in charge of these men?"

Her warm, sultry voice flowed over him like peat-warmed air. And if she stepped closer, would he catch her scent? That of a sun-warmed field of heather? Or the crisp, cool water flowing down a burn? "Aye," Giric replied, irritated this one slip of a woman, an Englishwoman at that, evoked such a deep response.

"Until I give further instruction, you and your men are offered shelter within Rancourt Castle." After a perfunctory glance over the rest of his party, she started toward the keep.

Dismissed! He bit back a string of oaths. With him staring at her like a green lad, 'twas nay wonder she treated him with such disregard. "My lady!"

Her pace remained steady, the whirl of snow consuming her as she strode toward the keep.

Never, in all of his years, had any dared to ignore him so deliberately. Giric dismounted in one controlled move. "Lady Sarra, I—"

"Sir Knight." The priest intercepted him, then shot a concerned look toward the lady of Rancourt Castle before turning toward Giric. Wind tugged at his cloak, and he drew his hood tighter. "Please, you and your men come inside the keep and warm yourselves. Lady Sarra will speak with you once you have eaten and rested."

Giric started to correct the priest of his improper address, then remained silent.

A knight.

With his lingering status as an outlaw in the Western Marches and the shame of serving as an escort to earn gold, he'd decided to conceal his title of Earl of Terrick during this mission.

Now, he must play the part.

The priest frowned at the exiting woman.

Curious at the priest's reaction, Giric studied the fading figure through the whirls of snow. Escorting Lady Sarra to her betrothed in Scotland was to be a simple deed. Yet, it appeared the bride was displeased by the match. "My thanks for your hospitality."

The priest signaled toward the stable.

A lad ran from the structure and halted before his horse. "I will take your mounts."

After one last glance toward the keep outlined in the increasing fall of white, Giric nodded and waved for his men to dismount. Warmth and food were his first priority. There would be enough time later to speculate on Rancourt Castle's intriguing mistress.

Three days later, Giric, along with his men, sat around the trencher table at supper. He kept his hands clasped together, his head bowed, and waited until the priest finished the blessing. But the hearty fare of venison, onions, and sage did little to ease a temper that had grown shorter with each passing day.

While rich tones of a prayer echoed throughout the great hall, he covertly glanced toward the dais. Lady Sarra sat rigid in her chair and stared straight ahead. As during every other meal, she neither bowed her head nor clasped her hands in prayer in a show of respect for which the occasion demanded.

Her indifference troubled him. If she was displeased by the match, 'twould seem she would seek answers in prayer. Yet, her lips remained still and naught about her countenance portrayed a hint of divine appeal.

If she indeed shunned the church and its beliefs, then why upon his arrival to Rancourt Castle had she sought out the priest to accompany her to meet him? Whatever her reason, it did nae excuse her poor manners. Each morning since their arrival, he'd sent her a request for an audience, all which she'd ignored.

Though they'd yet to speak, her distrustful looks when he caught her glance served to aggravate his temper. He looked toward her again, damning his body's tightening as he took in her slender frame, beauty of an angel, and rich golden hair. She was a task, nay more.

He studied the priest who dealt with the mistress of Rancourt Castle on a daily basis, and his respect for the cleric rose a notch. The day Giric delivered his wary charge to her betrothed in Scotland and left her far in his wake would be one to celebrate.

After making the sign of the cross, the priest ended his blessing.

The servants stepped to the tables with trenchers of bread as a page sliced off portions of venison roasting over the fire.

Another lad carrying a large platter of food halted beside Giric. "Sir Knight?"

Giric nodded and the lad placed a hunk of meat upon his trencher. Then he scooped onions and carrots alongside.

Once finished, the boy stepped to his right where a large, tawny-haired man sat. "Sir Knight?"

Colyne MacKerran, Giric's longtime friend and the Earl of Strathcliff, nodded.

The page filled his trencher then moved down the table.

Colyne speared the meat with his dagger and took several bites before glancing toward Giric. "'Tis fine fare."

How could he let Colyne join him in this mayhem? Blast it, both of them nobles, yet playing the roles of knights. The matter was his to take care of, but Colyne had insisted to come along. "Better than gruel."

Colyne eyed him a moment, then laughed. "Aye, 'tis at that. Though with your surly temper, you would be deserving such."

With a grunt, Giric carved a bite.

Colyne reached for his goblet. "If asked, I would say your foul mood began with the arrival of Lady—"

"I did nae ask."

Humor flickered in his friend's eyes. "You did nae, but it has been overlong since I have witnessed a woman who has sparked more than a brief glance from you."

"My interest is in the coin this task will provide, naught more." He had enough to do in rebuilding Wolfhaven Castle. He didna need a wayward heiress to keep reined in as well.

"She has a fine figure."

Giric stabbed his dagger into the tender venison. "And the warmth of ice."

"I have known you to melt a few maidens' hearts in your days," Colyne said with lazy enjoyment.

"Even if the lady in question appealed to me, which she does nae, she is betrothed."

His friend gave a resigned sigh. Then a glint of mischief sparked in his eyes. "But could be wooed for a wee kiss."

"You are a bloody pain in the arse." His appetite gone, Giric shoved away the half-eaten trencher. "I have nae figured out why I brought you along."

With a hearty laugh and his dimples giving a fine show, Colyne raised his cup in a toast. "Why, to keep you out of trouble, *Sir Giric*."

At his friend's emphasis on his title, Giric's irritation fell away. He was right, 'twas best to remember the humility of his position until he'd delivered Lady Sarra to her betrothed.

The clank of tankards melded with the voices of the men around him. Smoke, thick and pungent, sifted overhead. "I am ready for this journey to be over," Giric said. "'Tis long past time to return home."

"But it will be quiet without your sister, Elizabet, in residence."

"Aye, but she is safe. Though English and sworn to serve King Edward, Sir Nicholas has proven to be a good husband and fair to the bordering Scots." Though Colyne nodded, Giric didna miss the shadow of hurt that crossed his face. Over the years when his friend had visited Wolfhaven Castle, the love Colyne held for his sister hadna escaped him, nor his intent to offer her marriage.

Except, true to her unconventional manner, Elizabet had fallen in love and wed a man who by rights should be their enemy. And blast if Giric didn't like the Sassenach.

In these troubled times, where rumors of war between England and Scotland rumbled as often as thunder, that his sister had found a man worthy of her love, made their union all the more precious.

He glanced at Lady Sarra who maintained her regal pose upon the dais and toyed with her food. Regret sifted through his mind. It appeared she, like most women, would marry for obligation.

A knight slammed his fist upon the table several lengths away and laughter broke out around him.

Lady Sarra turned toward the warrior, then her gaze shifted to Giric.

Their eyes locked.

Anger flared in her gaze as she stared at him. For a split second, they darkened with awareness, then her mouth parted in surprise.

Heat stormed Giric's body. The temptation of how her mouth would feel beneath his shoved his need up another notch.

Her finger touched her lips as if she could read his thoughts. Then, the heat in her gaze iced, and her tempting mouth thinned in a haughty line.

An air of challenge snapped between them, and at her clear dismissal of him, Giric's regrets of moments ago faded.

But nae his desire.

He held her gaze, refusing to be the first to look away. Her contempt toward him, for God knows whatever reason, was her affair. Like it or nae, if she agreed to her guardian's writ, they would be traveling together.

A long moment passed.

Redness crept up her face, but from the hard set of her expression, it wasna from embarrassment.

Giric narrowed his gaze.

She tilted her head in defiance, almost daring. Then, her nostrils gave a slight flare and she looked away.

His body thrummed with unspent energy, unsure if he should be pleased or aggravated by her bravado.

After a sip from her goblet, she leaned over and whispered to the priest, then pushed her chair back and stood.

"You will nae avoid me this time," he muttered beneath his breath. Giric snatched the cloth nearby, wiped the grease from his mouth and hands, tossed it aside.

Colyne laughed as he watched the heiress depart. "Methinks the rose has thorns."

"A bloody bushel of them." Giric shoved to his feet. Rushes crunched under his boots as he strode after her. He kept his pace steady. Nae too fast as to alert the guards or her of his intent, but enough to keep her in sight.

Three blasted days now she'd made him and his men wait, and if she had her way, the lass would make it four. By God, he would speak with her this night!

Once shielded from the great hall, he took the steps up the turret two at a time. As he ascended, the light scent of heather mingled with the moors and the night. A wisp of her ivory linen gown twisted ahead of him with an elusive swirl as she made to take a step, then was lost in the shadows.

Giric rounded the corner and caught her figure clearly silhouetted from the torch in the wall sconce. "Lady Sarra."

Leather kid slippers scraped over stone as she whirled to face him. The flutter of flames outlined her like a dark angel. Wariness flared in her eyes.

He took a step closer, damning her beauty, lured by her spirit.

Her hand slid to the side of her gown. With a flick of her wrist, she withdrew a slim dagger from the folds. "Halt." Her ominous warning echoed in the darkened void, edged with a hint of fear.

Giric dismissed the knife. Did the lass think she could hold her own against him with a mere blade? "I mean you no harm, my lady. I wish but a brief moment of your time."

That small pert nose lifted a fraction, like a warrior would raise his shield. "How dare you steal about and corner me in my own home."

"If you had talked to me instead of avoided me, I would nae have had to resort to such extreme measures."

A sliver of torchlight glinted off the dagger in her hands. "Leave me. I will grant you an audience when I deem the time appropriate."

If she believed he could be swayed by flashing a weapon before him or a terse command, she was about to learn otherwise. He wasna one of her servants she could order about. He took a step closer. "We need to discuss our departure."

She flinched, but she held her ground.

Determined to keep his temper, he took a slow breath and started again. "My Lady, our acquaintance has begun poorly." Her narrowing eyes chinked at his hard-won control, and the fact that she hadna lowered the blade didna help either, but he pressed on. "Let us begin anew, this time in the proper manner. Let me introduce my—"

"No!" She stepped forward, the dagger tight in her grip. "I will leave Rancourt Castle at my discretion. Your name as well as your demands are of little consequence. Try my patience further, Sir Knight, and you will find yourself housed within my dungeon this night instead of on a pallet of straw." As regal as a queen, she sheathed her dagger and strode up the steps.

Fury slammed through Giric. He was wrong. With a woman like her, nae even a saint could keep his temper in check.

On a curse he bolted up the steps.

The angry scrape of the knight's steps gave Sarra a second's warning as the Scot caught her arm, spun her around, and pinned her against the wall.

Pressed in a firm hold, the coldness of the stone seeped through every pore as the heat of his hard, sculpted body leaned inches from hers. She stared at the large hand clasped on her arm, lined with scars and calloused by hours of maneuvering a sword. On an unsteady breath, she looked up.

His large frame blocked the light, leaving his face partially shadowed. Hard, unforgiving angles that served a fitting canvas for ice-blue eyes that held no quarter. And his devil's black hair added an ominous edge to his dark looks.

Fear surged through her, a hard brutal force that threatened to undermine her hard-won control. The man was dangerous, a fact she'd noted from the first. What had possessed her this evening to challenge him on any level?

But she knew.

So caught up in her anger over her guardian's news of her betrothal, she'd ignored the knight's requests for a meeting. But, once in her chamber and with time settling her thoughts, she faced the reality that once she left her home, if Lord Bretane denied her request and forced her to marry his son, she might never return to Rancourt Castle.

And her intent to depart immediately to confront her guardian had become smothered by fear. She hated her indecision, it but postponed her inevitable fate.

Shame filled Sarra at her poor manners. The knight was hired to perform a task. He didn't deserve her dismissal. Except his dark presence churned up painful memories of the reivers who'd murdered her parents, and reminded her of her future promised to a Scot she abhorred.

"Apologize," he breathed.

His voice, as potent as thunder, rattled through her senses, jerking her thoughts back to the fore. Sarra shoved against his muscled chest.

He didn't move.

"Release me." At his noncompliance, her mouth grew dry. She licked her lips; his eyes followed the act.

The knight muttered a soft curse, and a new worry shot through her. Oh, God. She glanced past him down the spiral steps to where her men ate, oblivious to her peril.

The knight tilted his head and fragments of light spilled over his angled face. Anger still raged within his ice-blue eyes, but now desire churned as well.

Stunned by his boldness, she shoved harder. "Comply or I will order you hanged!"

The knight loosened his grip, but he didn't let go. "Rest assured, my lady, I have no personal intentions. A boar would offer more warmth than you."

"Ho—How dare you!"

"And how dare you stand before me in judgment, casting aspersions on my person when you know naught of me."

He was right, but he didn't understand her aversion to his people or what they represented to her. "My decisions are those of the mistress of Rancourt Castle. And 'twas not I who skulked through the castle without permission."

He leaned an inch forward. "'Twas your rudeness that forced my hand."

"I am firm but fair."

He arched a skeptical brow. "Have you deluded yourself into believing that as well?"

The coldness of the night seeped through her skin, leaving her chilled. "You know naught about me."

"Then we are even, are we nae?"

Again she shoved against his chest. To her surprise, this time he released her, but he didn't step away. His gaze shifted to her lips. Raw hunger burned in his eyes as they lifted to hers. Then they grew cold, distant.

A sense of loss infused her, followed by shame at her untoward thoughts. For a moment, trapped within this rogue's embrace, she'd wanted his touch.

God help her.

She looked away, but the sense of loss remained.

"Yell." His challenge, as hard as seductive, ripped through her tangled emotions and threw her further off balance.

Sarra met his gaze, confused by the urgent roughness of his voice.

He caught a lock of her hair and threaded it through his fingers. "Call for your guards to come and rescue their fair maiden." With devastating slowness, he lifted the tendril to his lips.

Silence clattered between them. She should be afraid. Terrified. Never before had a man dared touch her so. But she remained still, as intrigued as afraid.

" 'Tis what you are good at, is it nae?" he pressed. "Ignoring those you do nae wish to see. Allowing others to deal with issues you canna, or that you refuse to face?"

The coldness of his words shattered her delusions of desire. Humiliated to have been so easily seduced, she felt heat steal up her cheeks.

The Scot held his position, one hand pressed against the wall where he'd held her trapped moments ago, his ice-blue eyes riveted upon her.

The image of a wolf flashed in her mind. Dark. Wild. Untamed.

A tremor rocked her, then another. Her knees wobbled and threatened to give. Refusing to allow him the satisfaction of knowing he'd unnerved her, she tilted her chin in defiance. An error as it brought their faces within a hand's breath.

Shaken by everything this warrior made her feel, she drew a steadying breath. "My doubts have left me indecisive. Once I leave, fate may never allow me to return."

"So you ignore me? Refuse to explain your reasons?"

What did he know about her and what did she care? "My reasons are not your concern." With as much dignity as she could muster, she walked up the stairs. The lonely shuffle of her slippers on the stone steps echoed around her, but she sensed he still watched.

Waited.

Though the writ from her guardian had tossed her organized life into chaos, it appeared with the arrival of the Scottish knight, fate had thrown in another curve as well.

Whatever lay between them was far from over.

A retired Navy Chief, AGC(AW), Diana Cosby is an international bestselling author of Scottish medieval romantic suspense. Diana has spoken at the Library of Congress, appeared at Lady Jane's Salon NYC, in *Woman's Day*, in *Texoma Living* magazine, *USA Today's* romance blog, "Happily Ever After," and MSN.com.

After retiring from the Navy, Diana dove into her passion—writing romance novels. With thirty-four moves behind her, she was anxious to create characters who reflected the amazing cultures and people she's met throughout the world. In August 2012, she released her story in the anthology *Born to Bite*, with Hannah Howell and Erica Ridley.

With the release of her sixth book in the bestselling MacGruder Brothers series, Diana is now working on the Scottish medieval The Oath trilogy. In addition, she's excited about the upcoming release of the MacGruder Brother series box set early in 2015.

Diana looks forward to the years of writing ahead and meeting the remarkable people who will share this journey.

www.dianacosby.com

Love Diana Cosby?

Be sure to check out

The MacGruder Brothers series!

Keep reading to learn more

HIS CAPTIVE

With a wastrel brother and a treacherous former fiancé, Lady Nichola Westcott hardly expects the dangerously seductive Scot who kidnaps her to be a man of his word. Though Sir Alexander MacGruder promises not to hurt her, Nichola's only value is as a pawn to be ransomed.

Alexander's goal is to avenge his father's murder, not to become entangled with the enemy. But his desire to keep Nichola with him, in his home—in his bed—unwittingly makes her a target for those who have no qualms about shedding English blood.

Now Nichola is trapped—by her powerful attraction to a man whose touch shakes her to the core. Unwilling and unable to resist each other, can Nichola and Alexander save a love that has enslaved them both?

SPECIAL
PRICE
$4.99
$5.99 CAN

"Diana Cosby
is superbly talented."
—Cathy Maxwell,
New York Times
Bestselling Author

His Woman

Some passions are too powerful to forget...

DIANA COSBY

HIS WOMAN

Lady Isabel Adair is the last woman Sir Duncan MacGruder wants to see again, much less be obliged to save. Three years ago, Isabel broke their engagement to become the Earl of Frasyer's mistress, shattering Duncan's heart and hopes in one painful blow. But Duncan's promise to Isabel's dying brother compels him to rescue her from those determined to bring down Scottish rebel Sir William Wallace.

Betraying the man she loved was the only way for Isabel to save her father, but every moment she spends with Duncan reminds her how much she sacrificed. No one could blame him for despising her, yet Duncan's misgivings cannot withstand a desire that has grown wilder with time. Now, on a perilous journey through Scotland, two wary lovers must confront both the enemies who will stop at nothing to hunt them down, and the secret legacy that threatens their passion and their lives. . . .

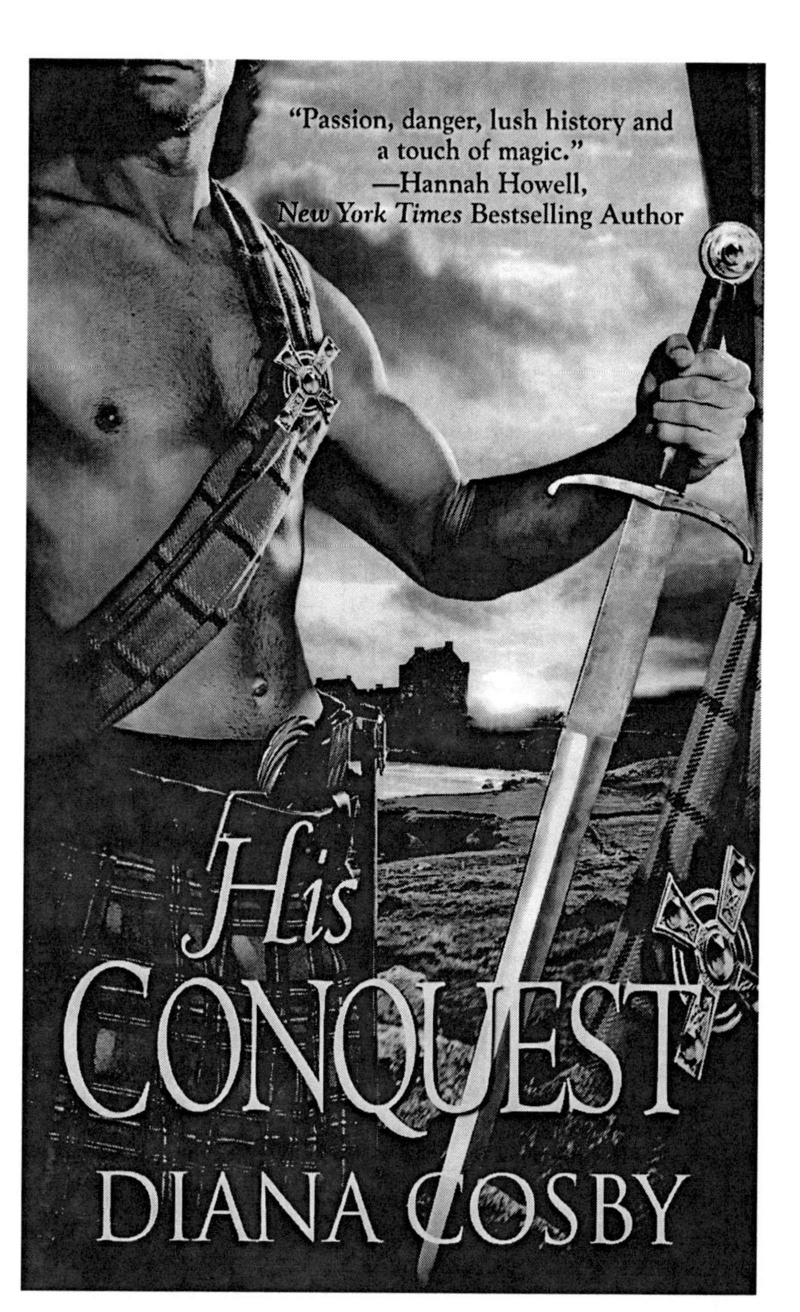
"Passion, danger, lush history and
a touch of magic."
—Hannah Howell,
New York Times Bestselling Author
His
CONQUEST
DIANA COSBY

HIS CONQUEST

Linet Dancort will not be sold. But that's essentially what her brother intends to do—to trade her like so much chattel to widen his already vast scope of influence. Linet will seize any opportunity to escape her fate—and opportunity comes in the form of a rebel prisoner locked in her brother's dungeon, predatory and fearsome, and sentenced to hang in the morning.

Seathan MacGruder, Earl of Grey, is not unused to cheating death. But even this legendary Scottish warrior is surprised when a beautiful Englishwoman creeps to his cell and offers him his freedom. What Linet wants in exchange, though—safe passage to the Highlands—is a steep price to pay. For the only thing more dangerous than the journey through embattled Scotland is the desire that smolders between these two fugitives the first time they touch. . . .

DIANA
COSBY
His
DESTINY
"Medieval Scotland roars to life in this fabulous series."
—Pam Palmer, *New York Times* Bestselling Author

HIS DESTINY

As one of England's most capable mercenaries, Emma Astyn can charm an enemy and brandish a knife with unmatched finesse. Assigned to befriend Dubh Duer, an infamous Scottish rebel, she assumes the guise of innocent damsel Christina Moffat to intercept the writ he's carrying to a traitorous bishop. But as she gains the dark hero's confidence and realizes they share a tattered past, compassion—and passion—distract her from the task at hand. . . .

His legendary slaying of English knights has won him the name Dubh Duer, but Sir Patrik Cleary MacGruder is driven by duty and honor, not heroics. Rescuing Christina from the clutches of four such knights is a matter of obligation for the Scot. But there's something alluring about her fiery spirit, even if he has misgivings about her tragic history. Together, they'll endure a perilous journey of love and betrayal, and a harrowing fight for their lives. . . .

DIANA COSBY

His SEDUCTION

"Medieval Scotland roars to life in this fabulous series."
—Pamela Palmer, *New York Times* bestselling author

HIS SEDUCTION

Lady Rois Drummond is fiercely devoted to her widowed father, the respected Scottish Earl of Brom. So when she believes he is about to be exposed as a traitor to England, she must think quickly. Desperate, Rois makes a shocking claim against the suspected accuser, Sir Griffin Westcott. But her impetuous lie leaves her in an outrageous circumstance: hastily married to the enemy. Yet Griffin is far from the man Rois thinks he is—and much closer to the man of her dreams. . . .

Griffin may be an Englishman, but in truth he leads a clandestine life as a spy for Scotland. Refusing to endanger any woman, he has endured the loneliness of his mission. But Rois's absurd charge has suddenly changed all that. Now, with his cover in jeopardy, Griffin must find a way to keep his secret while keeping his distance from his spirited and tempting new wife—a task that proves more difficult than he ever imagined. . . .

DIANA
COSBY
"Medieval Scotland roars to
life in this fabulous series."
—Pamela Palmer, New York
Times Bestselling Author
His
ENCHANTMENT
The MacGruder Brothers

HIS ENCHANTMENT

Lady Catarine MacLaren is a fairy princess, duty-bound to eschew the human world. But the line between the two realms is beginning to blur. English knights have launched an assault on the MacLarens, just as the families of Comyn have captured the Scottish king and queen. Now, Catarine is torn between loyalty to her people and helping the handsome, rust-haired Lord Trálin rescue the Scottish king. . . .

As guard to King Alexander, Lord Trálin MacGruder will stop at nothing to defend the Scottish crown against the Comyns. And he finds a sympathetic, and gorgeous, ally in the enigmatic Princess Catarine. As they plot to rescue the kidnapped king and queen, Trálin and Catarine will discover a love made all but impossible by her obligations to the Otherworld. But a passion this extraordinary may be worth the irreversible sacrifices it demands. . . .

CPSIA information can be obtained
at www.ICGtesting.com
Printed in the USA
LVOW12s1531120517
534312LV00001B/102/P